# Love of My Life: Love Turns Deadly

Michael Harbut and Michael Anderson

Published by Michael Harbut, 2023.

LOVE OF MY LIFE: LOVE TURNS DEADLY

**First edition. December 7, 2023.**

ISBN: 979-8218338947

Written by Michael Harbut and Michael Anderson.

# Also by Michael Harbut

Love of My Life: Love Turns Deadly

Watch for more at https://bottom2thatopentertainment.com.

# Also by Michael Anderson

Love of My Life: Love Turns Deadly

This work is respectfully devoted to my parents, siblings, extended family, dedicated team, and cherished offspring – Chrishawn, Michaela, Jaaizh, and Michael. Their steadfast support, boundless love, and inspirational encouragement have been the cornerstone of this literary journey. This book wouldn't exist without them. My love for each of you transcends the limitations of language.

Love of My Life: Love Turns Deadly

# Chapter 1: Serendipitous Encounter

Chapter 1: Serendipitous Encounter

In the heart of the bustling city of Alderidge, Emily Carter lived a life marked by a comforting routine. As a dedicated art teacher in a local high school, her days were filled with vibrant colors and the creative energy of her students. Her world, though not expensive, was rich with the simplicity and contentment of her passions.

One crisp October evening, as the city was draped in the golden hues of autumn, Emily's path intersected with that of Michael Harrison. Michael, a graphic designer with a penchant for capturing life's moments through his lens, was in Alderidge on an assignment to document the city's autumnal charm. His camera inadvertently captured Emily, her figure set against the backdrop of the city park, her auburn hair dancing in the gentle breeze.

Their eyes met, and in that brief exchange, a connection sparked between them. It was as if destiny had orchestrated this moment, setting in motion a series of events that would redefine their lives.

In the days that followed, Emily and Michael found themselves inexplicably drawn to each other. They met frequently, sometimes in the park where their paths first crossed, other times in quaint cafes where their conversations flowed as freely as the coffee they sipped. The connection they shared was undeniable, a rare blend of intellectual compatibility and emotional resonance.

Emily, who had always been cautious with her heart, found herself gradually opening up to Michael. He listened to her dreams, her aspirations, and her subtle fears with an intensity that made her feel deeply understood. Michael, with his warm smile and eyes that seemed to reflect a world of stories, brought a sense of adventure into her life. He shared tales of his travels, of sunsets in distant lands, and of the myriad people he had encountered along his journey.

Their romance blossomed naturally, beautifully. Casual strolls in the park evolved into cozy movie nights, and coffee dates deepened into long, intimate conversations under the stars. They shared their favorite books, music, and fragments of their souls, intertwining their lives in the most delicate manner.

Emily's friends noticed the transformation in her. There was a newfound lightness in her step, a melody in her voice that spoke of newfound happiness. Her eyes sparkled when she spoke of Michael, her laughter filling the room with a warmth that was palpable. In Michael, Emily had found not just a lover but a kindred spirit, someone who understood her silences as profoundly as her words.

For Michael, Emily was like a serene melody, calming the chaos that often accompanied his creative mind. Her presence was a balm to his restless spirit, offering a sense of peace he hadn't realized he was seeking. In her, he found not only a romantic partner but also a companion, a confidante, a source of unwavering support.

As autumn's vibrant display gave way to the first snow of winter, their love continued to flourish. They celebrated their first Christmas together, exchanging gifts that were thoughtful reflections of their deep understanding and affection for each other. Emily gifted Michael a vintage camera, acknowledging his passion for photography. Michael, in turn, presented Emily with a beautifully illustrated edition of her favorite novel, its pages echoing tales of adventure and romance.

Their relationship, though filled with love, was not without its challenges. They navigated through differences and misunderstandings, each obstacle bringing them closer, fortifying their bond. They learned the art of compromise and the importance of listening not just to respond but to understand truly.

As they sat by the fireplace in Emily's apartment, watching the snow gently blanket the world outside, their fingers entwined, they spoke of future dreams and aspirations. In each other, they had found a love that felt as timeless as the stars and as fresh as the morning dew.

Unbeknownst to them, the winds of change were stirring, poised to test the strength of their bond. But for now, they reveled in the warmth of their love, oblivious to the impending storm that loomed on the horizon.

As winter's chill enveloped Alderidge, Emily and Michael's relationship continued to deepen. They spent evenings wrapped in blankets, sharing stories and dreams by the glow of the fireplace. Michael introduced Emily to the world of photography, teaching her to capture moments through the lens with the same passion he felt. Emily, in turn, shared her love for art, guiding Michael's hands in creating brushstrokes that brought canvases to life.

Their weekends were filled with small adventures. They explored the hidden gems of Alderidge, from quaint bookshops tucked away in narrow lanes to cozy, little-known cafes that became their sanctuaries. They visited art galleries and museums, where they admired the works of masters, each piece telling a story that fueled their conversations.

As the city thawed into spring, their love blossomed further. They celebrated Valentine's Day with a homemade dinner in Emily's apartment, surrounded by candles and the soft strumming of a guitar as Michael serenaded Emily with her favorite songs. It was a simple yet profoundly intimate celebration, emblematic of the depth of their connection.

The arrival of spring brought new adventures. They planted a small garden on Emily's balcony, where flowers and herbs grew under their joint care, a symbol of their nurturing love. Weekends were spent cycling through the countryside, the fresh, floral-scented air filling their lungs as they discovered scenic routes and shared laughter and joy.

Emily's family, who lived a few hours away, welcomed Michael with open arms. Her parents saw the happiness he brought to their daughter's life and appreciated his respectful, caring nature. Dinners with her family became a regular occurrence, where stories and jokes were shared, further intertwining Michael into the fabric of her life.

Meanwhile, Michael introduced Emily to his circle of friends, a diverse group of creative souls who embraced her warmly. They attended gatherings where music, art, and lively debates filled the air, and Emily found herself seamlessly fitting into Michael's world.

As summer approached, they planned their first vacation together – a road trip along the coast. The excitement of planning their journey, of selecting destinations and activities, brought them even closer. They talked about visiting small coastal towns, spending nights under the stars, and experiencing the thrill of the open road together.

However, beneath the surface of their idyllic love story, subtle undercurrents began to emerge. Michael, often lost in his work, began to show signs of restlessness. Emily noticed moments of distraction, a faraway look in his eyes that hadn't been there before. She attributed it to the stress of his demanding career and did her best to provide support and understanding.

As they prepared for their road trip, Emily couldn't shake off a niggling sense of unease. She pushed these thoughts aside, attributing them to pre-trip jitters. After all, they were about to embark on a beautiful journey together, a chance to create unforgettable memories.

Little did Emily know the journey they were about to undertake would test the very foundations of their relationship. The road ahead was filled with unforeseen twists and turns, and the strength of their bond was about to be challenged in ways they never imagined.

For now, they stood on the brink of a summer filled with promise, their hearts intertwined, yet unaware of the shadows that lurked just around the corner.

The eagerly anticipated road trip began under a canopy of clear blue skies, with the sun casting a warm glow over the landscape. Emily and Michael set off in high spirits, the car packed with essentials and a playlist of their favorite songs filling the air. The open road symbolized freedom, an escape from the mundane, a journey into shared experiences, and deeper bonding.

Their first stop was a picturesque coastal town, where they strolled hand in hand along the beach, the sand cool under their feet and the sound of waves a soothing backdrop. They captured moments in photographs, with Emily's newly acquired skills impressing Michael. Laughter and conversation flowed effortlessly as they dined in small seafront restaurants, tasting local delicacies and toasting to their love.

As they traveled from one town to another, each day unraveled new sights and experiences. They hiked to hidden waterfalls, picnicked in lush meadows, and watched sunsets that painted the sky in brilliant oranges and pinks. At night, they lay under the stars, sharing whispers and dreams, the world around them fading into insignificance.

However, as the days passed, Emily sensed a subtle shift in Michael. He became increasingly distant, his thoughts seemingly preoccupied. Conversations that once flowed naturally now had pauses filled with unspoken words. Emily tried to bridge the gap, attributing Michael's change in demeanor to the exhaustion of travel or perhaps some unresolved work issues.

One evening, as they sat by a campfire, Emily broached the subject. Michael reassured her that everything was fine, attributing his quietness to tiredness. Yet, Emily couldn't shake off the feeling that something remained unsaid, a hidden concern that Michael wasn't sharing.

Despite these undercurrents, they continued their journey, making the most of their time together. They visited a famous lighthouse, its beam of guiding light in the darkness, and explored quaint villages where time seemed to stand still. They met locals who shared stories of the sea, of storms weathered and calm waters cherished.

As the trip neared its end, they arrived at a small town known for its vibrant art scene. Here, Emily felt a renewed sense of connection with Michael as they immersed themselves in the world of art. They attended a local art fair, where Emily's enthusiasm and knowledge shone. Michael watched her with a mixture of admiration and something else, a complexity in his gaze that Emily couldn't decipher.

On the last night of their trip, as they sat overlooking the ocean, a sense of melancholy enveloped Emily. The trip had been beautiful, yet marred by the subtle changes in Michael's behavior. She longed to return to the simplicity and joy of their early days, to the time when their love seemed unshakeable.

As they drove back to Aldridge, the silence in the car was a stark contrast to the beginning of their journey. Emily pondered over the right words to say and the right questions to ask. She hoped that once back in the familiarity of their city, they could address the unspoken tension that had slowly crept into their relationship.

Unbeknownst to Emily, the return to Alderidge would mark the beginning of a tumultuous phase in their lives. The journey they had embarked upon was more than a physical one; it was a journey into the depths of their relationship, a prelude to challenges and revelations that lay ahead.

In Alderidge, Emily and Michael's return from their coastal road trip marked a stark shift in their relationship. The comforting familiarity of the city did little to alleviate the growing tension between them. Emily, resuming her teaching, sought refuge in her students' creativity, while Michael, absorbed in his photography work, became increasingly distant. Their home, once a haven of shared dreams and laughter, now echoed with silence and strained conversations.

As weeks passed, Emily's attempts to rekindle their connection felt futile, like temporary fixes to a deepening wound. The warmth and affection that once defined Michael's gaze had faded, replaced by a distant, troubled look. Desperate for answers, Emily confronted him one evening, only to receive vague assurances of work-related stress. Yet, she sensed an unspoken truth lurking beneath his evasive responses.

Conflicted emotions plagued Emily; doubt cast shadows over her once joyful relationship. Michael's erratic behavior and evasive answers only deepened her sense of disconnection. As autumn's chill set in, mirroring the coldness in their relationship, Emily resolved to seek the truth, regardless of the pain it might bring. This decision propelled her onto a path of challenging revelations, marking the beginning of a tumultuous new chapter in their once-idyllic love story.

# Chapter 2: Building a Life Together

In the heart of spring, Emily and Michael's relationship blossomed with a newfound depth. The city of Alderidge, with its vibrant streets and blooming gardens, mirrored the flourishing love between them. They spent their days exploring the nooks and crannies of the city, each adventure bringing them closer, weaving a tapestry of shared experiences.

Michael's affection for Emily was evident in his every action. He would surprise her with impromptu picnics in the park, where they lay under the sky, talking about everything and nothing. Emily, in turn, brought warmth and stability to Michael's life, often grounding him when the chaos of his creative pursuits overwhelmed him.

Their evenings were spent in Michael's apartment, which slowly transformed into a cozy haven for the couple. Emily's artistic touch merged with Michael's minimalist style, creating a space that was uniquely theirs. They cooked together, the kitchen bustling with laughter and the clinking of dishes, as they experimented with recipes and occasionally indulged in playful food fights.

It was during one of these ordinary yet magical evenings that Emily realized she was pregnant. The discovery came as a surprise, a curveball neither of them had anticipated. The initial shock quickly gave way to a whirlwind of emotions – fear, excitement, uncertainty, and above all, a profound sense of connection.

Michael's reaction mirrored Emily's complex emotions. He was stunned, but as the reality sank in, his face lit up with a joy that was contagious. They embraced, a silent promise passing between them, a commitment to each other and the life they were about to bring into the world.

The following weeks were a blur of activity and anticipation. They attended doctor's appointments, where the sound of the baby's heartbeat filled them with awe. They read books on parenting, often laughing at the conflicting advice yet eagerly absorbing every bit of information.

As Emily's body began to change, so did their relationship. It deepened, rooted in a shared purpose. They discussed baby names, each suggestion sparking stories and debates. They decorated the nursery, choosing colors and themes, imagining the laughter and joy that would soon fill the room.

Their conversations at night became more profound, often centered around their hopes and fears for the future. They spoke of the values they wanted to instill in their child, of the lessons they hoped to teach, and the world they wished to show them.

Michael, ever the romantic, would often hold Emily, whispering promises and dreams into the night. He spoke of the places they would show their children and the experiences they would share as a family. Emily, her heart full of love and gratitude, would listen, her hand resting on her growing belly, feeling the flutter of life within.

Their love, already deep, took on new dimensions, colored by the anticipation and joy of the life they were creating together. They stood at the threshold of a new chapter, hand in hand, hearts intertwined, ready to face the joys and challenges of parenthood. The future, once a distant concept, was now a tangible, exciting reality filled with endless possibilities and the promise of shared adventures.

As summer unfurled its warmth over Aldridge, Emily's pregnancy progressed, weaving new patterns into the fabric of their lives. The couple, once spontaneous in their outings, now found joy in quieter, more intimate moments. Evenings were spent on the balcony, watching the sunset paint the sky in hues of orange and pink while they shared dreams for their future family.

Michael became increasingly attentive, his care for Emily evident in small, everyday gestures. He would often return home with fresh flowers or her favorite snacks, his eyes lighting up at her smile of appreciation. Emily, glowing with the radiance of impending motherhood, found comfort in Michael's unwavering support and affection.

Together, they attended prenatal classes, an experience that brought them even closer. They learned about childbirth and parenting, often exchanging amused glances at the new and unfamiliar territory they were navigating. These classes were not just about preparation; they were a testament to their commitment to each other and their baby.

The city of Alderidge, with its bustling streets and tranquil parks, became a backdrop to their growing bond. They would take leisurely walks, Emily's hand resting gently on her belly, as they talked about the kind of parents they wanted to be. Michael's excitement was palpable; he would often talk to the baby, his words a mix of humor and tenderness.

As the due date approached, the couple began to prepare in earnest. The nursery, once an empty room, was now a sanctuary of comfort and love, adorned with soft colors and filled with toys and books. They meticulously assembled the crib, the task turning into an afternoon of laughter and playful bickering.

Their friends and family surrounded them with love and support. A baby shower was organized, a joyous celebration that brought together their loved ones. Gifts were unwrapped, advice was shared, and the air was filled with laughter and well-wishes. Emily felt a profound sense of gratitude for the community that would be part of their child's life.

Despite the happiness and anticipation, Emily couldn't shake off a subtle undercurrent of anxiety. She worried about the unknowns of childbirth and motherhood, the responsibility of nurturing a life. Michael, sensing her unease, would reassure her with words of encouragement, reminding her of her strength and the journey they were on together.

Their nights were often spent in quiet contemplation, the couple lying awake, sharing their thoughts and fears. They spoke of the changes that were coming, the challenges they might face, and the strength they found in each other. These moments of vulnerability only strengthened their bond, their love a beacon guiding them through the uncertainties.

As summer gave way to autumn, the anticipation reached its zenith. The baby's arrival was imminent, a thought that filled them with a mix of excitement and nervousness. They stood on the cusp of a new life, a new beginning that would redefine their love and partnership.

Emily and Michael, hand in hand, hearts full of love, awaited the arrival of their child. The journey they had embarked upon was about to take its most significant turn, a turn that would lead them into the uncharted territories of parenthood, with all its joys, challenges, and endless possibilities.

Autumn's arrival in Alderidge brought a kaleidoscope of changing leaves and a crispness in the air, mirroring the changes in Emily and Michael's life as they awaited their child's birth. The city, with its amber hues and gentle breezes, seemed to be in sync with their growing anticipation and excitement.

During this period, their home became a hive of activity. Friends and family visited often, each bringing gifts and sharing their own experiences of parenthood. These visits were filled with laughter and sometimes overwhelming advice, creating a tapestry of support and love around the couple.

Emily, now in the final stages of her pregnancy, found a serene strength within herself. She spent hours in the nursery, folding tiny clothes and arranging toys, each action filled with love and care. Michael, ever the doting partner, was always by her side, assisting with the preparations and ensuring Emily was comfortable and stress-free.

The couple also used this time to strengthen their bond. They knew that the arrival of their baby would bring joyous upheaval, so they cherished their moments together. Quiet dinners, gentle strolls in the park, and cozy movie nights became precious, a calm before the beautiful storm of parenthood.

As the due date drew closer, Emily and Michael attended their final prenatal appointments. The doctor's reassuring words and the ultrasound images of their baby brought a sense of awe and reality to the impending arrival. They were about to meet the little person who had been growing inside Emily, a realization that filled them with an indescribable mix of emotions.

One evening, as they sat together, Michael presented Emily with a handmade photo album. It was filled with pictures documenting their journey – from their early days as a couple to Emily's pregnancy. Each photo told a story of love, growth, and anticipation. Emily, moved by the gesture, realized how far they had come and how much they had grown together.

Their conversations now often revolved around the baby. They speculated about whether they would have a boy or a girl, what traits the baby might inherit from each of them, and how they would navigate the challenges of raising a child in the modern world. These discussions, sometimes light-hearted and sometimes serious, brought them even closer, solidifying their partnership and shared values.

As autumn deepened, Emily and Michael finalized their birth plan with the hospital. They packed a hospital bag, ensuring everything they might need was ready. The reality of their situation was exhilarating and, at times, daunting. They were about to embark on the most significant journey of their lives, one that would change them in ways they couldn't yet fathom.

In the quiet of the night, they would often lie awake, feeling the baby move. These moments were intimate and profound, a shared experience that only deepened their connection. They talked to the baby, sharing their hopes and dreams, creating a bond that transcended the physical.

As the leaves continued to fall and the city of Alderidge prepared for the onset of winter, Emily and Michael stood on the brink of a new chapter in their lives. The journey of pregnancy had been one of growth, love, and preparation. Now, they waited with bated breath for the moment that would transform their lives forever – the arrival of their child, the embodiment of their love, and the beginning of a new, extraordinary chapter.

The final days before the baby's arrival were a blend of serene anticipation and bursts of nervous energy. Emily and Michael, now on the threshold of parenthood, found themselves reflecting on their journey. The city of Alderidge, with its early winter chill and quiet streets, seemed to be holding its breath along with them.

Emily, her body a testament to the miracle of life, moved with grace and resilience that amazed Michael. He watched her in awe, her maternal glow a constant reminder of the strength and beauty of their love. Their home, once a place for two, was ready to welcome its newest member, the nursery, a cocoon of warmth and safety.

In these final moments, their relationship took on a new depth. They found strength in each other's presence, a silent understanding that they were about to face life's most profound change together. Their conversations, once filled with playful banter, now carried a weight of earnestness. They discussed their hopes and fears, not just for the birth but for the years to come, envisioning the life they would build for their child.

One quiet evening, as they sat together, Emily felt the first signs of labor. The realization that their baby was on its way brought a rush of emotions. Excitement, fear, and an overwhelming sense of love enveloped them. They held each other, knowing that the next time they embraced, they would be parents.

The journey to the hospital was a blur, the streets of Alderidge passing by as they focused on the imminent arrival. At the hospital, amidst the flurry of activity, Emily and Michael found their oasis of calm in each other. Each contraction brought them closer to meeting their child, and Michael was there every step of the way, offering words of encouragement and love.

The labor was a testament to Emily's strength and Michael's unwavering support. As they worked together through each contraction, their bond solidified, a partnership in its truest form. The hours passed, a mix of intensity and anticipation, until finally, with one last push, their baby was born.

The sound of their baby's first cry was a symphony, a culmination of their journey. As the nurse placed the baby in Emily's arms, their world shifted. Tears of joy and relief streamed down their faces as they gazed at the tiny life they had created. Michael, overcome with emotion, held Emily and their baby close, his heart full of indescribable love.

In those first moments as a family, time stood still. The challenges and joys of the past nine months faded into the background, replaced by the overwhelming reality of their new life. They whispered promises and dreams to their baby, vowing to provide a world filled with love, laughter, and endless opportunities.

As they left the hospital, stepping out into the crisp air of Alderidge, Emily and Michael embarked on their greatest adventure yet. Parenthood promised to be a journey of endless learning, of sleepless nights and boundless joy, of challenges and triumphs. Together, they stepped into this new chapter, their hearts and lives forever intertwined with the tiny, perfect being they held in their arms. The story of their love, now shared with their child, was just beginning.

# Chapter 3: The Disappearance

In the wake of their blissful journey into parenthood, Emily and Michael's life in Alderidge seemed to embody a perfect harmony. However, as autumn's leaves began to wither, a disquieting change loomed. Michael's sudden disappearance shattered the tranquility of their existence.

One ordinary Thursday, under a sky heavy with unshed rain, Michael left for work as usual. His parting words, a casual "See you tonight," echoed in the now eerily silent apartment. Hours turned into a night fraught with worry as Michael did not return, nor did he answer his phone. Emily's heart, once filled with love and trust, now pounded with anxiety and confusion.

The following morning brought no relief. Michael's phone went straight to voicemail, and his colleagues at the design studio were equally baffled by his absence. They confirmed he hadn't been at work the previous day. This revelation sent a cold shiver down Emily's spine. Her mind raced with possibilities, each more frightening than the last.

Emily's initial response was to consider plausible explanations. Perhaps an urgent issue had arisen, or maybe Michael had lost his phone. Yet, as hours turned into days with no word from him, her worry deepened into a profound sense of dread. She contacted hospitals, local authorities, and friends, but no one had seen or heard from Michael.

The apartment, once a haven of shared dreams and laughter, now felt hollow. Emily wandered through the rooms, each corner a reminder of Michael's absence. His belongings, scattered as if he would return any moment, served as a stark contrast to the grim reality. The silence was oppressive, broken only by the occasional coo of their baby, oblivious to the turmoil.

Emily's mind was a whirlwind of questions with no answers. Had Michael met with an accident? Was he in trouble? Or, a thought she dared not entertain, had he left willingly? The uncertainty was maddening. She found herself staring at the door, longing for it to open and reveal Michael safe and sound.

As days passed, Emily's initial confusion gave way to a deep worry. She struggled to maintain a semblance of normalcy for their child, but the strain of Michael's unexplained absence was overwhelming. Sleep eluded her, and when it did come, it was fitful and haunted by nightmares of dire possibilities.

The community of Alderidge, initially sympathetic, began to whisper theories and speculations. Friends offered support, but their words often felt hollow against the magnitude of her distress. Emily felt a growing isolation, a sense that she was navigating this harrowing experience alone.

Amidst this turmoil, Emily grappled with the practicalities of daily life. Financial concerns began to surface. Michael had been the primary breadwinner, and his sudden disappearance left Emily facing a precarious financial situation. She delved into their savings, but the uncertainty of how long it would need to last weighed heavily on her.

The police, involved from the first day of Michael's disappearance, had little to report. Their investigation revealed no signs of foul play nor any indication that Michael had planned to leave. His bank accounts and credit cards remained untouched, deepening the mystery.

As Emily faced each day with a brave front, her internal world crumbled. The man she loved, the father of her child, had vanished without a trace, leaving a gaping hole in their lives. The absence of closure, the not knowing, was a relentless torment.

In this first part of her ordeal, Emily oscillated between hope and despair. Each morning brought a renewed sense of hope, which faded as the sun set with no news of Michael. Her emotions were a tumultuous sea, ebbing and flowing with each passing day.

The weight of single parenthood, coupled with the agony of uncertainty, began to take its toll. Emily's once vibrant spirit dimmed, her energy consumed by the effort to keep going for the sake of their child. The joy of motherhood, so recently discovered, was now overshadowed by the specter of her partner's unexplained absence.

As the first part of this chapter in her life drew to a close, Emily stood at a crossroads. She could succumb to despair or muster the strength to seek answers. The path ahead was fraught with uncertainty, but for her own sake and that of her child, she knew she had to confront whatever lay ahead.

As weeks turned into a month since Michael's disappearance, the initial shock that had gripped Emily began to morph into a relentless quest for answers. She could no longer remain passive, waiting for news that never came. Driven by a mixture of desperation and determination, Emily embarked on her own investigation.

Her first step was to meticulously retrace Michael's steps. She visited his workplace, speaking with anyone who might have noticed unusual behavior or conversations in the days leading up to his disappearance. These inquiries, however, yielded nothing but sympathetic shrugs and confused looks. Michael, it seemed, had been his usual self, his colleagues remarked, dedicated and seemingly content.

Undeterred, Emily delved deeper. She scoured through Michael's emails and social media accounts, searching for any clue, any anomaly that might shed light on his whereabouts. This digital excavation brought her into a world she barely knew – Michael's private thoughts and interactions. Yet, even this intimate probe into his digital footprint revealed nothing out of the ordinary.

As she navigated this challenging period, Emily's resilience was put to the test. She balanced her investigation with the demands of motherhood, often running on little sleep and a lot of coffee. Her friends and family rallied around her, offering to babysit and providing emotional support. Yet, in the quiet moments alone with her child, Emily felt the full weight of her situation. The joy of watching her baby reach new milestones was tinged with sadness as she wished for Michael to share these moments.

The police, meanwhile, continued their investigation but with diminishing urgency as leads dried up. They reassured Emily that cases like these sometimes resolved unexpectedly, but as days turned into weeks, their reassurances rang hollow.

In a bid to reignite public interest, Emily organized a community search. Flyers with Michael's face were distributed, and a group of volunteers combed the local areas he frequented. Local media covered the story, casting a spotlight on the mystery of Michael's disappearance. Yet, despite these efforts, no new information surfaced.

The strain of the situation began to manifest in Emily's health. Dark circles formed under her eyes, and her once steady hands now trembled with fatigue. She found solace in her art, often losing herself in painting, a temporary escape from the relentless cycle of hope and despair.

As autumn gave way to a harsh winter, the reality of her circumstances settled in. Emily faced the daunting prospect of moving forward without Michael. She began to make difficult decisions, adjusting her lifestyle to accommodate the financial strain. She returned to teaching part-time, the familiar environment of the school offering a semblance of normalcy.

Yet, even as she took these steps, Emily clung to a sliver of hope. She kept Michael's belongings untouched, his side of the bed made as if expecting him to return at any moment. She spoke of him often to their child, determined to keep his memory alive.

During this period, Emily's resilience was both tested and fortified. She discovered a strength within herself she never knew existed. Her love for her child became the anchor that kept her grounded, even as the storm of uncertainty raged around her.

As the second part of this chapter drew to a close, Emily found herself at a crossroads. She could either remain anchored in the past, shackled by the mystery of Michael's disappearance, or she could attempt to forge a new path, one filled with uncertainty but also with the possibility of healing and new beginnings. The choice was daunting, but Emily knew she owed it to herself and her child to find a way to live again, even in the shadow of unanswered questions.

Emily's journey through the labyrinth of uncertainty and grief took a new turn as the harsh winter began to thaw into spring. The change of seasons seemed to mirror a subtle shift within her. Though the mystery of Michael's disappearance remained unsolved, the icy grip of perpetual despair began to loosen, giving way to a cautious acceptance.

This phase of Emily's journey was marked by introspection and a gradual reconnection with the world around her. She started attending a support group for people who had lost loved ones in ambiguous circumstances. Here, amidst strangers sharing their stories of loss and resilience, Emily found a sense of solidarity. Their shared experiences, though uniquely painful, wove a tapestry of collective strength that helped Emily to feel less isolated in her struggle.

Simultaneously, Emily's role as a mother provided a vital source of purpose and joy. Her child, now more aware and interactive, brought a daily dose of wonder and love into her life. Emily found solace in their shared moments, from the morning cuddles to the bedtime stories. These routines, once shared with Michael, now became sacred rituals between mother and child, imbued with love and a poignant sense of continuity.

In her professional life, Emily's return to teaching art became more than a financial necessity; it evolved into a therapeutic outlet. She poured her emotions into her teaching, fostering a creative sanctuary not only for her students but also for herself. The art room became a place where she could express and process her emotions without the need for words.

During this time, Emily also began to explore new avenues of self-expression. She took up journaling, a practice that allowed her to articulate her thoughts and feelings in a private, unfiltered way. This practice became a nightly ritual, a space where she could converse with her inner self and, in a way, with Michael. Through these written dialogues, she began to process her grief, her anger, and her myriad unanswered questions.

The community around Emily remained a pillar of support. Her friends and family, while unsure of how to navigate her complex emotional landscape, provided a steady presence. They offered practical help, like babysitting and meals, and a listening ear when she needed to voice her fears and frustrations.

As spring blossomed, Emily found herself taking small but significant steps toward rebuilding her life. She initiated a project at school, a mural that symbolized hope and renewal. This project, involving her students and colleagues, became a symbol of communal healing and resilience. It was a testament to Emily's belief in the power of art to heal and connect people.

However, the journey was not without its setbacks. There were days when the weight of Michael's absence felt unbearable, when the unanswered questions loomed large, casting a shadow over her hard-won progress. On these days, Emily allowed herself to grieve, to feel the full extent of her loss. Yet, she no longer let these moments define her. Instead, they became part of the complex tapestry of her healing process.

As the third part of this chapter unfolded, Emily's journey through the landscape of loss and resilience continued. She began to understand that while the mystery of Michael's disappearance might never be solved, her life could still be filled with meaning and joy. This realization did not diminish her love for Michael or the depth of her loss, but it allowed her to view her future through a lens of cautious hope.

In this newfound state of being, Emily stood at the precipice of a new chapter. She recognized that while the past would always be a part of her, it did not have to dictate her future. With this understanding, she began to envision a life that honored her past, embraced her present, and was open to the possibilities of the future.

As the first anniversary of Michael's disappearance neared, Emily faced this poignant milestone with a blend of sorrow and resilience. She chose to commemorate the day not with despair but as a tribute to the love and life she once shared with Michael. A small gathering at her home brought together friends and family. They reminisced, sharing stories that painted a vivid picture of Michael, each memory a precious thread in the tapestry of their past. Laughter mingled with tears, echoing the complex emotions that had become a part of Emily's journey.

In a serene moment, Emily led her guests to the garden. Here, she revealed a sculpture, a creation born from her grief and love. It was an abstract piece, intertwining elements of Michael's photography with her artistic expression, symbolizing their intertwined lives and passions. This act of creation was Emily's way of transforming her grief into something tangible, a testament to the enduring impact of their love.

With the passing seasons, Emily's life continued to evolve. Her child, now a toddler, was a source of boundless energy and joy. Emily found profound purpose in motherhood, often sharing stories of Michael with her child, keeping his spirit alive in their daily lives.

Professionally, Emily's commitment to teaching and art began to bear fruit. She participated in a city-wide art exhibition, a prestigious event that celebrated local talent. Her submission, a series of paintings inspired by her journey through grief and healing, garnered critical acclaim. This recognition was more than a professional accolade; it was a personal victory, showcasing her ability to transform adversity into art.

In her personal life, Emily gradually opened herself to new experiences. She attended social gatherings, finding joy in moments of companionship and laughter. While the prospect of romantic love still seemed distant, she learned to appreciate the various forms of love and support that surrounded her.

As this part of her life unfolded, Emily stood at a significant crossroads. The mystery of Michael's disappearance remained, a story without closure. Yet, she had reached a place of acceptance where the absence of answers no longer consumed her. She had learned to live with the questions, finding a semblance of peace in the unknown.

# Chapter 4: Shattered Illusions

Emily's discovery of Michael's secret life came as a shock that shattered her world. It was a mundane Tuesday when the truth unveiled itself. While scrolling through social media, a mutual friend's post caught her eye. There, in a candid photograph, was Michael, unmistakably older yet familiar, his arm wrapped around a woman she didn't recognize. The caption read, "Celebrating Michael and Clara's first anniversary!" The image, so jarringly normal yet inconceivable, sent a wave of disbelief coursing through her.

The initial shock gave way to a torrent of emotions. Confusion reigned supreme, followed closely by a sense of betrayal so profound it took her breath away. Questions raced through her mind. How? Why? Was their entire relationship a lie? The life they had built, the dreams they had shared, now seemed like a fragile illusion, easily discarded.

Emily's thoughts turned to Clara, the woman beside Michael. Who was she? How had their paths crossed? The need for answers consumed her, leading her down a rabbit hole of online searches. She discovered Clara was an artist, like herself, but from a different city. Their social media profiles painted a picture of a life that paralleled the one she had lived with Michael. There were photos of trips, celebrations, and quiet domestic moments, all eerily similar to her own memories with him.

The revelation that Michael had not only left but had built a life with another woman was a blow that resonated through every aspect of Emily's life. Her home, filled with remnants of their shared past, now felt like a museum of a life that was never truly hers. The art they had created together, once a source of pride, now mocked her from the walls.

In the days that followed, Emily grappled with a myriad of emotions. Anger surged through her, a righteous indignation at the deceit and the years stolen from her. Yet, beneath the anger lay a deep, pervasive sadness. The man she had loved, the father of her child, was a stranger, his actions eroding the foundation of their shared history.

Her friends and family rallied around her, offering support and comfort. They listened as she poured out her heart, her words a mix of grief and disbelief. They offered advice, some suggesting legal action, others advocating for emotional closure. But for Emily, no words could soothe the sting of betrayal; no advice could navigate her through this labyrinth of pain.

As she processed this new reality, Emily's role as a mother became her anchor. Her child, innocent and unaware of the turmoil, provided a sense of purpose amidst the chaos. She found strength in her child's laughter, a balm for her wounded heart. Her resolve to protect and nurture her child became a guiding light, pulling her through the darkest moments.

Professionally, Emily's work began to reflect her inner turmoil. Her art, once vibrant and full of life, took on a darker, more introspective tone. She poured her emotions onto the canvas, each stroke a release of the pain and confusion that engulfed her. Her students, sensing a change, responded with their own creativity, their art becoming a dialogue of shared human experiences.

In her personal life, Emily withdrew from social engagements, finding it difficult to face the world with her newfound burden. The trust she had placed in Michael had been a cornerstone of her identity, and its collapse left her questioning her judgment, her worthiness of love, and the very nature of trust itself.

As weeks turned into months, Emily's journey through this landscape of betrayal and pain was marked by small victories and setbacks. She sought therapy, a space where she could unravel her emotions without fear of judgment. The sessions were challenging, often leaving her emotionally drained, but they provided a framework to understand and process her feelings.

The path to healing was neither linear nor easy. There were days when anger and sadness threatened to overwhelm her and others when acceptance seemed within reach. Through it all, Emily clung to the love for her child and the support of those who stood by her, slowly piecing together the fragments of her shattered illusions.

As Emily navigated the turbulent waters of betrayal, her sense of self underwent a profound transformation. The revelation of Michael's duplicity not only shattered her trust in him but also sparked a deep introspection about her own identity. She began to question the choices she had made, the signs she might have ignored, and the parts of herself she had lost or compromised in the name of love.

This period of self-reflection was painful yet necessary. Emily delved into her past, revisiting the early days of her relationship with Michael. She recalled the red flags she had dismissed, the subtle inconsistencies in his stories, and the times she had rationalized his absences. With the clarity of hindsight, these memories took on new meanings, revealing a pattern of deception she had been too in love to recognize.

Amidst this painful reckoning, Emily found solace in her art. Her studio became her sanctuary, a place where she could express her inner turmoil without words. The canvases bore witness to her journey, each piece a testament to her evolving emotions. Her art, once characterized by bright colors and bold strokes, now explored the darker shades of the human experience. It was through this creative process that she began to reclaim parts of herself that had been overshadowed by her relationship with Michael.

Emily's relationship with her child also deepened during this time. She became fiercely protective, determined to provide a stable and loving environment amidst the personal chaos. Her child's innocence and unconditional love were a constant reminder of the purity and resilience of the human spirit. In her child's eyes, she saw hope, a future untainted by the past's shadows.

The support of her friends and family was invaluable during this period. They provided a safety net, catching her when she faltered and celebrating her small victories. Their unwavering presence helped Emily slowly rebuild her trust in others, a process that was both challenging and healing.

As the months passed, Emily's journey of self-discovery led her to new understandings. She recognized the strength that lay in vulnerability and the importance of setting boundaries. She learned to forgive herself for the choices she had made in love, understanding that blame and regret would only anchor her to the past.

Professionally, Emily's art began to gain recognition for its raw, emotional depth. Galleries showed interest, and her work resonated with those who had experienced similar heartaches. This professional validation was a bittersweet reminder of the growth that often comes from pain.

In her personal life, Emily cautiously reopened herself to the idea of new relationships. She understood that trust would be a slow process, a journey of small steps and setbacks. But she also recognized the importance of remaining open to love despite the risks it entailed.

As the seasons changed, so did Emily. The pain of betrayal, though still a part of her, began to transform into a source of strength and wisdom. She emerged from this chapter of her life with a deeper understanding of herself, a renewed sense of purpose, and a cautious optimism for the future. Her heart, once shattered, was slowly mending, its cracks a testament to her resilience and capacity for growth.

In this phase of her journey, Emily's focus shifted towards healing and empowerment. She embraced activities and pursuits that fostered her individual growth, distancing herself from the shadow of Michael's betrayal. This period was marked by a series of small yet significant steps that collectively symbolized her path to recovery and self-discovery.

Emily's relationship with her child remained the cornerstone of her existence. She found immense joy and purpose in motherhood, cherishing each moment spent with her child. Their bond, strengthened by the trials they had faced, became a source of constant comfort and motivation for Emily. She dedicated herself to being a role model, instilling values of resilience, honesty, and compassion in her child.

Simultaneously, Emily sought to expand her social circle beyond the confines of past associations linked to Michael. She joined local community groups, attended art workshops, and participated in events that aligned with her interests. These new connections brought fresh perspectives and experiences into her life, helping her to rebuild her sense of community and belonging.

Professionally, Emily's art continued to evolve. She experimented with new mediums and techniques, pushing the boundaries of her creativity. Her work, reflective of her personal journey, garnered attention for its authenticity and emotional depth. Exhibitions and collaborations with other artists opened up new avenues for her career, providing a sense of accomplishment and independence.

In this process of rebuilding her life, Emily also embarked on a journey of self-care and wellness. She recognized the importance of looking after her mental and physical health, especially in the wake of the emotional turmoil she had experienced. Yoga, meditation, and nature walks became regular practices, offering her moments of tranquility and reflection.

As she healed, Emily began to reflect on her past relationship with a newfound clarity. She acknowledged the lessons learned and the strength gained from her experiences. This introspection led to a gradual release of anger and resentment towards Michael, as she understood that holding onto these emotions only hindered her progress.

Emily's transformation was not just internal. Her friends and family noticed a visible change in her demeanor. She carried herself with quiet confidence, a testament to the inner peace she was cultivating. Her laughter, once rare and restrained, became more frequent and genuine, echoing the joy she was rediscovering in her life.

During this period, Emily also revisited her passion for teaching. She returned to the classroom with a renewed sense of purpose, sharing her love for art with her students. Her experiences enriched her teaching, allowing her to connect with her students on a deeper level. She became a mentor and a source of inspiration for young minds, encouraging them to express themselves through art.

As the year drew to a close, Emily found herself reflecting on the journey she had undertaken. The pain of betrayal had been transformed into a journey of self-discovery and growth. She had navigated through the darkest of times to emerge stronger and more self-aware. The future, once a source of uncertainty and fear, now held promise and potential.

Emily's story was one of resilience, a narrative of overcoming adversity and finding strength in vulnerability. Her journey was a testament to the human spirit's ability to heal and grow, even in the aftermath of profound betrayal. As she looked forward to the new year, Emily felt a sense of hope and excitement for the chapters yet to be written in her life's story.

# Chapter 5: Downward Spiral

Emily's life, once full of stability and contentment, began to unravel in a series of unfortunate events. The first blow came unexpectedly when she received a notice of eviction. The apartment building, her home for years and a sanctuary for her and her child was to be demolished for new development. The news struck Emily like a physical blow, leaving her reeling in disbelief and uncertainty.

In the weeks that followed, Emily scrambled to find a new home. Her search was fraught with challenges, exacerbated by her limited budget and the need for a child-friendly environment. Each rejection added to her growing sense of despair. The stability she had worked so hard to build for her child seemed to be slipping away, piece by piece.

Amidst this turmoil, another misfortune struck. Emily's car, an old model that had faithfully served her for years, broke down beyond repair. The cost of fixing it was exorbitant, far beyond her dwindling savings. The loss of her car meant more than just a mode of transportation; it was a lifeline to her job, her child's school, and the semblance of normalcy she desperately tried to maintain.

These twin calamities plunged Emily into a state of constant anxiety. She found herself struggling to cope with the new reality, each day a battle against rising tides of despair. Her once orderly life was now marked by chaos and uncertainty, leaving her emotionally and physically drained.

The impact of these events was not just logistical but deeply emotional. Emily's sense of independence, a trait she had always prided herself on, was now in jeopardy. The prospect of relying on others for basic needs like transportation and housing was a bitter pill to swallow. It challenged her self-perception and forced her to confront vulnerabilities she had long kept at bay.

Her role as a mother added an additional layer of pressure. Emily's primary concern was the well-being and stability of her child. She grappled with feelings of guilt and inadequacy, fearing that she was failing as a parent. The bright, carefree laughter of her child, once a source of joy, now served as a poignant reminder of the security she struggled to provide.

In her professional life, Emily's challenges began to seep into her teaching. She found it increasingly difficult to maintain her usual level of engagement and enthusiasm in the classroom. Her students, sensitive to the change, responded with a mix of concern and confusion. Emily, who had always been a pillar of strength and inspiration for her students, now found herself on shaky ground, struggling to impart lessons she herself was grappling with.

Financial strain compounded her emotional turmoil. With each passing day, Emily's savings dwindled, consumed by the costs of daily living and the search for a new home. She began to cut back on non-essential expenses, but the financial pressure continued to mount. The fear of not being able to provide for her child's basic needs loomed large, casting a shadow over her every decision.

Amidst this chaos, Emily's social support network became both a blessing and a challenge. Friends and family offered help, but Emily found it difficult to accept assistance. Her pride and desire for independence often clashed with the practical need for support. This internal struggle only added to her emotional burden, creating a sense of isolation at a time when she needed connection the most.

As Emily navigated this tumultuous period, her resilience was tested in ways she had never imagined. The downward spiral seemed relentless, each day bringing new challenges and setbacks. Yet, in the depths of despair, Emily clung to a flicker of hope, a belief that she would find a way to rise above the trials and rebuild the life she and her child deserved. This belief, fragile yet unyielding, was her beacon in the darkest of times.

In the ensuing weeks, Emily's situation grew increasingly dire. The deadline for vacating her apartment loomed, yet she had not secured a new residence. Each day was a relentless cycle of searching for affordable housing, juggling her teaching responsibilities, and caring for her child. The stress was unrelenting, casting a shadow over her once vibrant spirit.

Emily's interactions with her friends and family began to change. She withdrew, feeling a mix of shame and frustration at her circumstances. Invitations to social gatherings were declined; phone calls and messages were often left unanswered. Emily, once the heart of her social circle, now found solace in solitude, a place where her struggles remained unseen.

Her professional life also suffered. Emily's once exemplary teaching performance faltered. Lesson plans, once crafted with meticulous care, were now put together hastily. Her students' artwork, which she used to praise with genuine enthusiasm, received only cursory attention. The school administration took notice, expressing concern over her well-being and the noticeable shift in her performance.

Financial pressures reached a breaking point. Emily sold most of her valuables, including some cherished art supplies, to cover living expenses. She started taking public transportation, a time-consuming endeavor that added hours to her daily commute. Her life became a constant battle against time, money, and the overwhelming sense of being trapped in a situation with no clear way out.

Amidst these hardships, Emily's role as a mother became her sole source of strength. Her child's laughter was a balm to her weary soul, a reminder of what truly mattered. She shielded her child from the harsh realities, maintaining a facade of normalcy. Bedtime stories were still read with the same tenderness, and mornings were greeted with a forced smile, hiding her inner turmoil.

However, the strain of her circumstances was not lost on her child. Children, with their innate sensitivity, can sense when something is amiss. Her child's once carefree demeanor began to mirror Emily's anxiety, manifesting in quietness and a reluctance to leave her side. This change in her child was perhaps the most painful blow for Emily, a stark reminder of the impact her situation had on the most important person in her life.

As the eviction date approached, Emily's sense of desperation grew. She visited numerous apartments, but each one was either too expensive or unsuitable for a child. The reality of possibly having to stay in a shelter became increasingly likely, a prospect that filled her with dread and fear.

In a final attempt to secure housing, Emily reached out to a distant relative, an aunt she hadn't spoken to in years. The call was difficult, her pride battling against the necessity of her situation. Her aunt, surprised by the call, listened with a mix of concern and hesitation. She offered Emily and her child a temporary place to stay, a small room in her suburban home. It was far from ideal, but it was a refuge from the imminent threat of homelessness.

Accepting this offer was a humbling experience for Emily. It meant uprooting her child from their familiar surroundings and admitting to her own inability to solve her problems alone. Yet, this decision marked a turning point. It was an acknowledgment of her vulnerability and a step towards accepting help, however difficult that might be.

As Emily packed her belongings, a mix of relief and sorrow washed over her. The life she had known was being packed away in boxes, a tangible representation of her loss and upheaval. Yet, in this moment of profound change, Emily found a glimmer of resilience within herself, a determination to rebuild her life from the ashes of her shattered illusions. This resilience, though tested and weary, was the ember that she clung to, a promise to herself and her child that they would rise again.

During her stay at her aunt's house, Emily's life took on a starkly different rhythm. The once familiar landscape of the city was replaced by the quiet, monotonous suburbs. Her days were filled with job searches, long commutes to work, and the constant challenge of adapting to a new environment. The comfort of her own home, with its cherished memories and personal touch, was now a distant memory.

The small room they occupied at her aunt's house was cramped but clean. Emily tried to make it feel like home, decorating it with a few personal items she had managed to keep. Her child seemed to adjust better than she had anticipated, finding joy in the small backyard and the new surroundings. This adaptability, often inherent in children, was a source of comfort for Emily.

Financial constraints continued to be a pressing issue. Emily's salary as a teacher was barely enough to cover their basic needs. She often found herself calculating every expense, cutting corners wherever possible. The lack of financial freedom was stifling, a constant reminder of her precarious situation.

Her social interactions dwindled to almost nothing. Conversations with colleagues were brief and focused on work. The vibrant social life she once enjoyed seemed like a relic of a past life. Her friends, though sympathetic, could not fully grasp the depth of her struggle. Emily felt isolated, trapped in a world where she was constantly battling to keep her head above water.

Amidst these challenges, Emily's bond with her child remained her beacon of hope. She found solace in their nightly routine – reading stories, sharing quiet conversations, and watching her child drift into sleep. These moments were a balm to her weary heart, a reminder of the love that remained constant in her life.

However, the stress of her situation began to take a toll on her health. Emily's sleep was often restless, plagued by worries and anxiety about the future. She lost weight, her face reflecting the fatigue that had become her constant companion. Her once vibrant energy was now replaced by quiet, persistent exhaustion.

The school where she taught became her only escape from the harsh realities of her personal life. She poured her energy into her work, finding a sense of purpose in her students' progress and creativity. Yet, even at work, her thoughts were never far from her struggles, a silent undercurrent that colored every aspect of her life.

One particularly challenging day, Emily received a call from her child's school. Her child, usually well-behaved and cheerful, had gotten into a minor altercation with a classmate. This incident was out of character, and it shook Emily. It was a stark reminder of how her circumstances were affecting her child, an innocent bystander in the turmoil of their lives.

That evening, as Emily sat in the small room, her child asleep beside her, she allowed herself to truly feel the weight of her situation. Tears streamed down her face, a release of the pent-up emotions she had been holding back. In this moment of vulnerability, she allowed herself to grieve – for the loss of her relationship, her home, her sense of security, and the life she had envisioned for herself and her child.

Yet, amidst the grief, a flicker of determination remained. Emily knew she had to find a way out of this downward spiral, not just for her sake but for her child's as well. She resolved to take small, tangible steps towards rebuilding their lives. This resolution, born out of her darkest moment, was a testament to her resilience, a quality that had been tested time and again but remained unbroken. It was this resilience that would become the foundation upon which she would start to rebuild, slowly but surely, a new life for herself and her child.

# Chapter 6: Unveiling the Past

In the unfolding narrative, attention shifts to Michael and the history he shared with Clara. Their story, though less tumultuous than Emily's current predicament, held its own complexities and secrets. Michael and Clara's relationship, spanning over a decade, was marked by its own set of trials and tribulations.

Michael met Clara during his college years. She was a year his junior, studying art history, a subject that fascinated Michael despite his major in business. Their initial encounters were casual, often in the bustling university cafeteria or at mutual friends' gatherings. However, as time progressed, their interactions grew more frequent and intimate.

Clara was different from anyone Michael had known. Her passion for art was infectious, and her perspective on life was refreshingly unconventional. She challenged Michael's views, making him question his own beliefs and aspirations. It was this intellectual stimulation, coupled with a growing emotional connection, that drew Michael closer to Clara.

Their relationship blossomed swiftly. They shared a love for quiet evenings, discussing everything from art to philosophy, often losing track of time. These moments forged a deep bond between them, a connection that seemed unbreakable. After graduation, they decided to move in together, a step that felt natural given the intensity of their relationship.

Two years into their cohabitation, Clara announced her pregnancy. The news was unexpected, and it sent ripples through their relationship. Michael, though initially shocked, embraced the idea of fatherhood with cautious optimism. Clara, however, was apprehensive, fearing that motherhood might impede her aspirations as an artist.

Despite these fears, they welcomed their first child, a daughter they named Lily. Lily's arrival brought a new dynamic to their relationship. Michael found himself juggling his burgeoning career with fatherhood, a balancing act that proved more challenging than he had anticipated. Clara, on the other hand, struggled with her new role as a mother. Her art took a backseat, a sacrifice that weighed heavily on her.

Four years later, they had a second child, a son named Ethan. Ethan's birth seemed to stabilize the family dynamic. Michael had advanced in his career, providing a comfortable life for his family. Clara, too, had found a way to reignite her passion for art, balancing her time between her children and her work.

However, beneath the surface of this seemingly idyllic family life, tensions simmered. Michael's career demanded more of his time, often leaving Clara to manage the household and the children's needs. Resentment began to build as Clara felt her own dreams and aspirations being overshadowed by Michael's career.

Their relationship, once marked by deep conversations and shared dreams, had evolved into a pragmatic partnership, focused more on the logistics of family life than on the emotional connection that had once defined them. This shift created a distance between them, a gap that widened with each passing year.

As Michael's absence in Emily's life became more pronounced, his home life with Clara and their children also began to unravel. The once strong bond he shared with Clara was now frayed, strained by years of unspoken grievances and neglected emotional needs.

In this backdrop, the story delves deeper into the complexities of Michael and Clara's relationship. It explores the challenges they faced as individuals and as a couple, shedding light on the circumstances that led to the current state of their marriage. This exploration serves as a crucial piece in understanding the intricate web of relationships and events that have shaped the lives of Emily, Michael, and Clara.

As the narrative delves deeper into Michael and Clara's past, the focus shifts to the underlying issues that gradually erode their once-strong bond. Their life, outwardly stable and content, was internally marred by growing disconnect and unfulfilled aspirations.

Clara, once a vibrant and ambitious art student, found herself increasingly confined within the roles of motherhood and domesticity. Her art, which was not just a passion but a vital part of her identity, took a backseat as family responsibilities grew. She watched as her dreams were slowly overshadowed by the demands of raising Lily and Ethan. This gradual sidelining of her aspirations created a simmering resentment towards Michael, who, in her eyes, had not sacrificed as much.

Michael, for his part, was largely oblivious to Clara's growing discontent. Engrossed in his career, he viewed his professional success as a means to provide for his family, unaware that his prolonged absences were contributing to a widening rift. He mistook Clara's quiet acquiescence for contentment, not realizing the depth of her unspoken frustrations.

The birth of their children, while a source of joy, also brought new challenges. Lily, a spirited and curious child, demanded constant attention, her inquisitive nature often leaving Clara exhausted. Ethan, quieter and more introspective, required a different approach, often feeling overshadowed by his older sister's vibrant personality. Clara, juggling the needs of two very different children, often felt overwhelmed, her own identity slipping further away with each passing day.

As the children grew, so did the distance between Michael and Clara. Their conversations, once filled with dreams and intellectual debates, became transactional and focused on the logistics of daily life. Romantic gestures and shared laughter became rare, replaced by a functional coexistence. The couple, once inseparable, now lived parallel lives under the same roof.

This growing chasm was not lost on Lily and Ethan. They sensed the tension, the lack of warmth that had once defined their family. Lily, in her teenage years, became more rebellious, often challenging her parents and seeking solace in her friends and hobbies. Ethan, more sensitive to the undercurrents of discord, retreated into his own world, finding comfort in books and solitary activities.

Amidst this familial discord, Michael's chance encounter with Emily offered an escape, a reminder of a life unburdened by the weight of unmet expectations and silent resentments. Emily, with her passion for art and her refreshing outlook on life, mirrored the younger Clara, reigniting a spark that Michael thought had long been extinguished.

This affair, however, was not just a simple escape for Michael but a manifestation of his own unaddressed desires and frustrations. He found in Emily a listener, someone who seemed to understand and appreciate him in ways he felt Clara no longer did. This emotional connection, coupled with the physical attraction, led him down a path that would eventually cause immense pain and upheaval.

As the story unfolds, the complexities of Michael's relationships with Clara and Emily become increasingly evident. His actions, driven by a mix of escapism and a quest for lost parts of himself, set in motion a series of events that would have far-reaching consequences for everyone involved. The narrative thus paints a picture of a man caught between his past and present, his responsibilities and desires, leading to choices that would alter the lives of those closest to him.

Michael's history with Clara, once shrouded in mystery, gradually comes into sharper focus. Years before his serendipitous meeting with Emily, Michael and Clara's marriage had already begun to fray at the seams. Clara, once a vibrant artist, had slowly receded into the shadows of their family life, her canvases gathering dust, her dreams shelved amidst the demands of motherhood and domesticity.

The turning point came on a particularly tense evening. Clara, overwhelmed by a sense of loss for her forgotten art, confronted Michael. Her voice, usually calm and measured, trembled with a mixture of anger and despair. "You never see me!" she exclaimed, her words echoing through the walls of their home. "Not as I am now, not as the artist I used to be. I'm just a shadow in your life, Michael."

Michael, stunned, could barely muster a response. He had always considered himself a supportive husband, but Clara's outburst laid bare the painful truth. He had been so engrossed in his own world that he had failed to notice Clara's growing unhappiness. That night, as Clara's sobs filled the silence, Michael realized the extent of the emotional chasm that had developed between them.

In the days that followed, Michael attempted to bridge the gap. He encouraged Clara to return to her art, promising to shoulder more responsibilities at home. Clara, initially hesitant, gradually found her way back to her easel. The smell of oil paint and turpentine began to permeate their home once again, a reminder of the woman she once was.

But the years of emotional neglect had taken their toll. Clara's return to art provided a temporary solace, but it could not fully heal the rift that had grown between them. Their conversations, once filled with shared dreams and laughter, now felt strained, the silences longer and more frequent.

Their children, Lily and Ethan, responded in their own ways to the changing dynamics at home. Lily's behavior became more rebellious, her actions a reflection of the turmoil she sensed within the family. Ethan, quieter and more sensitive, tried in his own way to mend the fraying threads of their family fabric, often feeling helpless in the face of his parents' growing distance.

It was during this period of quiet familial disintegration that Michael's path crossed with Emily's. His affair with Emily was not just a betrayal of his marital vows but also an escape from the complexities of his life with Clara. Emily represented a breath of fresh air, a connection untainted by the disappointments and routine of his marriage.

Michael's relationship with Emily, though deeply flawed, was a manifestation of his unmet emotional needs and a longing for a part of himself that he felt he had lost. This affair, while providing a temporary escape, set in motion a series of events that would eventually bring the hidden fractures of his life with Clara to the surface.

As the story of Michael and Clara's past unfolds, it paints a picture of a marriage caught in the web of unspoken grievances and unfulfilled dreams. The revelation of Michael's affair with Emily and its impact on the family adds a layer of complexity to the narrative, highlighting the intricate and often painful interplay of human relationships and choices.

In the wake of the revelations, Clara, with Lily and Ethan in tow, departs from the home she shared with Michael. Her decision, though heart-wrenching, emanates from a deep need for self-preservation and a desire to shield her children from further emotional turmoil. The house, once brimming with familial warmth, stands silent, a stark testament to the consequences of Michael's duplicity.

Clara finds solace in her parent's home, a haven where she attempts to mend the emotional fractures within herself and her children. Lily's anger and confusion manifest in her rebellious behavior, challenging Clara's already strained resilience. Ethan, quieter, internalizes his pain, his youthful innocence clouded by the family's upheaval.

Meanwhile, Michael confronts profound loneliness in the empty house. The absence of his family's presence is a constant reminder of the cost of his actions. His thoughts frequently drift to Emily, the other victim of his deceit. He grapples with guilt, realizing the depth of the pain he has inflicted on both families.

Emily, on the other hand, navigates through a storm of betrayal. The revelation of Michael's other life shatters her trust and the future she had envisioned. She finds herself questioning the authenticity of every moment they shared, each memory now tainted with the sting of deception.

In this turmoil, Michael reaches out to Emily, seeking forgiveness and a chance to explain. But Emily, engulfed in her sense of betrayal, is not ready to hear his apologies or excuses. She cuts off all communication, leaving Michael to stew in his own remorse.

Clara, in her quest for healing, begins attending therapy sessions. She encourages Lily and Ethan to join her, hoping to provide them with a space to voice their feelings and begin the process of healing. Slowly, through these sessions, the family starts to untangle the web of emotions that the revelation has spun around them.

Lily's rebelliousness begins to wane as she starts to understand the complexities of adult relationships and the pain of betrayal. Ethan, through therapy, finds a way to express his confusion and hurt, gradually coming out of his shell.

As for Emily, the path to recovery is solitary but necessary. She immerses herself in her art, using it as a conduit for her emotions. Her paintings become more profound, reflecting the turmoil and eventual acceptance of her situation. Friends and family rally around her, providing support and strength.

Michael, left to reflect on the ruins of his choices, begins a journey of self-discovery. He seeks therapy, confronting the reasons behind his actions and the impact they have had on those he loved.

Through this introspective journey, he starts to understand the gravity of his mistakes and learns to live with the consequences.

# Chapter 7: Gathering Storm

Emily, her heart still heavy with the weight of betrayal, resolves to seek answers. She can no longer remain in the shadows of uncertainty and confusion. Her journey for truth leads her to the quaint, bustling streets of her hometown, where memories lurk around every corner.

In this familiar yet altered landscape, Emily encounters Ava, an old friend from high school. Ava, now a vibrant figure in the local LGBTQ community, runs a cozy bookstore-café hybrid, a haven for those seeking solace in literature and warm conversation. Their reunion, filled with nostalgia and new revelations, rekindles their friendship. Ava becomes a pillar of support for Emily, offering a listening ear and insightful perspectives.

As Emily delves deeper into her quest for understanding, she uncovers layers of her own past. She revisits places that hold significance to her and Michael's relationship, each location a piece in the puzzle of their shared history. These explorations lead her to unexpected encounters and revelations about Michael's life that she had been oblivious to.

Meanwhile, Ava's life presents a subplot of its own. She grapples with family dynamics that challenge her identity and choices. Her parents, traditional in their views, struggle to fully accept her sexuality. This conflict, juxtaposed with Emily's turmoil, adds depth to the narrative, showcasing diverse struggles and the quest for acceptance.

In parallel, Emily's interactions with her own family reveal strained relationships. Her parents, though loving, have always been distant, wrapped up in their own worlds. Her younger brother, Alex, emerges as a key character, his own life marred by challenges. Alex's journey, dealing with unemployment and a failing marriage, intersects with Emily's, creating a tapestry of familial complexities.

As Emily and Ava's friendship strengthens, they become confidantes, sharing not just their current predicaments but also their aspirations. Ava's resilience in the face of societal and familial pressures inspires Emily. She begins to see her own situation through a different lens, one that offers a glimmer of hope amidst despair.

The narrative weaves through these personal journeys, exploring themes of identity, acceptance, and the enduring power of friendship. Emily, through her interactions with Ava and her family, starts to piece together a clearer picture of her past with Michael and the reasons behind his deceit.

This part of the story, rich with emotional depth and character development, sets the stage for further revelations and confrontations. Emily's quest for answers is not just about understanding Michael's actions but also about rediscovering herself and her place in a world that has drastically shifted beneath her feet.

As the storm of emotions and revelations gathers, Emily stands at the precipice of major decisions. Her journey, intertwined with the lives of those around her, promises to lead her to a place of greater understanding and, hopefully, peace.

Emily's world, once clouded by confusion and betrayal, began to brighten with the presence of Ava. Their conversations, often deep into the night, were a balm to Emily's wounded heart. Ava, with her own tales of struggle and triumph within the LGBTQ community, instilled in Emily a newfound resilience. It was as if Ava's strength seeped into Emily, urging her to view her challenges not as insurmountable obstacles but as pathways to personal growth.

During this transformative period, Leo entered Emily's life. A friend of Ava's, Leo's charisma was matched only by his insight. As a transgender man, he had navigated a complex journey towards self-acceptance, a journey that resonated deeply with Emily. His stories, filled with both pain and triumph, offered Emily a fresh perspective on identity and love.

Conversations with Leo prompted Emily to reflect on her own identity. She saw parallels between her quest for the truth about Michael and Leo's journey towards self-acceptance. This introspection marked the beginning of a significant transformation in Emily as she started to embrace the complexities of her own identity.

Meanwhile, Emily's family dynamics took a turn. Her brother Alex, struggling with his marriage, sought her advice. Their discussions unearthed long-standing family issues: communication barriers, unmet emotional needs, and a general sense of disconnect. These revelations shed light on Emily's upbringing, offering her a clearer understanding of the impact it had on her relationships.

As Emily navigated these personal journeys, she found herself at the heart of a healing process. She and her family began to address their past misunderstandings and grievances. This path of reconciliation mirrored Ava's efforts to balance her identity with her family's expectations.

Emily's bond with Ava and Leo grew stronger, evolving into a pillar of support and understanding. Their shared experiences, though diverse, created a foundation of trust and empathy. This support system enabled Emily to confront her feelings about Michael with newfound clarity.

The mosaic of Emily's life was becoming increasingly vivid. Each character's story, interwoven with hers, painted a complex picture of human experience. The challenges they faced, though varied, echoed universal themes of identity, acceptance, and belonging.

As Emily prepared to confront her past with Michael, she did so with a sense of clarity and strength, bolstered by the insights and support of her friends and family. This preparation marked a significant turning point, setting the stage for a confrontation that promised to be both revealing and transformative.

In her journey, Emily's world had transformed from a place of solitude and confusion to one rich with emotional depth and interconnected relationships. At the center of this narrative storm, she stood ready to face her past and embrace a future filled with understanding and hope.

Amidst her journey of self-discovery, Emily encountered Grace, a vibrant figure in the local LGBTQ community. Grace's story, marked by a relentless fight for acceptance and equality, resonated with Emily. Their conversations often revolved around the challenges of societal norms and the courage to defy them. Grace, with her unwavering spirit, became another beacon of inspiration for Emily.

As Emily's social circle expanded, she found herself increasingly involved in community events. These gatherings were not just celebrations of diversity but also platforms for advocacy and awareness. Emily, once a bystander in such discussions, now found herself actively participating, her voice growing stronger with each conversation.

Simultaneously, Emily's relationship with her family began to evolve. Her parents, initially distant and uncomprehending of her turmoil, started to show signs of empathy. This change was gradual, often punctuated by moments of misunderstanding, but it was progress nonetheless. Emily's newfound confidence allowed her to express her feelings more openly, bridging gaps that had long seemed insurmountable.

In these family gatherings, Emily noticed subtle shifts. Her mother, traditionally reserved, began to share stories of her own youth, revealing struggles Emily had never known. Her father, a man of few words, started to ask questions, genuinely interested in understanding his daughter's world. These moments, small yet significant, marked a turning point in their family dynamics.

Meanwhile, Emily's quest for answers about Michael continued. Her resolve to confront him was bolstered by the support of her friends and the newfound understanding within her family. She realized that this confrontation was not just about seeking answers but also about asserting her newfound sense of self.

As the day of the confrontation approached, Emily reflected on her journey. She thought of Ava's resilience, Leo's wisdom, Grace's passion, and her family's gradual acceptance. Each of these relationships had contributed to her growth, transforming her from a woman shrouded in confusion to one radiating strength and purpose.

The night before she was to meet Michael, Emily sat with her thoughts. She pondered over what she would say, how she would feel, and what revelations might come. This meeting, she knew, was more than a closure; it was a testament to her journey, a culmination of her struggles and triumphs.

In this reflective state, Emily realized that regardless of the outcome, she had already emerged victorious. She had navigated through a storm of emotions, faced her fears, and had come out stronger. The Emily who would confront Michael was vastly different from the one who had been shattered by his disappearance.

As dawn broke, Emily stood before her mirror, a mix of anticipation and resolve in her eyes. Today, she would face her past, armed with the lessons of her present and the hopes for her future. This confrontation was not just an end to a chapter but the beginning of a new narrative in Emily's life, one where she was the author of her own story.

Emily's resolve to confront Michael was unwavering, yet as the day approached, a storm of emotions brewed within her. Each step she took felt like a journey through the chapters of her past, leading her to a crossroads of her future. She was no longer the person who had been left in the shadows of Michael's departure; she had emerged stronger and more self-aware.

On the eve of the confrontation, Emily found solace in the company of her friends. Ava, with her unyielding spirit, reminded Emily of the strength she had within. Leo, ever the voice of reason, provided a calming perspective, ensuring Emily's emotions did not cloud her judgment. Grace, with her infectious optimism, instilled a sense of hope. These friends, once strangers, had become her pillars of support.

As they gathered around, sharing stories and laughter, Emily felt a sense of belonging. This was her chosen family, a tapestry of souls woven together by shared experiences and mutual respect. Their presence was a reminder of the diverse paths that had converged in her journey, each adding color and depth to her life.

In these moments of camaraderie, Emily's thoughts drifted to her family. The recent thaw in their relationship had brought a gentle warmth to her heart. She pondered on the intricate dynamics that defined families, the unspoken bonds that could withstand the tests of time and turmoil. Her family's gradual acceptance was a balm to her long-held wounds.

The night deepened, and the conversations mellowed. Emily found herself reflecting on the myriad emotions that had led her to this point. Anger, betrayal, sorrow, and confusion had been her companions, but now, they were joined by understanding, forgiveness, and hope. This emotional tapestry was complex, yet it was hers, a testament to her resilience.

As her friends departed, each leaving behind words of encouragement, Emily felt a surge of gratitude. Life had thrown her into turbulent waters, but it had also provided her with lifelines, unexpected yet steadfast. She realized that every encounter, every challenge, had been a stepping stone, leading her to this very moment.

Alone with her thoughts, Emily contemplated the upcoming confrontation with Michael. This was not just about seeking answers or closure; it was about reclaiming her narrative. She was no longer a character in Michael's story; she was the protagonist of her own.

The night gave way to a pensive dawn. Emily stood at her window, watching the first light of daybreak on the horizon. Today, she would face Michael, not as a victim of his actions, but as a survivor of her own journey. She was ready to close this chapter, not with bitterness, but with the dignity and grace of someone who had traversed through darkness and emerged into light.

With a deep breath, Emily stepped away from the window. She was ready to face the day, ready to face Michael. This meeting was more than a confrontation; it was a declaration of her newfound self, a celebration of her journey from the shadows of betrayal to the light of self-discovery. Today, Emily would not just confront Michael; she would confront her past, ready to embrace her future with open arms.

The day of reckoning had arrived. Emily's heart raced as she approached the café where she would finally confront Michael. Each step felt heavy yet purposeful, a physical manifestation of the emotional journey she had traversed. The café, once a haven of shared memories, now stood as a battleground for truth and closure.

Inside, she spotted Michael, his presence instantly reigniting a myriad of emotions. He looked up, his expression a mix of surprise and apprehension. Emily steadied herself, drawing strength from the resolve that had been simmering within her. This was her moment, a culmination of pain, growth, and resilience.

As they sat, an uneasy silence enveloped them. Emily's eyes once filled with affection for Michael, now bore the weight of betrayal and disappointment. Michael's gaze, evasive at first, slowly met hers. At that moment, Emily realized the power dynamics had shifted; she was no longer the one left in the dark, seeking answers.

The conversation began tentative and fraught with tension. Emily's voice, firm yet measured, conveyed her quest for truth. She recounted the pain of his disappearance, the agony of not knowing, and the betrayal she felt upon discovering his life with Clara. Her words were not just a recounting of events; they were an articulation of her shattered trust and the strength it took to rebuild herself.

Michael's responses were a mix of apologies, explanations, and admissions. He spoke of his own confusion, his struggles, and the choices that led him down this path. Yet, as he spoke, Emily realized that his words, no matter how sincere, could not undo the past. They were mere echoes of a relationship that had crumbled under the weight of deceit.

As the conversation delved deeper, Emily introduced the narratives of her friends and family, highlighting how their support had been her anchor. She spoke of Ava's unwavering support, Leo's wise counsel, and Grace's optimism. She shared the journey of reconnecting with her family, the slow healing of old wounds, and the acceptance that had brought them closer.

In these revelations, Michael saw not just the woman he had left but the person Emily had become. Strong, self-assured, and surrounded by a community of love and support. He realized that Emily sitting before him was no longer defined by their past but was the architect of her own future.

As the conversation drew to a close, Emily felt a sense of catharsis. This was not a fairy-tale ending, nor was it a reconciliation. It was an acknowledgment of the past and a release from its hold. She stood up, her heart lighter, her spirit unburdened. She had sought answers and, in doing so, had found her peace.

Emily walked out of the café, not with the gait of someone who had lost, but with the stride of someone who had triumphed over her own trials. The sky above was a canvas of twilight hues, reflecting the storm that had passed and the calm that now reigned.

As she walked away, Emily knew that this chapter of her life was complete. Ahead lay a path of new beginnings, uncharted yet promising. She stepped forward, not as a victim of her past, but as a victor of her present, ready to embrace whatever the future held with courage, dignity, and an open heart.

# Chapter 8: Crossroads

Emily stood outside the café, her mind a whirlwind of thoughts and emotions. The confrontation with Michael had been both cathartic and unsettling, leaving her at a crossroads in her life. The evening air was crisp, a gentle reminder of the changing seasons, much like the changes she was experiencing in her own life.

As she walked, the rhythmic sound of her footsteps on the pavement echoed the tumultuous beat of her heart. The conversation with Michael had closed a painful chapter, yet it opened a myriad of questions about her future. What path should she take now? The comfort of the familiar or the uncertainty of new beginnings?

Her mind wandered back to the café, to the moment she had stood up to leave. There was a finality in that action, a silent declaration of her newfound strength and independence. Yet, as she moved forward, the shadows of doubt and fear loomed large. Could she truly leave behind the remnants of her past and forge a new identity?

The city around her was alive with the buzz of evening activity. People hurried past, lost in their own worlds, oblivious to the internal struggle raging within Emily. She felt a kinship with the city, its vibrancy, and resilience mirroring her own journey.

As she continued her walk, her thoughts shifted to the people who had stood by her through her darkest times. Ava, with her unwavering support and wisdom; Leo, whose humor and insight had often been a balm to her wounded soul; Grace, whose optimism had been a constant source of inspiration. They had been her pillars, her guiding lights in the storm.

Yet, even with their support, Emily knew the journey ahead was hers alone to traverse. The decisions she made now would shape the course of her life. She pondered over her career, her passions, and her dreams. What did she truly want from life? The answer seemed to dance just beyond her grasp, a tantalizing glimpse of possibilities yet unexplored.

As she walked, the city lights cast long shadows on the streets, a visual metaphor for the impending conflicts she sensed on the horizon. Her relationship with her family, once strained, was now on the mend, but the path to complete healing was fraught with challenges. Her career, which had taken a backseat during her tumultuous relationship with Michael, now demanded her attention and dedication.

Moreover, there was the question of love and trust. Could she open her heart again after the betrayal she had experienced? The thought of venturing into new relationships was both exciting and terrifying. The scars of the past were still tender, yet the human heart's capacity for love and forgiveness was boundless.

As the night deepened, Emily found herself at a familiar park. The moon cast a gentle glow over the landscape, transforming the ordinary into something ethereal. She sat on a bench, and her gaze lost in the dance of the leaves in the gentle breeze. This place had always been a sanctuary for her, a space where she could think and dream.

Here, amidst the tranquility of nature, Emily allowed herself to contemplate her next steps. She envisioned a future where she was not defined by her past but empowered by it. A future where her dreams were not just fleeting thoughts but tangible goals.

Yet, in the quiet of the night, a sense of foreboding crept into her heart. She could not shake off the feeling that the peace she was experiencing was the calm before a storm. There were conflicts on the horizon, challenges that would test her resolve and her growth.

As she sat there, lost in thought, the night whispered its secrets. Emily knew that the crossroads she faced were not just about choosing a path but about embracing the journey, with all its twists and turns. The road ahead was uncertain, but she was ready to face it with courage and hope. For in the heart of the storm, she would find her true strength.

In the days that followed, Emily's resolve to forge a new path grew stronger. She spent hours revisiting her old sketches and designs, reigniting a passion for art that had been dimmed by life's trials. Each stroke of her brush on the canvas was a step towards reclaiming her identity, a declaration of her independence from the shadows of her past.

Her newfound determination also led her to reconnect with old colleagues and mentors. Conversations brimming with potential collaborations and opportunities rekindled her ambition. The art world, once a distant dream, now seemed within reach, a canvas awaiting her unique imprint.

However, this period of self-discovery was not without its challenges. Financial constraints, a lingering consequence of her past, loomed over her like a dark cloud. The loss of her car and eviction had left deep scars, reminders of how quickly life could unravel. She juggled part-time jobs, each a stepping stone towards stability, yet the path was fraught with uncertainty.

Amidst these personal battles, Emily found solace in her growing circle of friends. Ava, ever the confidante, provided not just emotional support but practical advice, helping Emily navigate the complexities of rebuilding her life. Leo, with his infectious enthusiasm, encouraged her to explore new avenues to see life through a lens of possibilities rather than limitations.

It was during a casual evening at Ava's apartment that Emily met Maya, a vibrant character with a story as compelling as her own. Maya, a transgender woman, shared her journey with a candor that resonated deeply with Emily. Her struggles, her triumphs, and her unyielding spirit in the face of adversity were both inspiring and humbling.

This encounter sparked a new subplot in Emily's life, one where the themes of acceptance, identity, and transformation took center stage. Conversations with Maya opened Emily's eyes to the diverse tapestry of human experiences, each thread a story of resilience and courage.

Meanwhile, Emily's family dynamics underwent a subtle transformation. Her parents, once distant and critical, began to show signs of understanding and support. Phone calls became more frequent, and the conversations less strained. It was a slow process, the mending of old wounds, but each small gesture of reconciliation was a step towards healing.

As Emily navigated these personal and professional crossroads, the narrative of her life grew more complex. The introduction of new characters, each with their own struggles and triumphs, added layers to her story, enriching it with their perspectives and experiences.

Yet, amidst this growth and change, the foreshadowing of impending conflicts was ever-present. The art world, with its allure and challenges, was a battlefield of its own. Competition was fierce, and success was as much about talent as it was about connections and timing.

Moreover, the specter of her past relationship with Michael lingered. The revelation of his marriage to Clara and the subsequent emotional turmoil had left a void, a sense of betrayal that was hard to shake off. The question of whether to confront him or to seek closure in other ways was a dilemma that weighed heavily on her mind.

As Emily stood at these crossroads, the choices before her were as daunting as they were exciting. Each decision, each step, was a thread in the tapestry of her life, weaving a story of resilience, growth, and the relentless pursuit of dreams. The path ahead was uncertain, but Emily was ready to embrace it, armed with hope, courage, and an unyielding spirit.

Emily's journey through the crossroads of her life brought her to a pivotal moment. She found herself at the threshold of a significant art exhibition, an event that could potentially launch her career to new heights. The gallery, bathed in soft, ambient light, was a haven for artists and art enthusiasts alike, a place where dreams and creativity converged.

As she mingled among the crowd, her eyes absorbing the myriad of colors and forms that adorned the walls, Emily felt a surge of belonging. Here, amidst the buzz of conversation and the clinking of glasses, her aspirations seemed tangible, within reach. Her own artwork, a series of abstract pieces reflecting her tumultuous journey, hung proudly, each canvas a testament to her resilience.

However, this moment of triumph was tinged with apprehension. The art world was a maelstrom of talent and ambition, where recognition was as elusive as it was coveted. Emily knew that the road ahead was fraught with challenges and that each opportunity was a stepping stone that required tenacity and perseverance.

Her thoughts were interrupted by the approach of a well-known art critic whose opinions could make or break careers. The critic's gaze lingered on Emily's work, a mix of scrutiny and curiosity. Their conversation, initially marked by formalities, gradually delved into a deeper discourse on art and expression. Emily found herself defending her artistic choices, her voice a blend of passion and vulnerability.

This encounter, though brief, left Emily with a profound realization. Her art was not just a reflection of her past but a dialogue with the present, a conversation that extended beyond the canvas. It was her voice in a world often too loud, a world where being heard was as important as the message itself.

Meanwhile, the narrative of Emily's life continued to evolve with the introduction of new characters. Among them was Chris, a fellow artist whose experiences as a gay man in a conservative community added yet another layer to the story. His friendship with Emily, forged through shared struggles and mutual respect, became a source of strength and inspiration.

Their conversations, often late into the night, were a blend of humor and depth, touching upon themes of identity, acceptance, and the pursuit of one's truth. Chris's journey, much like Maya's, was a beacon for Emily, a reminder that every path, though fraught with obstacles, was unique and worthy.

Back in the realm of her personal life, Emily's relationship with her family continued to mend. Her father, once a figure of authority and distance, began to show a softer side. He took an interest in her art, his questions a tentative bridge across years of misunderstanding. Her mother, too, seemed more receptive, her words less critical, more curious.

This gradual transformation in her family dynamics was a source of quiet comfort for Emily. It was a healing process, one that required patience and the willingness to embrace change, both in herself and in her loved ones.

As Emily navigated these various facets of her life, the narrative was rich with the interplay of emotions and experiences. Each character, each subplot, added depth to her story, painting a picture of a life in flux, a life being rebuilt piece by piece.

Yet, amidst this tapestry of change, the foreshadowing of impending conflicts remained. The art world, with its promise and perils, was a constant reminder of the challenges ahead. And the unresolved feelings towards Michael and the lingering sense of betrayal continued to cast a shadow over her newfound happiness.

With each step forward, Emily was acutely aware of the delicate balance she was striving to maintain. Her journey was a testament to the power of resilience, the beauty of self-discovery, and the unending quest for a place in the world. As she stood at this crossroads, the path ahead was shrouded in uncertainty, but her resolve to forge ahead, undeterred by the storms that lay in wait, remained unshaken.

In the heart of the bustling city, Emily found herself at a crossroads, both literally and metaphorically. The streets, alive with the hum of activity, mirrored the tumult within her. Each step she took was a dance with uncertainty, a negotiation with her own aspirations and fears.

Her recent successes in the art world had brought a sense of accomplishment, yet they also ushered in new challenges. The recognition she craved now felt like a double-edged sword, offering validation but also exposing her to scrutiny and doubt. Her artwork, once a sanctuary, had become a battleground where her deepest insecurities clashed with her boldest dreams.

Amidst this whirlwind of emotions, Emily's thoughts often drifted to Michael. The revelation of his marriage to Clara had left a wound that time had yet to heal. His presence, though absent, lingered like a shadow, a constant reminder of a betrayal that had reshaped her world. Yet, in the depths of her heart, a flicker of unresolved feelings persisted, complicating her journey toward closure.

As she navigated these turbulent waters, Emily found solace in her growing circle of friends and allies. Chris, with his unwavering support and insightful perspectives, had become a pillar in her life. Their conversations, rich with empathy and understanding, were a balm to her soul. Similarly, Maya's presence, a beacon of strength and resilience, inspired Emily to embrace her own vulnerabilities.

These relationships, each unique in their depth and significance, were more than mere companionships; they were reflections of Emily's own journey towards self-acceptance and growth. Through them, she learned the value of diverse experiences and the strength that comes from embracing one's truth.

However, the tranquility of these newfound connections was often disrupted by the undercurrents of impending conflicts. The art world, with its capricious nature, continued to be a source of both exhilaration and anxiety. Emily's rise in prominence brought not only opportunities but also rivalries and expectations that weighed heavily on her.

Moreover, the complexities of her family dynamics, though improving, remained a labyrinth of emotions and old wounds. Her parents' gradual acceptance and support were a welcome change, yet the journey towards complete understanding and reconciliation was far from over.

In this landscape of shifting realities, Emily's resolve was tested time and again. Each decision she made, each path she chose, was a step towards defining her identity and her place in the world. The crossroads she faced were not just about choosing between different directions but about reconciling the various facets of her life into a harmonious whole.

As this chapter of her life drew to a close, the foreshadowing of future conflicts and challenges was palpable. The art exhibition, a milestone in her career, was also a harbinger of the trials that lay ahead. The unresolved feelings for Michael, the complexities of her family and friendships, and the unpredictable nature of her artistic journey were threads that wove together the tapestry of her story.

Yet, amidst the uncertainty and the storms that loomed on the horizon, Emily's spirit remained undaunted. Her journey, marked by resilience and the pursuit of authenticity, was a testament to the enduring power of hope and the unyielding quest for self-discovery. As she stood at the crossroads, her eyes set on the future, Emily embraced the unknown with a heart full of courage and a mind open to the endless possibilities that lay ahead.

# Chapter 9: Unraveling Secrets

Emily's quest to unearth the hidden chapters of Michael's life led her down a path filled with unexpected twists and revelations. Her first clue surfaced during a seemingly mundane coffee shop encounter with an old acquaintance of Michael's. The conversation, initially light and superficial, took a sharp turn when Michael's past struggles with substance abuse were inadvertently revealed. This information struck Emily like a bolt of lightning, illuminating aspects of Michael's behavior that she had previously dismissed or misunderstood.

The more Emily probed into Michael's history, the more she uncovered about his tumultuous relationship with Clara. Their union, far from the idyllic partnership she had imagined, was marred by cycles of addiction and episodes of domestic violence. This stark revelation shattered Emily's perception of the man she had loved, replacing it with a complex, troubled figure.

As she delved deeper, Emily's understanding of Michael transformed. She learned of his repeated attempts to conquer his demons, each relapse into addiction more devastating than the last. These discoveries painted a portrait of a man in a constant battle with himself, a battle that had profound impacts on his relationships.

Amidst these personal revelations, Emily's professional life was undergoing its own transformation. Her art, once a source of solace, began to reflect the turmoil and complexity of her emotional journey. Her latest series, raw and unfiltered, resonated with an audience that found a connection to the vulnerability and truth in her work.

Despite her professional success, Emily's personal life felt increasingly isolated. The revelations about Michael created a chasm between her and the life she once knew. In this period of upheaval, the support of her friends became her anchor. Chris, always a reliable confidant, offered empathy and stability, while Maya provided a sense of solidarity and understanding.

Yet, the support of friends couldn't fully alleviate the loneliness that enveloped Emily. The path of discovery she walked was hers alone, each step revealing more about Michael's past and, inadvertently, about herself. With every uncovered secret, Emily faced her own vulnerabilities and fears, confronting the reality of a love that was far more complex than she had ever realized.

This journey was not just about piecing together Michael's past; it was about Emily redefining her own identity in the wake of these revelations. Each secret brought a painful clarity, forcing her to confront uncomfortable truths about herself and the nature of her relationship with Michael.

Through this process of discovery and self-reflection, Emily was not only uncovering the past but also shaping her future. She was learning to navigate the complexities of human relationships and her own inner landscape, a journey that was as much about healing as it was about understanding. In this quest for truth, Emily was slowly but surely laying the foundation for a new chapter in her life, one built on a deeper, more nuanced understanding of love, loss, and the resilience of the human spirit.

Emily's journey into the labyrinth of Michael's past continued, each revelation more unsettling than the last. Her discovery of his struggles with substance abuse and the volatile nature of his relationship with Clara had already shaken her, but what she learned next was even more disturbing. Through conversations with Michael's estranged friends and a few of Clara's acquaintances, Emily pieced together a narrative of domestic turmoil and emotional upheaval.

One evening, in a dimly lit corner of a local bar, Emily met with one of Michael's former colleagues, a man who had witnessed the deterioration of Michael's marriage first-hand. Over the course of their conversation, he painted a picture of a relationship fraught with tension, mistrust, and bouts of aggression. This insight into Michael's life was a far cry from the loving, gentle person Emily thought she knew. The colleague spoke of incidents where Michael's frustration had escalated into physical altercations, leaving Clara bruised and broken. These stories were a stark contrast to the Michael Emily had loved, a man she believed incapable of such violence.

As Emily absorbed these harrowing accounts, her sense of betrayal deepened. She grappled with feelings of anger and confusion, struggling to reconcile the Michael she had known with the man emerging from these stories. This internal conflict was exacerbated by her own experiences of vulnerability in the relationship, moments she had previously dismissed as insignificant but now saw in a different light.

Amidst this emotional turmoil, Emily's art became her refuge. Her studio, once a place of joy and creativity, transformed into a sanctuary where she could process her feelings. Her latest pieces were visceral, a raw expression of the pain and confusion she felt. The colors were darker, the strokes more aggressive, a reflection of the tumult in her heart.

In these moments of artistic expression, Emily found a semblance of peace. The act of creating allowed her to externalize her inner turmoil, giving form to emotions that were too complex to articulate. Her art became a dialogue between her past and present, a way to make sense of the chaos that had engulfed her life.

As Emily continued to navigate this storm of revelations, she found unexpected solace in her growing friendship with Maya. Maya's own experiences with loss and betrayal provided a shared ground, a mutual understanding that went beyond words. Their conversations, often late into the night, were a source of comfort and strength for Emily.

Through these interactions, Emily began to see her situation through a different lens. She realized that her journey was not just about uncovering Michael's secrets; it was about understanding the nature of human frailty and the capacity for change. This realization brought a new level of complexity to her feelings for Michael. She began to see him not just as a perpetrator of pain, but as a flawed individual grappling with his own demons.

This shift in perspective was not an absolution of Michael's actions, but rather an acknowledgment of the multifaceted nature of human behavior. Emily's journey was teaching her the difficult lesson that love and pain often coexist, intertwined in the complexities of human relationships. As she continued to unravel the threads of Michael's past, Emily was also weaving a new narrative for herself, one that embraced the full spectrum of human emotion and experience.

As Emily delved further into the tangled web of Michael's past, she encountered a myriad of emotions and revelations that challenged her understanding of their relationship. Her discovery of Michael's struggles with substance abuse and his turbulent marriage to Clara had already cast a shadow over her memories, but the deeper she probed, the more complex the picture became.

One afternoon, Emily found herself in the quiet confines of a local library, poring over old newspaper articles and public records. It was here that she stumbled upon a crucial piece of the puzzle – a police report detailing an incident of domestic violence involving Michael and Clara. The stark, factual language of the report sent a chill down her spine. It was one thing to hear about Michael's violent outbursts from others, but seeing it documented in black and white made it undeniably real.

This revelation forced Emily to confront the uncomfortable truth that the man she had loved was capable of causing great harm. She grappled with feelings of guilt and confusion, wondering how she could have been so blind to this side of him. The more she learned, the more she questioned her own judgment and the nature of her relationship with Michael.

Amidst this internal struggle, Emily's friendship with Maya continued to deepen. Maya's unwavering support and understanding provided a much-needed anchor in the storm. Their conversations, often filled with shared experiences and insights, became a source of strength and clarity for Emily.

During one such conversation, Maya shared her own story of overcoming a tumultuous relationship. Her words resonated with Emily, offering a glimpse of hope amidst the chaos. Maya's journey of healing and self-discovery inspired Emily to look beyond her current pain and envision a future where she could find peace and closure.

This newfound perspective was reflected in Emily's art. Her latest pieces were more introspective, exploring themes of resilience and transformation. The colors were brighter, the lines more fluid, symbolizing a shift from turmoil to tranquility. Her art became a visual diary, charting her journey from darkness into light.

As Emily continued to piece together the fragments of Michael's past, she also began to rebuild her own sense of self. She realized that her identity was not defined by her relationship with Michael but by her own strengths and vulnerabilities. This epiphany marked a turning point in her journey, a step towards reclaiming her independence and self-worth.

In parallel to Emily's personal growth, the narrative introduced a new subplot involving Maya's brother, Lucas, who was navigating his own challenges as a member of the LGBTQ community. Lucas's story added another layer of complexity to the narrative, exploring themes of identity, acceptance, and the search for belonging.

Lucas's struggles and triumphs mirrored Emily's in many ways, highlighting the universal nature of their experiences. Their stories, though different in context, were connected by a common thread of resilience and the human capacity for growth.

As Emily and Lucas's paths intersected, their friendship blossomed into a source of mutual support and understanding. Together, they navigated the complexities of their respective journeys, finding solace in their shared experiences and the knowledge that they were not alone in their struggles.

This convergence of paths not only enriched the narrative but also underscored the importance of community and connection in the face of adversity. As Emily and Lucas forged ahead, their stories became a testament to the power of human resilience and the enduring spirit of hope.

In the midst of her quest for truth, Emily encountered an unexpected ally in Clara's sister, Sophie. Sophie, having distanced herself from Clara and Michael due to their tumultuous relationship, reached out to Emily after learning of her investigation. Their meeting, in a quaint café tucked away in a serene corner of the city, opened a new chapter in Emily's search for answers.

Sophie's revelations about Michael and Clara's marriage were eye-opening. She spoke of the volatile dynamics, the constant battles, and the shadow of substance abuse that loomed large over their household. Her words painted a picture of a deeply troubled relationship, far removed from the idealized version that Emily had once believed in.

As Sophie recounted her experiences, Emily listened intently, her mind racing to connect the dots. She learned of incidents that had never made it to the public eye, of nights filled with arguments and days marked by a tense silence. Sophie's perspective added depth to Emily's understanding of Michael, revealing layers of complexity in his character and the life he had led.

This encounter left Emily with a mix of emotions. She felt a sense of solidarity with Sophie, yet also a profound sadness for the pain that both women had endured. The conversation was a stark reminder of the ripple effects of troubled relationships, affecting not just the individuals involved but also those around them.

Amidst these revelations, Emily's own journey of self-discovery continued. She found solace in her art, channeling her emotions into her paintings. Each stroke of her brush was a step towards healing, a way to process the myriad feelings that her investigation had unearthed.

Her latest series of paintings, inspired by her conversations with Sophie and Maya, were more than just art; they were visual narratives of struggle, resilience, and hope. They resonated with viewers, drawing them into a world where pain and beauty coexisted, where darkness gave way to light.

As Emily delved deeper into her art, she also found herself reconnecting with her family. Her relationship with her parents, strained in the past, began to mend. They offered support and understanding, acknowledging the challenges she had faced and admiring her courage in confronting them.

This rekindled family bond provided Emily with a newfound sense of belonging and stability. It was a reminder that, despite the trials and tribulations, she was not alone. Her family's presence was a comforting constant in the ever-changing landscape of her life.

Meanwhile, the subplot involving Lucas took a significant turn. He found himself at a crossroads, grappling with decisions that would shape his future. His story, paralleling Emily's, highlighted the universal themes of identity and self-acceptance.

Lucas's journey was a mirror to Emily's, each reflecting the other's struggles and triumphs. Their parallel paths underscored the interconnectedness of their experiences, weaving a tapestry of human emotion and resilience.

As the narrative progressed, Emily's and Lucas's stories converged, their lives intertwining in unexpected ways. Their shared experiences forged a bond that transcended their individual journeys, uniting them in their quest for understanding and acceptance.

This convergence of paths not only enriched their lives but also added depth to the narrative, creating a multifaceted tapestry of human experience. Their stories, though unique in their own right, were united by a common thread of resilience, hope, and the enduring power of the human spirit.

In the heart of the night, Emily sat alone in her dimly lit room, surrounded by the scattered pages of Michael's journals. Each word she read unraveled more of the man she once believed she knew. His confessions, scribbled in a hurried hand, spoke of a life marred by shadows, a stark contrast to the Michael she had loved.

Outside, the world was silent, but inside, Emily's mind was a cacophony of emotions. She felt betrayed, yet her heart ached for the pain that Michael had endured in solitude. The revelations about his struggles with substance abuse and the cycle of domestic violence he couldn't escape painted a harrowing picture.

Amidst the chaos of her thoughts, Emily's eyes fell upon a series of entries about a night that changed everything. Michael had written about an altercation, a night where things had spiraled out of control, leading to tragic consequences. The details were murky, but the remorse in his words was palpable.

As dawn broke, Emily knew she couldn't carry the weight of these revelations alone. She reached out to Lucas, seeking solace in his understanding. Over cups of steaming coffee, she shared the contents of the journals. Lucas listened, his expression a mix of shock and empathy.

Their conversation took a turn when Lucas shared his own struggles, his journey of coming out to his family, and the challenges he faced in finding his place in the world. His story, though different, resonated with Emily. It was a reminder of the diverse tapestries of human experience, each thread interwoven with its own set of trials and triumphs.

As they talked, Emily's perspective began to shift. She realized that her quest for understanding Michael was not just about uncovering his secrets but also about confronting her own inner turmoil. Her journey was as much about self-discovery as it was about understanding Michael.

Later, Emily found herself in her studio, her sanctuary where emotions transformed into art. Her latest piece was a chaotic blend of dark and light strokes, mirroring the tumultuous journey she was on. Each brushstroke was a release, a way to process the myriad of feelings that Michael's revelations had stirred within her.

In the midst of her painting, Emily received an unexpected visitor. Clara, Michael's wife, stood at her doorstep, her eyes holding a story yet untold. The air was thick with unspoken words as they faced each other, two women bound by their connection to a man who was an enigma to both.

Clara's visit opened another chapter in Emily's quest. She listened as Clara recounted her own experiences with Michael, a narrative filled with love, pain, and regret. Their conversation was a tapestry of shared sorrows and unfulfilled dreams, revealing the complex layers of Michael's life and the impact he had on those around him.

As Clara left, Emily felt a sense of solidarity with her. Their stories were different, yet they shared a common thread of love and loss. This encounter was a poignant reminder of the interconnectedness of lives and the unseen threads that bind us together in the tapestry of human experience.

Emily's journey was far from over, but with each revelation, she was piecing together a puzzle that was larger and more intricate than she had ever imagined. It was a journey through the shadows of the past, a quest for truth that was slowly leading her towards the light of understanding and acceptance.

Emily's quest for understanding led her to a small, unassuming house on the outskirts of town. This was where Michael had spent his childhood, a place he had mentioned only in passing, with a tone of unmistakable pain. Standing before the weathered door, Emily felt a surge of apprehension, yet she knew this was a necessary step in her journey.

She knocked, and an elderly woman answered, her eyes reflecting years of life's joys and sorrows. This was Michael's mother, a key to the past he had so carefully hidden. Invited in, Emily found herself in a living room that seemed frozen in time, pictures of a young Michael smiling innocently from the walls.

Over tea, Michael's mother spoke of her son with a mixture of pride and regret. She recounted tales of a bright, sensitive boy who slowly became ensnared in a web of challenges too daunting for his young soul. Her words painted a picture of a family struggling under the weight of unspoken issues, where love was present but overshadowed by darker forces.

As they talked, Emily learned of Michael's father, a man whose own battle with substance abuse had cast a long shadow over the family. The cycle of violence and addiction that Michael had fought so hard to escape had begun here, in this very house, passed down like a tragic inheritance.

The revelation of this family history was a missing piece in the puzzle of Michael's life. Emily realized that his struggles were not born in isolation but were part of a generational saga of pain and resilience. It was a profound insight into the man she had loved, a realization that his battles were deeply rooted in a troubled past.

Leaving the house, Emily felt a mix of sadness and clarity. The visit had been emotionally taxing, yet it had given her a deeper understanding of Michael's journey. She now saw him not just as the man who had left her but as a victim of circumstances that had shaped his life from the very beginning.

In the days that followed, Emily found herself reflecting on the interconnectedness of lives and the unseen forces that shape our paths. She pondered over the concept of fate and free will, the delicate balance between the legacy we inherit and the choices we make.

Her art became a reflection of this introspection, each piece a dialogue between the past and the present, between darkness and light. She poured her newfound understanding into her work, creating pieces that were not just visually striking but emotionally resonant.

One evening, as she painted, Emily received a call from Lucas. He spoke with urgency, revealing that he had uncovered something crucial about the night of the altercation mentioned in Michael's journals. His discovery promised to shed new light on the events that had changed the course of Michael's life.

Emily felt a jolt of anticipation. This new information could be the key to unraveling the final mysteries of Michael's story. It was a chance to understand the full truth, to bring closure to the questions that had haunted her.

As she set down her brush, Emily knew that the next step in her journey was upon her. With Lucas's discovery, she was poised on the brink of a revelation that could change everything she thought she knew about Michael, about their love, and about the intricate tapestry of life itself.

# Chapter 10: Allies and Enemies

Emily's journey took a new turn as she found herself forming alliances with those she had never expected to be her allies. Among them was Clara, Michael's wife, a woman she had once viewed only as a rival. Their initial meeting was fraught with tension, but as they talked, a surprising bond began to form, rooted in their shared connection to Michael and the mysteries surrounding him.

Clara revealed her own struggles, painting a picture of a marriage fraught with complexities and unspoken truths. She spoke of Michael's increasingly erratic behavior, his periods of withdrawal, and the secrets he kept locked away. It became clear to Emily that Clara, too, was a victim of the circumstances, caught in the web of Michael's troubled past.

Together, they began to piece together the puzzle of Michael's life, each revelation bringing them closer to understanding the man they both loved. They pored over old letters, diary entries, and photographs, each item a piece of the intricate mosaic of Michael's existence.

As they delved deeper, Emily found herself confronting not just the mysteries of Michael's life but also the shadows in her own past. She was forced to confront her own vulnerabilities, the fears and insecurities that had shaped her relationship with Michael. It was a painful but necessary part of her journey, a confrontation with the inner demons that had long haunted her.

Meanwhile, Lucas, Emily's steadfast friend, continued his own investigations. He dug into the darker aspects of Michael's life, uncovering connections to figures from the criminal underworld. These revelations painted a disturbing picture of a man caught in a dangerous game, one that had potentially led to his downfall.

Emily also faced obstacles from those who wished to keep Michael's secrets buried. She encountered veiled threats and mysterious warnings, signs that there were those who would stop at nothing to prevent the truth from coming to light. These enemies, hidden in the shadows, added a sense of danger to her quest, a reminder that the path to understanding was fraught with peril.

Despite these challenges, Emily's resolve only strengthened. She was determined to uncover the truth, to bring to light the hidden aspects of Michael's life that had led to his tragic end. Her journey was no longer just about finding closure for herself but about seeking justice for Michael, a man whose life had been a tapestry of pain and secrets.

As she navigated this complex web of alliances and enmities, Emily found herself transformed. She was no longer the woman who had been shattered by Michael's disappearance. She had become a seeker of truth, a woman on a mission to unravel the mysteries of a life that had touched hers in profound and irrevocable ways.

Her quest was far from over, but Emily knew that she was on the right path. With each step, she was moving closer to understanding, to a resolution that would bring peace to both her and Michael's troubled soul. The journey was arduous, but Emily was ready to face whatever lay ahead, armed with newfound strength and a determination to uncover the truth, no matter the cost.

Emily's alliance with Clara, initially formed out of shared confusion and betrayal, evolved into a formidable partnership in their quest for truth. Together, they unearthed a trove of cryptic correspondences between Michael and an enigmatic figure. These letters, laced with coded language, hinted at a clandestine life Michael had led, one that was shrouded in mystery and danger.

While Emily delved deeper into Michael's secrets, her own life teetered on the brink of chaos. Financial burdens escalated as she poured her energy into this personal investigation. Her days were a relentless cycle of work and fleeting rest, while her nights were dedicated to piecing together Michael's enigmatic past.

Lucas, Emily's steadfast friend, ventured into the perilous realms of Michael's criminal connections. His forays into this underworld unearthed unsettling links to shadowy figures, revealing a network that was both alarming and essential to understanding Michael's double life.

The bond between Emily and Clara, forged in the fires of shared trauma, blossomed into a deep friendship. This unexpected camaraderie became a source of strength for Emily, a light in the darkness of her journey. Together, they faced the escalating threats and intimidation that came with their discoveries, a testament to the danger of the truths they were unearthing.

Amidst these external challenges, Emily's personal life underwent a transformation. She reconnected with her estranged family, navigating a labyrinth of old wounds and misunderstandings. These reunions, though emotionally charged, were pivotal in her path to healing and self-discovery. Her family's history, once a closed book, now opened up new perspectives on her past decisions and her relationship with Michael.

Emily's world expanded beyond her immediate quest. She encountered individuals from various walks of life, each with their own narratives of adversity and resilience. These stories, particularly those from the LGBTQ community, resonated with her, echoing themes of identity, acceptance, and the universal quest for understanding.

With each challenge she faced, Emily's resilience grew. Her journey became more than a quest to unravel Michael's secrets; it was a path to her own empowerment. She was no longer defined by her past with Michael but by her own strength and determination.

As the web of Michael's secrets began to unravel, the narrative neared its zenith. The mysteries of his life, once impenetrable, started to yield their truths, revealing a complex tapestry of deception and redemption. Emily, now a far cry from the woman who had been blindsided by Michael's disappearance, stood ready to face the final revelations. These truths promised to illuminate not just the enigmatic life Michael had led but also the path to Emily's own liberation and understanding.

In this phase of her journey, Emily encountered a myriad of obstacles, each more daunting than the last. Her relentless pursuit of the truth about Michael's life led her into confrontations with figures from his hidden world. These encounters were fraught with peril, yet they revealed the depth of Michael's entanglements in activities far removed from the life he had shared with her.

Clara, once a rival in love, now stood by Emily's side as an unwavering ally. Their combined efforts uncovered layers of deceit woven into the fabric of Michael's existence. This alliance, born out of shared betrayal, grew into a bond of sisterhood, empowering them both in their quest.

The investigation took a dramatic turn when Emily and Clara stumbled upon a cache of documents. These papers, carefully hidden away in one of Michael's secret hideouts, contained startling revelations about his dealings. The documents painted a picture of a man deeply involved in illicit activities, a stark contrast to the Michael Emily thought she knew.

As Emily delved deeper into the labyrinth of Michael's life, she grappled with the emotional turmoil of her discoveries. Each revelation about his secret activities, his double life, and his criminal connections was a blow to her understanding of their shared past. The man she had loved appeared to be a mere facade, masking a reality far more complex and disturbing.

Amidst these revelations, Emily's personal growth continued. Her experiences had forged her into a woman of formidable strength and resilience. She found solace in her renewed relationships with her family and the friendships she had cultivated along her journey.

These connections provided her with the emotional support she needed to face the challenges that lay ahead.

The narrative took a poignant turn as Emily began to understand the full extent of Michael's duplicity. His actions, once shrouded in mystery, now came into sharp focus, revealing a man torn between different worlds, different lives. This understanding, while painful, was crucial in Emily's journey towards closure and healing.

As the story progressed, Emily's resolve was tested time and again. She faced threats from those who wished to keep Michael's secrets buried. Yet, with each challenge, her determination only grew stronger. She was no longer just seeking answers about Michael; she was fighting for her own sense of self, her own truth.

The culmination of Emily's quest was fast approaching. The pieces of the puzzle that was Michael's life were coming together, forming a picture that was as shocking as it was enlightening. Emily stood on the brink of uncovering the ultimate truth, a revelation that promised to change everything she thought she knew about the man she had loved and the life they had shared.

Emily's journey led her to a clandestine meeting with a figure from Michael's past, a man known only as "The Broker." This enigmatic character, shrouded in mystery, held keys to many of Michael's secrets. The Broker, with his own agenda, offered Emily a glimpse into the dark underbelly of Michael's world, a world filled with dangerous liaisons and illicit dealings.

In a dimly lit room, The Broker unveiled a series of recordings - conversations between Michael and various shadowy figures. These recordings, laced with cryptic references and veiled threats, shed light on the depth of Michael's involvement in a network of criminal activities. Emily listened, her heart pounding, as the man she once loved was revealed to be a master manipulator, his charm a tool wielded with precision.

As Emily absorbed this new information, her resolve hardened. She knew that bringing Michael's deeds to light would be fraught with danger, but she was no longer the woman who had been blindsided by his disappearance. She was a warrior, battle-hardened by the trials she had faced.

Meanwhile, Clara, who had become more than an ally to Emily, was fighting her own battles. Clara's journey of self-discovery, intertwined with Emily's quest, brought to light her own strengths and vulnerabilities. Together, they formed an unbreakable bond, a sisterhood forged in the fires of shared betrayal and a mutual quest for truth.

Their next move was a daring one. Emily and Clara planned to confront one of Michael's associates, a key player in the network. This confrontation was risky, but it was a necessary step in unraveling the web of deceit that Michael had woven. As they prepared, Emily felt a surge of adrenaline, a mix of fear and exhilaration. This was her moment of truth, the point of no return in her quest for justice.

The meeting was tense, fraught with danger. Words were exchanged, accusations hurled, and in that heated exchange, Emily's courage shone. She stood her ground, her voice steady, her eyes unflinching. The associate, taken aback by her tenacity, revealed crucial information - the location of a safe house where Michael had kept his most guarded secrets.

Armed with this new knowledge, Emily and Clara embarked on what would be the most perilous part of their journey. They approached the safe house under the cover of darkness, their hearts racing with anticipation and fear. Inside, they hoped to find the final pieces of the puzzle, the evidence that would bring Michael's house of cards crashing down.

As they entered the safe house, they were met with a scene of chaos. Papers strewn about, files opened and discarded, it was clear that someone had been there before them, someone who knew what they were looking for. Amidst the disarray, Emily found a photograph, a picture that took her breath away. It was a photo of Michael, but not the Michael she knew. This Michael was different, harder, colder, a stranger in the guise of the man she had loved.

This photograph was more than just an image; it was a symbol of the shattered illusions that had once blinded Emily. It represented the final breaking point, the moment when the last vestiges of her old life fell away, leaving her to face a new, harsher reality. But in this moment of revelation, Emily found not despair, but a fierce determination. She would not let Michael's deceptions define her. She would rise from the ashes of her broken dreams, stronger, more resilient, and more determined than ever to seek justice.

In the wake of the discovery at the safe house, Emily and Clara meticulously sifted through the scattered documents, searching for anything that could serve as incontrovertible evidence against Michael. Amongst the chaos, they unearthed a series of encrypted files, each one a piece of the intricate puzzle that was Michael's double life. With each file they decoded, the extent of his deception became increasingly apparent, painting a picture of a man far removed from the one Emily had known.

As they delved deeper, they stumbled upon a set of financial records, meticulously detailed, revealing a network of offshore accounts and illicit transactions. These records were the smoking gun they needed, the undeniable proof of Michael's criminal activities. With this evidence in hand, Emily felt a surge of vindication. Her journey, fraught with obstacles and heartache, was finally yielding results.

Meanwhile, the narrative shifted to focus on the secondary characters, each with their own subplot intricately woven into the main storyline. Among these was Lucas, a young man grappling with his identity in a conservative family, his story a poignant exploration of the struggles faced by LGBTQ individuals. Lucas's journey of self-acceptance and his fight for acceptance from his family added a layer of emotional depth to the narrative.

Another subplot revolved around Sarah, Emily's best friend, who was dealing with the complexities of a failing marriage. Sarah's story, though separate, was a mirror to Emily's, reflecting the universal themes of love, betrayal, and the quest for self-discovery. Through these subplots, the narrative painted a rich tapestry of human experience, each thread contributing to the overarching story.

As Emily and Clara continued their quest, they encountered a myriad of challenges. They faced threats from unknown adversaries, each one more menacing than the last, a clear indication that they were getting closer to the truth. But with each obstacle they overcame, their resolve only strengthened, their bond deepened.

In a pivotal moment, Emily received an unexpected message from an anonymous source. The message contained a clue, a cryptic reference to a location where they could find the final piece of evidence they needed. With cautious optimism, Emily and Clara set out to this location, unaware of the dangers that awaited them.

Their journey led them to a remote cabin, nestled deep in the woods. As they approached, the air was thick with tension, the silence ominous. Inside the cabin, they found a trove of documents, each one more incriminating than the last. But it was a series of audio recordings that proved to be the most damning. These recordings, conversations between Michael and his associates, were the irrefutable evidence of his guilt.

As they listened to the recordings, Emily's emotions were a whirlwind of anger, sadness, and relief. The man she had loved, the man she had trusted, was a stranger, his life a web of lies. But amidst the turmoil, she felt a sense of closure. The truth was out, and with it, the weight of uncertainty lifted from her shoulders.

With the evidence in hand, Emily and Clara prepared to take their findings to the authorities. They knew that the road ahead would be fraught with legal battles and public scrutiny, but they were ready. They had faced the storm and emerged stronger, their spirits unbroken.

As the narrative drew to a close, Emily stood at a crossroads, her past behind her, her future uncertain. But she was no longer the woman who had been blindsided by Michael's disappearance. She was a survivor, a woman who had faced the darkest depths of betrayal and emerged with a newfound strength. Her journey was a testament to the resilience of the human spirit, a reminder that even in the darkest of times, there is always a path forward.

With the evidence securely in their possession, Emily and Clara made their way to the authorities, their hearts heavy yet determined. As they navigated the labyrinthine legal system, they encountered skepticism and bureaucratic hurdles, but their resolve never wavered. They were on a mission to bring Michael to justice, to expose his duplicity for the world to see.

In the midst of this tumultuous journey, Emily found solace in her newfound allies. Lucas, with his quiet strength and unwavering support, became a pillar of strength for her. His own battles with acceptance in his family paralleled Emily's struggle for truth, creating a bond forged in adversity. Sarah, too, stood by Emily, her own marital woes a stark reminder of the fragility of relationships and the strength required to rebuild one's life from the ashes of betrayal.

As the legal proceedings commenced, Emily was thrust into the public eye, her story a subject of media frenzy. Reporters clamored for interviews, eager to unravel the sordid details of Michael's double life. Amidst this chaos, Emily remained steadfast, her focus singular: to see justice served.

The trial was a spectacle, a clash of legal titans as evidence was presented and testimonies heard. Michael, once a figure of charm and charisma, now sat sullen and defeated, the weight of his transgressions laid bare for all to see. The audio recordings were particularly damning, their contents echoing through the courtroom, irrefutable proof of his guilt.

Throughout the trial, Emily grappled with a maelstrom of emotions. Anger, betrayal, and heartache swirled within her, yet there was also a growing sense of liberation. With each passing day, the shackles of her past loosened, giving way to a future filled with possibilities.

As the trial neared its conclusion, Emily took the stand, her testimony a powerful account of the man she thought she knew and the reality she came to face. Her words resonated with the jury, a poignant reminder of the human cost of Michael's actions.

In the end, justice was served. Michael was found guilty, his sentence a reflection of the gravity of his crimes. As he was led away, Emily felt a chapter of her life close, the pain of the past giving way to a sense of closure.

Outside the courtroom, the world continued to spin, life moving forward with relentless momentum. Emily, once ensnared in the web of Michael's deceit, now stood free, her spirit unburdened. She had confronted her demons, faced her fears, and emerged victorious.

In the aftermath of the trial, Emily's journey was far from over. She embarked on a path of self-discovery, exploring the depths of her own strength and resilience. The experience had changed her, shaping her into a woman of fortitude and grace.

Lucas, too, found his own path, his story a beacon of hope for those struggling with their identity. His journey with his family reached a resolution, acceptance slowly taking root in the once unfertile ground of misunderstanding. Sarah's story, a parallel to Emily's, reached a turning point. She found the courage to end her unhappy marriage, embarking on a journey of self-reliance and empowerment.

As the narrative drew to a close, Emily stood at the precipice of a new beginning. The storm had passed, leaving in its wake a landscape of possibility. She had faced the darkest night and emerged into the dawn, her spirit a testament to the enduring power of hope and the unyielding strength of the human heart.

In the days following the trial, Emily's life took on a new rhythm, one marked by introspection and healing. She spent long hours walking in the park, the natural beauty a balm for her wounded soul. Each step was a movement towards recovery, a journey back to herself.

Her evenings were often spent with Clara, their bond strengthened by the ordeal they had endured together. They shared stories, laughter, and tears, finding solace in their shared experience. Clara, once a symbol of Emily's pain, had become a dear friend, a sister in arms.

Lucas and Sarah were frequent companions on these evenings, their presence a source of comfort and joy. Together, they formed a tapestry of support, each thread interwoven with strength and compassion.

As Emily rebuilt her life, she found a new purpose in advocacy. She became a voice for those who had suffered in silence, her story a beacon of hope for others facing the darkness of betrayal and deceit. She spoke at events, participated in support groups, and wrote articles, her words a testament to her journey from victim to survivor.

Her work brought her into contact with a myriad of individuals, each with their own story of resilience. Among them was a young man named Alex, whose struggle with substance abuse and recovery mirrored the hidden battles Michael had faced. Alex's story was a poignant reminder of the complexities of the human condition, the fine line between vice and vulnerability.

Emily's relationship with her parents, once strained by distance and misunderstanding, began to mend. They reached out to her, their conversations tentative at first, but gradually growing in warmth and understanding. Forgiveness and reconciliation, once distant concepts, became tangible realities, healing old wounds.

As autumn gave way to winter, Emily found herself at a crossroads. The path behind her was marked by pain and struggle, but also growth and triumph. Ahead lay a road untraveled, its destination unknown but filled with promise.

She pondered her next steps, her heart torn between the comfort of the familiar and the allure of the unknown. Her advocacy work was fulfilling, but part of her yearned for something more, a new challenge to conquer.

It was during a quiet evening, the city cloaked in a blanket of snow, that Emily made her decision. She would write a book, a memoir of her journey through the labyrinth of Michael's deception and her path to empowerment. It would be a legacy of her experience, a guide for others navigating the treacherous waters of betrayal.

With renewed purpose, Emily set to work. She poured her heart and soul into the pages, her words a tapestry of pain, hope, and redemption. The process was cathartic, each sentence a step towards healing.

As she wrote, Emily reflected on the myriad of people who had touched her life. Clara, Lucas, Sarah, Alex, her parents - each had played a role in her journey, their stories intertwined with her own.

The book, once completed, was a mosaic of human experience, a narrative that transcended her own story. It was a testament to the resilience of the human spirit, a reminder that even in the darkest of times, there is light to be found.

Emily's journey had begun with a disappearance, a shattering of illusions. It had taken her through a downward spiral, a journey into the past, and a gathering of storms. Now, at this crossroad, she stood poised to embark on a new chapter, her spirit unbroken, her heart open to the endless possibilities that lay ahead.

Emily's book launch was a momentous occasion, a culmination of her journey from despair to empowerment. The event was held in a cozy bookstore, its walls lined with volumes of hope and wisdom. Friends, family, and supporters filled the room, their faces a tapestry of anticipation and pride.

As Emily spoke, her voice resonated with strength and vulnerability. She recounted her story, not just as her own, but as a shared narrative of struggle and resilience. Her words echoed in the hearts of those present, a reminder of the power of truth and the beauty of healing.

The response to her book was overwhelming. Readers from all walks of life reached out, sharing their own stories of betrayal and recovery. Emily's journey had become a beacon of hope, a guide for those navigating the treacherous waters of personal turmoil.

In the weeks that followed, Emily found herself at the center of a growing movement. She was invited to speak at conferences, participate in panel discussions, and lead workshops. Her message of resilience and empowerment resonated with many, her story a catalyst for change and healing.

Among the many who reached out was a young woman named Maya. Maya's story mirrored Emily's in many ways, her life marked by a similar pattern of deception and betrayal. Emily saw in Maya a kindred spirit, a fellow traveler on the road to recovery.

They formed a close bond, their friendship a source of mutual support and understanding. Maya became an integral part of Emily's advocacy work, her insights and experiences adding depth and perspective to their efforts.

As Emily's influence grew, so did her network of allies. She collaborated with other advocates, forming partnerships that spanned continents and cultures. Together, they worked towards a common goal - to bring light to the hidden corners of human experience, to give voice to those who had suffered in silence.

Amidst this whirlwind of activity, Emily's personal life underwent a quiet transformation. She found solace in simple pleasures - long walks in the park, quiet evenings with friends, moments of solitude and reflection.

Her relationship with her parents blossomed into a deep and abiding bond, the wounds of the past healed by time and understanding. They became a source of strength and support, their love a constant in her ever-changing world.

As the seasons changed, Emily found herself reflecting on the journey she had undertaken. She had confronted her past, formed unexpected alliances, and emerged as a voice for the voiceless. Her life, once shattered by betrayal, had been rebuilt on a foundation of strength and purpose.

Now, at this juncture, Emily stood ready to embark on a new chapter. Her heart was open to the possibilities that lay ahead, her spirit undaunted by the challenges that might arise.

Her story was one of many, a single thread in the vast tapestry of human experience. But it was a thread woven with courage and resilience, a testament to the enduring power of the human spirit.

# Chapter 11: In Too Deep

Emily's quest for truth had become an all-consuming force, driving her deeper into a labyrinth of secrets and lies. Each revelation seemed to lead to more questions, the answers always just out of reach. Her days were spent poring over documents, her nights haunted by dreams of shadowy figures and whispered conversations.

In her relentless pursuit, Emily began to cross boundaries she had never imagined. She found herself engaging in covert activities, from clandestine meetings with informants to surreptitious gathering of evidence. The line between right and wrong blurred, her actions driven by a desperate need to uncover the full extent of Michael's deception.

Her obsession did not go unnoticed. Friends expressed concern over her increasingly erratic behavior, warning her of the dangers of delving too deep. But Emily was undeterred, her resolve only strengthened by their cautionary words.

As she delved further into Michael's past, Emily uncovered a web of corruption that extended far beyond her own personal tragedy. She discovered connections to powerful individuals, their influence reaching into the highest echelons of society. The realization that she was up against forces much larger than herself was both terrifying and exhilarating.

Amidst this turmoil, Emily's relationship with her family began to strain. Her parents, once her staunchest supporters, grew weary of her single-minded focus. They feared for her safety, concerned that her quest for truth would lead her down a dangerous path.

Despite these challenges, Emily found solace in her growing network of allies. Maya, ever her faithful companion, stood by her side, her own experiences providing valuable insight into the shadowy world they were navigating.

Together, they pieced together the puzzle of Michael's past, each discovery shedding light on the complex tapestry of deceit and manipulation. They uncovered evidence of financial malfeasance, illicit dealings, and a trail of broken lives left in Michael's wake.

As the pieces fell into place, Emily was faced with a daunting realization. Bringing Michael to justice would require more than just exposing his lies. It would mean challenging a system that had enabled his behavior, a system that valued power and wealth over truth and justice.

This realization brought with it a profound sense of responsibility. Emily knew that her actions could have far-reaching consequences, not just for herself, but for all those caught in Michael's web of deceit.

She wrestled with the moral implications of her quest, torn between her desire for justice and her fear of the collateral damage her revelations might cause. The weight of this responsibility was a heavy burden, one that tested the limits of her courage and conviction.

As Emily stood at this crossroads, she knew that the path she chose would define not just her own fate, but the fate of many others. Her journey had taken her into the depths of darkness, but it was in this darkness that she found her true strength.

In this maelstrom of moral quandaries, Emily's resolve was put to the test. She grappled with the enormity of her discoveries, each more unsettling than the last. Her investigation revealed not just financial improprieties and personal betrayals, but hinted at darker, more sinister activities.

The deeper Emily delved, the more she realized that Michael's actions were not merely those of a flawed individual, but part of a larger, more systemic problem. She uncovered connections to organized crime, money laundering, and even hints of political corruption. These revelations painted a picture of a man who was not just unfaithful and deceptive, but dangerously powerful and well-protected.

Amidst these revelations, Emily's personal life continued to unravel. Her obsession with the truth had cost her friendships, strained family ties, and left her isolated. She found herself questioning her own judgment, wondering if her quest was worth the price she was paying.

Yet, in the midst of her turmoil, Emily found unexpected allies. A group of journalists, intrigued by her findings, offered their support and resources. They saw in Emily's story not just a personal tragedy, but a tale of systemic corruption that needed to be exposed.

With their help, Emily began to piece together a comprehensive picture of Michael's activities. They worked tirelessly, sifting through financial records, tracking down leads, and conducting interviews with those who had been affected by Michael's actions.

As they worked, Emily began to see the potential impact of their findings. She realized that exposing Michael could bring about much-needed change, shining a light on the corrupt systems that had allowed his behavior to go unchecked.

However, with this realization came a new set of fears. Emily knew that going public with her findings would put her in the crosshairs of powerful individuals. She feared for her safety, and for the safety of those assisting her.

Despite these fears, Emily's determination only grew stronger. She was no longer driven by a desire for personal vengeance, but by a sense of duty to those who had suffered at Michael's hands. She knew that her actions could bring about real change, and this knowledge gave her the strength to continue.

As the investigation neared its conclusion, Emily prepared for the inevitable confrontation. She knew that exposing Michael would be a battle, one that would require all her courage and cunning.

She braced herself for the backlash, ready to face the consequences of her actions. For Emily, the journey had become about more than just uncovering the truth. It was about standing up to injustice, about fighting for those who had no voice.

In this fight, Emily found her purpose. She was no longer a victim of circumstance, but an agent of change. Her journey had transformed her, and she stepped into the fray, ready to face whatever challenges lay ahead.

As Emily and her newfound allies edged closer to unveiling the full extent of Michael's transgressions, the stakes escalated. They were now not just battling a single man's deceit, but a web of corruption that extended far beyond him.

The journalists, with their expertise in investigative reporting, unearthed connections that were both shocking and far-reaching. They discovered that Michael's financial misdeeds were tied to a network of influential figures, including politicians and business magnates. This network, it seemed, had been manipulating the levers of power for their own gain, with Michael as a key player.

Emily's role in the investigation took on a new dimension. She was no longer just a source of information; she had become an integral part of the team, her personal experience providing crucial context to the broader story. Her insights into Michael's character and their shared history lent a human element to the investigation, making the story not just about corruption, but about betrayal and the abuse of trust.

As they delved deeper, the team faced increasing pressure. They encountered threats, both veiled and overt, and it became clear that there were those who would go to great lengths to keep the truth buried. Emily's resolve was tested as she navigated this perilous landscape, her every move scrutinized by unseen adversaries.

Despite the dangers, Emily found strength in her mission. She was buoyed by the support of her allies and driven by a deep-seated

she felt a void. She pondered her next steps, aware that her life could never return to what it once was.

She sought solace in the support of her allies, the journalists, and activists who had become her friends and confidants. They celebrated their victory, but also acknowledged the challenges ahead. They knew that their work had just begun, that the fight against corruption and injustice was a never-ending battle.

Emily realized that her journey had changed her in profound ways. She was stronger, more resilient, and more committed to the cause of justice. She decided to continue working with the team, using her experience and insights to uncover and combat corruption in all its forms.

As she embarked on this new chapter, Emily felt a sense of purpose that she had never known before. She had faced her demons, confronted her past, and emerged as a champion of truth. Her story was one of pain and perseverance, of betrayal and redemption. It was a testament to the power of the human spirit to overcome adversity and to fight for what is right.

In the end, Emily's journey was not just about uncovering the secrets of one man's life, but about discovering her own strength and purpose. She had ventured into the depths of despair, only to rise, phoenix-like, from the ashes. Her story was a beacon of hope, a reminder that even in the darkest of times, the light of truth could prevail.

Emily's newfound resolve was tested as she delved deeper into the labyrinth of Michael's secrets. Each revelation brought more questions, painting a complex picture of a man she thought she knew. The deeper she dug, the more she realized that the truth was not just about exposing lies but also about understanding the human psyche's complexities.

Her investigation led her to a small, nondescript house on the outskirts of the city. Here, she uncovered a cache of letters and diaries, hidden away like forbidden treasures. These writings offered a glimpse into Michael's inner world, a place of turmoil and conflict. Emily read them with a mix of fascination and horror, each word revealing a new layer of Michael's persona.

The diaries spoke of his struggles with addiction, his battles with inner demons that drove him to the brink of self-destruction. They revealed a man torn between his desires and his duties, caught in a web of his own making. Emily's heart ached as she read his confessions, his moments of vulnerability laid bare on the page.

As she immersed herself in these writings, Emily began to see Michael not just as the villain of her story but as a tragic figure, a man who had lost his way in a world that offered no guidance. This realization did not excuse his actions, but it brought a sense of understanding, a recognition of the shared human frailty that binds us all.

Emily's quest for truth took her next to a rundown bar on the outskirts of town, a place where Michael was known to frequent in his darker days. The bar, with its dim lighting and the smell of stale beer, felt like a world away from Emily's own life. Yet, she stepped inside, driven by a resolve that had grown stronger with each revelation.

Inside, she found herself amidst a crowd of faces, each carrying their own untold stories. She struck up a conversation with the bartender, a middle-aged man with a kind face and tired eyes. He remembered Michael, remembered him as a troubled soul who often sought refuge in the bottom of a glass.

The bartender spoke of nights when Michael would sit alone at the end of the bar, muttering to himself, lost in a world of his own. He recalled one particular night when Michael had opened up about his life, his voice heavy with regret. He spoke of a love lost, a family torn apart, and a life that had spiraled out of control.

These confessions, shared in the anonymity of a dimly lit bar, painted a picture of a man tormented by his past and uncertain of his future. Emily listened, her heart heavy with a mix of pity and sorrow, as she realized the depth of Michael's despair.

Leaving the bar, Emily felt a chill in the air, a reminder of the cold, harsh realities that life sometimes presented. She walked through the deserted streets, her mind racing with thoughts of Michael, of the life he had led, and the pain he had endured.

She knew now that her search for the truth was not just about finding answers; it was about understanding the human heart, with all its capacity for love and its propensity for destruction. As she looked up at the starless sky, she felt a sense of kinship with the universe, a feeling of being intimately connected with the vast, complex web of human existence.

In the days that followed, Emily's investigation took her deeper into the labyrinth of Michael's past. Each discovery, each uncovered secret, seemed to add another layer of complexity to the man she thought she knew. Her journey led her to a small, cluttered apartment on the other side of town, where she met an old friend of Michael's, a woman named Sarah.

Sarah, with her weary eyes and a voice tinged with sadness, spoke of the Michael she knew, a man full of contradictions. He was charming yet distant, kind yet capable of sudden, inexplicable anger. She recounted stories of their youth, of wild nights and reckless adventures, a time when life seemed infinite and full of possibilities.

As they talked, Emily sensed a profound grief in Sarah, a sorrow born of years of watching a friend succumb to his inner demons. Sarah spoke of Michael's struggles with addiction, of his battles with unseen enemies that seemed to haunt him. She talked of his attempts to find solace, to escape the pain that seemed to cling to him like a shadow.

Listening to Sarah, Emily felt a growing sense of unease, a realization that the man she loved was far more complex and troubled than she had ever imagined. She left the apartment with a heavy heart, her mind a whirlwind of emotions.

The next day, Emily found herself at the local library, surrounded by stacks of books and the quiet hum of knowledge. She poured over old newspapers, searching for any mention of Michael, any clue that might shed light on his mysterious past.

Hours passed, and the library's clock ticked steadily in the background, a reminder of the relentless march of time. Emily's eyes grew tired, but her determination did not waver. She read about a tragic accident years ago, one that had claimed the life of a young woman, a woman who had been close to Michael.

This revelation hit Emily like a physical blow, a stark reminder of the fragility of life and the secrets that people carry with them. She sat there, amidst the silent books, feeling a profound connection to the past, to the lives that had intertwined with Michael's, each leaving their mark on his troubled soul.

As she left the library, the sun was setting, casting long shadows across the city. Emily walked slowly, lost in thought, her mind a tumult of emotions. She knew now that her search for the truth was more than just a quest for answers; it was a journey into the heart of human suffering, a journey that had only just begun.

Emily's quest for understanding led her next to a rundown bar on the outskirts of town, a place where Michael was known to frequent in his darker days. The air inside was thick with the smell of stale beer and cigarette smoke, a stark contrast to the sterile environment of the library where she had spent her afternoon.

She took a seat at the bar, her eyes scanning the dimly lit room, taking in the faces of the patrons, each absorbed in their own world of sorrows and secrets. The bartender, a middle-aged man with a grizzled beard, eyed her curiously as she ordered a drink.

As she sipped her drink, Emily struck up a conversation with the bartender, cautiously steering the topic towards Michael. The bartender's face changed at the mention of his name, a mix of recognition and something akin to pity. He spoke of Michael in a hushed tone, recounting tales of late nights and drunken confessions, of a man wrestling with inner demons that refused to be silenced.

The stories painted a picture of a man torn between two worlds, one of normalcy and love, the other a dark realm of addiction and despair. Emily listened, her heart heavy, as she began to understand the depth of Michael's struggle, the pain that he had so skillfully hidden behind a facade of normalcy.

Leaving the bar, Emily felt a chill in the air, a physical manifestation of the cold, hard truths she was beginning to uncover. She walked aimlessly through the streets, her mind racing with thoughts of Michael, of the man she loved and the stranger he had become.

The night grew darker, and the city's lights flickered in the distance, a reminder of the world that continued to move forward, oblivious to the personal tragedies unfolding in its shadows. Emily felt a sense of isolation, a realization that her journey was hers alone, a path that few could understand or follow.

As she wandered, her thoughts turned to the moral implications of her quest. Was she right to dig into Michael's past, to uncover secrets that he had chosen to bury? Was her search for truth a noble endeavor, or was it an invasion of the privacy of a man who was no longer able to defend himself?

These questions haunted Emily as she made her way back to her apartment, the city's noises fading into the background, replaced by the tumult of her own thoughts. She knew that her journey was far from over, that there were more secrets to uncover, more truths to face. But for now, she needed rest, a brief respite from the emotional turmoil that had become her constant companion.

Emily's quest for understanding led her to a small, unassuming coffee shop, a place where Michael had often sought solace. The barista, a middle-aged man with kind eyes, recognized Michael's photo immediately. He spoke of Michael with a fondness that surprised Emily, describing him as a regular who often came in to escape the world outside.

The barista's stories painted a picture of a different Michael, one who found comfort in the simple routine of a morning coffee, who listened to jazz music on rainy days, and who occasionally shared snippets of his life over a steaming cup. These moments of normalcy stood in stark contrast to the turbulent life Emily had been uncovering.

As she left the coffee shop, Emily felt a mix of emotions. The more she learned, the more complex Michael's character became, a tapestry of light and dark, of pain and moments of peace. It was as if she was getting to know him all over again, understanding the layers and contradictions that made up his life.

Her next stop was a small bookstore, a place Michael had mentioned in passing years ago. The owner, an elderly woman with a sharp memory, recalled Michael's visits. He was a voracious reader, she said, with a particular interest in poetry and philosophy. He would spend hours browsing the shelves, lost in the world of words.

This new revelation added another dimension to Michael's character. Emily imagined him in the quiet corners of the bookstore, seeking refuge in the pages of books, perhaps finding solace in the words of poets who spoke of love, loss, and the human condition.

As evening approached, Emily found herself at a local park, a place where she and Michael had often walked together. The familiarity of the surroundings brought a sense of nostalgia, a reminder of happier times before the complexities of life had pulled them apart.

Sitting on a bench, Emily watched the sunset, the sky a canvas of oranges and purples. She thought about the Michael she had known, the one she had loved, and the Michael she was now discovering. It was as if she was piecing together a puzzle, each piece a fragment of his life, some fitting easily, others requiring careful consideration.

Her phone buzzed with a message from an unknown number. Hesitantly, she opened it to find a photo of Michael, younger and seemingly carefree, his arm around a woman she didn't recognize. The message was cryptic, a simple question: "Do you really know who Michael was?"

The photo and message sent a shiver down her spine. It was a stark reminder that there were still aspects of Michael's life shrouded in mystery, parts of his past that remained hidden. Emily knew that her search for the truth was far from over, that there were more secrets waiting to be uncovered.

As the night enveloped the park, Emily made her way home, her mind a whirlwind of thoughts and emotions. She was determined to continue her search, to uncover the layers of Michael's life, no matter where it led her. The truth was out there, waiting to be found, and Emily was resolute in her quest to find it.

# Chapter 12: Tangled Webs

Under the first light of dawn, Emily approached the old lighthouse, its towering form casting a long shadow on the sand. The air was crisp, carrying the scent of the sea and the promise of revelations. She found a figure waiting for her, silhouetted against the rising sun. It was a man she had never seen before, his face weathered like the lighthouse itself. He introduced himself as Jonah, a former friend of Michael's. His voice was tinged with sorrow as he spoke of their friendship, a bond forged in youth but strained by time and secrets. Jonah revealed that Michael and Clara's relationship had been tumultuous from the start, marked by intense passion but also by deep-seated conflicts.

According to Jonah, Clara had struggled with her own demons, her life a tapestry of challenges and setbacks. Michael, drawn to her vulnerability, had tried to be her anchor, but their relationship had only served to amplify their struggles. Jonah spoke of heated arguments, of nights when Michael would seek refuge in his friend's home, his soul heavy with the weight of a love that was both his salvation and his curse.

Emily listened, her heart aching for the pain that both Michael and Clara must have endured. She realized that their relationship was far more complex than she had imagined, a labyrinth of emotions and unspoken truths. Jonah's words painted a picture of two people caught in a dance of love and pain, unable to break free from the patterns that bound them.

As Jonah spoke, Emily felt her own turmoil intensify. She grappled with feelings of betrayal, of having been kept in the dark about so much of Michael's life. Yet, she also felt a growing sense of empathy for both Michael and Clara. Their story was a reminder of the intricate complexities of human relationships, of how love can sometimes lead us into a maelstrom of emotions.

Jonah handed her a small, worn-out journal, its pages filled with Michael's handwriting. It was a window into his soul, his thoughts and feelings laid bare in ink. Emily held the journal, a sense of reverence washing over her. This was more than just a collection of words; it was a piece of Michael himself, a legacy of his innermost thoughts and dreams.

As she bid farewell to Jonah, Emily knew that her journey was far from over. The journal was a key to understanding Michael, but it also opened up a myriad of questions. She needed time to process everything, to unravel the tangled web of Michael and Clara's relationship.

She returned to her hotel, the journal clutched tightly in her hands. In the solitude of her room, she began to read, each page a step deeper into Michael's psyche. His words were raw and honest, filled with love, pain, and a yearning for something more. Emily felt as if she was walking alongside him, sharing in his journey of self-discovery and heartache.

The more she read, the more she understood the complexity of the man she had loved. Michael was not just a figure from her past; he was a mosaic of experiences and emotions, each piece a part of the whole. As the sun set, Emily continued to read, her heart heavy but her resolve strong. She would follow this path to its end, wherever it might lead.

Yet, even with this newfound resolve, Emily couldn't shake off a lingering sense of unease. The revelations about Michael and Clara's tumultuous relationship had opened a Pandora's box of emotions and questions. She pondered over the nature of their love, so intense yet fraught with such deep-rooted issues. It was a love that seemed to defy understanding, existing in a realm where passion and pain were inextricably linked.

In the midst of her contemplation, Emily's thoughts drifted to her own relationship with Michael. She reflected on the moments they shared, the promises made, and the dreams they had woven together. Now, those memories were tinged with a sense of betrayal, a realization that the man she loved was enshrouded in layers of complexity and secrets.

The more she thought about it, the more Emily felt a growing disconnect between the Michael she knew and the one who emerged from the pages of his journal. It was as if she had loved a ghost, a figment of her imagination that had been carefully crafted by Michael's omissions and half-truths.

This realization brought with it a profound sense of loss, not just for the relationship that was, but for the innocence and trust that had been irrevocably shattered. Emily mourned for the woman she was before, one who believed in the simplicity of love, unmarred by the shadows of hidden truths.

As these thoughts swirled in her mind, Emily knew that she could no longer view her past with Michael through rose-colored glasses. She needed to confront the reality of their relationship, to understand the role she played in this intricate dance of love and deception.

This introspection led Emily to a deeper understanding of herself. She recognized her own vulnerabilities, her desire to find love and acceptance, which had perhaps blinded her to the warning signs along the way. It was a painful acknowledgment, but one that brought with it a sense of empowerment.

With this newfound self-awareness, Emily felt a shift within her. She was no longer the passive recipient of Michael's narrative; she was now an active participant in her own story. She resolved to seek the truth, not just about Michael and Clara, but about herself and the choices that had led her to this point.

This determination marked a turning point for Emily. She was ready to face the complexities of her past, to unravel the tangled web of emotions and experiences that had brought her here. It was a journey fraught with uncertainty, but Emily was no longer afraid. She had found strength in her vulnerability, courage in her pain.

As the day drew to a close, Emily sat alone, the journal by her side. She felt a sense of peace amidst the turmoil, a quiet resolve to move forward. The path ahead was unclear, but Emily knew one thing for certain: she was ready to face whatever lay ahead, armed with the truth and a newfound understanding of herself.

Emily's resolve to seek the truth led her to unexpected places. She found herself revisiting old haunts, places she and Michael had frequented, hoping to glean some insight into the man he truly was. Each location was a memory, a piece of a puzzle she was desperately trying to solve. Yet, with each visit, the image of Michael that she held in her heart became increasingly blurred.

In her quest, Emily encountered individuals who had known Michael, but their accounts only added to her confusion. Some described him as a charismatic and kind-hearted man, while others hinted at a more complex, perhaps troubled, individual. These conflicting narratives left Emily feeling more isolated, struggling to reconcile the man she loved with the one emerging from the shadows of these stories.

Amidst this turmoil, Emily's own life began to unravel. Her job, which had once been a source of pride and stability, now felt like a hollow routine. She found it increasingly difficult to focus, her thoughts perpetually drifting to Michael and the web of lies that surrounded him. Her performance suffered, and she could sense her colleagues' growing concern, yet she felt powerless to stem the tide of her own unraveling.

Her personal life fared no better. Friends, once a source of comfort and joy, now seemed distant, unable to penetrate the wall of grief and obsession that Emily had built around herself. She felt adrift, untethered from the life she once knew, caught in the throes of a relentless quest for a truth that seemed ever out of reach.

In this state of isolation, Emily's thoughts turned inward. She began to question her own judgment, her decision to trust Michael, to love him. Had she been naïve, or was there something in her that needed to believe in the illusion he had created? These questions haunted her, eroding her confidence and leaving her feeling vulnerable and exposed.

Yet, it was in this vulnerability that Emily found a glimmer of hope. She realized that her quest for the truth about Michael was also a journey of self-discovery. Each step, each revelation, was a lesson, a chance to understand not just the man she loved, but herself as well.

This realization brought a sense of clarity. Emily understood that the answers she sought might not bring her peace, but the journey was necessary, a path she had to walk to find her way back to herself. She embraced this journey, not with the desperation that had initially fueled her, but with a quiet determination to face whatever truths lay ahead.

As Emily continued her search, she found herself drawn to places of significance in Michael's life. She visited his childhood home, walked the streets of his hometown, each step bringing her closer to understanding the man he was and the life he had lived before her.

These visits were painful, but necessary. Each location held a piece of Michael's story, fragments of a life that Emily had only glimpsed through the lens of their relationship. She began to see him not just as a lover, but as a complex individual shaped by experiences and choices far beyond the scope of their time together.

This broader perspective was both enlightening and heartbreaking. Emily mourned the loss of the simple narrative she had once believed, yet she also felt a growing sense of empathy for Michael. His actions, though hurtful, were part of a larger tapestry of his life, influenced by factors she was only beginning to understand.

With each revelation, Emily's anger and betrayal gave way to a more nuanced understanding of the man she had loved. She realized that the truth was not a simple dichotomy of right and wrong, but a complex interplay of emotions, experiences, and choices.

This understanding did not erase the pain of betrayal, but it allowed Emily to view Michael with a sense of compassion. She began to see him not as a villain in her story, but as a fellow traveler on a difficult journey, flawed and struggling in his own way.

As Emily delved deeper into Michael's past, she also began to confront her own. She reflected on her choices, her motivations, and the role she had played in their relationship. This introspection was challenging, but it brought a sense of empowerment. Emily was no longer a passive victim of Michael's deceit; she was an active participant in her own story, capable of growth and change.

This shift in perspective marked a turning point for Emily. She began to let go of the anger and hurt that had consumed her, focusing instead on her own journey of healing and self-discovery. She embraced the lessons of her past, using them as a foundation for a future built on self-awareness and authenticity.

As Emily moved forward, she carried with her the memories of her time with Michael, not as a burden, but as a testament to her resilience and capacity for growth. She stepped into the future with a sense of hope, ready to embrace the possibilities that lay ahead, armed with the wisdom gained from her journey through the tangled webs of love and deception.

Emily's journey through the remnants of Michael's past led her to a quaint, unassuming coffee shop in the heart of his hometown. It was here, amidst the aroma of freshly brewed coffee and the gentle hum of quiet conversations, that she met Anna, an old friend of Michael's from his high school days. Anna's insights offered Emily a new dimension to Michael's character, one that was both enlightening and disconcerting.

Anna spoke of a Michael that Emily had never known, a young man full of ambition and dreams, yet plagued by a restlessness that often led him into trouble. She recounted stories of their adventures, of moments where Michael's charm and charisma shone, drawing people to him effortlessly. Yet, there was a shadow to these tales, hints of a darker side to Michael, a propensity for risk-taking and a disregard for consequences.

As Emily listened, she felt a mix of emotions. There was a sense of sadness for the young man who had struggled with his own demons, a sense of frustration for the choices he had made, and a sense of empathy for the complexities of his life. Anna's stories painted a picture of a man caught in a perpetual struggle between his aspirations and his impulses.

This new understanding of Michael's past began to reshape Emily's perception of their relationship. She saw their time together in a different light, recognizing patterns she had previously overlooked. Michael's charm, which had once captivated her, now appeared as a façade, a mask he wore to hide his inner turmoil.

Emily's reflections on these revelations were interrupted by a chance encounter with a stranger at the coffee shop. This stranger, a middle-aged man with kind eyes and a gentle demeanor, overheard her conversation with Anna and approached her with a sense of familiarity. He introduced himself as David, a former colleague of Michael's.

David's account of Michael was different from Anna's. He spoke of Michael's professional achievements, of his dedication and hard work. Yet, even in these stories, there were hints of the same restlessness, a sense of dissatisfaction that seemed to follow Michael in all aspects of his life.

This juxtaposition of the personal and professional aspects of Michael's life left Emily with more questions than answers. She grappled with the complexities of his character, struggling to reconcile the different facets of the man she had loved.

In the midst of this turmoil, Emily found solace in her own growth. She realized that her quest for the truth about Michael was also a journey of self-discovery. Each revelation, each conversation, was a step towards understanding not just Michael, but herself as well.

Emily's journey was not just about uncovering the secrets of Michael's past; it was about confronting her own. She began to recognize her own patterns, her own vulnerabilities that had drawn her to Michael. This recognition was painful, yet it was also empowering. Emily was no longer the same person who had fallen in love with Michael. She had evolved, grown stronger and more self-aware through the crucible of her experiences.

As Emily left the coffee shop, she felt a sense of closure. Her journey had brought her face to face with the complexities of Michael's life, but more importantly, it had led her to a deeper understanding of herself. She walked away with a sense of peace, ready to face the future with a newfound resilience and a heart open to the lessons of the past.

In the days that followed, Emily's resolve to understand Michael's enigmatic life only intensified. She found herself delving deeper into his world, seeking out those who had known him in different capacities. Each person she met added another piece to the intricate puzzle of Michael's existence, revealing the multifaceted nature of his character.

Her next encounter was with a woman named Sarah, who had been Michael's neighbor for several years. Sarah's perspective was markedly different from the others. She spoke of Michael with a mixture of fondness and concern, describing him as a man who was often misunderstood, someone who struggled to fit into the expectations of society.

Sarah recalled instances where Michael had shown great kindness and compassion, helping her with household chores or offering a listening ear during tough times. Yet, there were also moments of inexplicable sadness in him, times when he seemed lost in his thoughts, burdened by an invisible weight.

These conversations were enlightening for Emily, but they also left her emotionally drained. The complexity of Michael's character was overwhelming, and she often found herself lost in a sea of conflicting emotions. She grappled with feelings of anger, betrayal, and sorrow, yet there was also a growing sense of empathy for Michael.

Amidst this emotional turmoil, Emily's own life was undergoing significant changes. She had started to rebuild her life, finding a new job and a new place to live. These changes, though challenging, brought a sense of stability and purpose to her life. She was no longer the same person who had been shattered by Michael's disappearance; she was stronger, more resilient.

As Emily navigated through this period of transformation, she also began to form new relationships. She found support and understanding in a small group of friends who had been through similar experiences. Their shared struggles and triumphs created a bond that was both healing and empowering.

One of these friends was Alex, a kind-hearted individual who had faced his own battles with loss and grief. Alex became a confidant for Emily, someone she could turn to when the weight of her journey became too much to bear alone. Their friendship blossomed into a source of strength and comfort for both of them.

Through her interactions with Alex and her other friends, Emily began to see the value of community and connection. She realized that healing was not a solitary journey, but one that was enriched by the presence and support of others.

As Emily continued to piece together the puzzle of Michael's life, she also started to focus on her own healing. She engaged in activities that brought her joy and fulfillment, such as painting and writing. These creative outlets became a form of therapy for her, a way to express her emotions and process her experiences.

Emily's journey was far from over, but she had come a long way from the broken-hearted woman who had first set out to uncover the truth about Michael. She had faced her fears, confronted her pain, and emerged stronger and more self-assured. Her quest for understanding had led her to a deeper appreciation of life's complexities and the resilience of the human spirit.

Emily's journey of self-discovery and understanding led her to a crucial realization: the answers she sought about Michael might not provide the closure she desired. She began to see that her quest was less about unraveling the mysteries surrounding him and more about confronting her own inner turmoil.

Her introspection brought forth a myriad of emotions. She grappled with the duality of her feelings for Michael – the love that once filled her heart now mingled with a sense of betrayal and disillusionment. Yet, amidst this emotional chaos, Emily found a surprising sense of liberation. She was no longer bound by the narrative she had constructed around their relationship. This newfound freedom was both exhilarating and daunting.

In her pursuit of understanding, Emily also encountered Clara's sister, Anne. Anne's insights into Clara and Michael's relationship were eye-opening. She painted a picture of a complex relationship, marked by intense passion and equally intense struggles. Anne's recollections suggested that Clara and Michael's marriage was far from the idyllic union that Emily had imagined.

Anne spoke of Clara's own battles with personal demons, her struggles with mental health, and how these issues had impacted her relationship with Michael. This revelation added another layer to

Emily's understanding of Michael. It became evident that his life was a tapestry of intricate and interwoven personal challenges, not just with Emily but also within his marriage to Clara.

As Emily absorbed these revelations, she began to see Michael in a different light. He was no longer just the man who had left her heartbroken; he was a deeply flawed individual, grappling with his complexities and vulnerabilities. This realization brought a sense of empathy to Emily's heart. She started to feel a sense of compassion for both Michael and Clara, recognizing the human frailties that defined their lives.

During this period, Emily also strengthened her bonds with her newfound friends. Their support became a cornerstone in her life, providing her with a sense of belonging and community that she had long craved. These relationships, built on mutual understanding and shared experiences, were a source of strength and comfort.

Emily's friendship with Alex, in particular, evolved into a deep and meaningful connection. They shared not only their personal struggles but also their hopes and dreams for the future. In Alex, Emily found a kindred spirit, someone who understood her journey and stood by her side.

As Emily navigated through these complex emotional landscapes, she also began to confront the ethical dilemmas that her quest for the truth had unearthed. She wrestled with questions about the right to privacy versus the need for closure. Her interactions with Michael's acquaintances and Clara's family members had opened a Pandora's box of moral quandaries.

These dilemmas forced Emily to reflect on her actions and motivations. She questioned whether her pursuit of the truth was justifiable or if it was an intrusion into the private lives of others. This introspection was challenging, but it was also a crucial step in her journey towards self-awareness and maturity.

Through all these experiences, Emily's character underwent a profound transformation. She emerged from her ordeal not just as a woman who had endured heartbreak and betrayal, but as someone who had grown in empathy, strength, and wisdom. Her journey was a testament to the resilience of the human spirit and the transformative power of confronting one's deepest fears and vulnerabilities.

As Emily's understanding deepened, so did her resolve to forge a new path for herself. She realized that her fixation on the past, particularly on Michael and Clara's relationship, was a way to avoid facing her own issues. This epiphany marked a turning point in her journey.

She began to invest more time in her personal growth, exploring interests and passions she had long neglected. Art, which had always been a source of solace for Emily, became a focal point of her life. She found herself spending hours painting, her emotions flowing onto the canvas in a riot of colors and shapes. This creative outlet provided her with a sense of peace and fulfillment that had been missing from her life.

In parallel, Emily's social circle expanded. She found herself gravitating towards individuals who shared her interests and values. These new friendships were built on mutual respect and understanding, offering her a sense of belonging that she had not felt in a long time.

Among these new friends was a woman named Sarah, a fellow artist who shared Emily's passion for painting. Sarah's vibrant personality and positive outlook on life were infectious. She encouraged Emily to step out of her comfort zone, to explore new artistic techniques, and to participate in local art exhibitions. This encouragement was instrumental in helping Emily regain her confidence.

As Emily's social and emotional landscape shifted, so did her perspective on her relationship with Michael. She began to see their time together not as a wasted chapter in her life but as a learning experience that had contributed to her growth. This shift in perspective was liberating, allowing her to let go of lingering resentment and pain.

Meanwhile, Emily's professional life also took a positive turn. She received an offer to work on a collaborative art project, a venture that promised not only creative satisfaction but also financial stability. This opportunity was a testament to her hard work and dedication to her craft.

However, just as Emily was finding her footing, an unexpected development threatened to unravel the progress she had made. A chance encounter with Michael brought back a flood of memories and emotions. Seeing him after all this time, Emily was confronted with a mix of nostalgia and unease.

Michael, looking more worn and tired than she remembered, seemed genuinely surprised to see her. Their conversation was awkward, filled with long pauses and hesitant exchanges. Emily could sense a deep sadness in Michael, a stark contrast to the confident man she once knew.

This encounter left Emily with a renewed sense of confusion. Part of her longed to reconnect with Michael, to find out what had happened to him since their last meeting. Yet, another part of her was hesitant, wary of reopening old wounds.

As Emily grappled with these conflicting emotions, she realized that her journey was far from over. While she had made significant strides in understanding herself and moving on from her past, the complexities of human relationships and emotions were ever-present challenges.

In the midst of this turmoil, Emily found solace in her art. She poured her conflicting emotions into her paintings, creating pieces that were more raw and expressive than anything she had done before. Her art became a reflection of her inner journey, a visual diary of her struggles and triumphs.

Through this process, Emily came to understand that life was not about finding definitive answers or achieving a state of perfect balance. Instead, it was about embracing the complexities, learning from experiences, and continually evolving as a person. This realization was both humbling and empowering, marking a new chapter in Emily's journey of self-discovery.

# Chapter 13: Breaking Point

The tension in Emily's life reached a crescendo, manifesting in a series of confrontations that tested her newfound resilience. The first of these confrontations occurred unexpectedly, during a visit to her favorite café. There, she encountered Clara, who had been a shadowy figure in her life for so long.

Clara, looking both defiant and uneasy, approached Emily. The air was thick with unspoken words, years of tension hanging between them. Clara's opening words were an apology, but her tone held an edge of defensiveness. She spoke of her own struggles, her voice laced with bitterness and regret.

Emily listened, her emotions a whirlwind of anger, pity, and disbelief. She realized that Clara, much like herself, was a victim of circumstances, yet she couldn't fully absolve her of the pain caused. The conversation ended abruptly, with Clara leaving in a huff, leaving Emily to grapple with a mix of relief and unresolved feelings.

This encounter was a catalyst for Emily, pushing her to confront her own inner turmoil. She began to question the narrative she had built around her relationship with Michael, recognizing the need to view things from a broader perspective.

Her introspection was interrupted by a crisis at work. A major project she had been leading was suddenly at risk due to unforeseen complications. Emily found herself at the center of a storm, with her team looking to her for guidance. The pressure was immense, but Emily rose to the challenge, her leadership skills coming to the fore. She worked tirelessly, coordinating with her team to find solutions, her focus unwavering despite the chaos around her.

This professional challenge brought a sense of clarity to Emily. She realized that her experiences, both personal and professional, had equipped her with a resilience she had not fully appreciated. She began to see her struggles not as insurmountable obstacles but as opportunities to learn and grow.

Amidst these challenges, Emily's social life took a back seat. Her friends, noticing her absence, reached out with concern. Emily found comfort in these gestures of friendship, reminded of the support system she had in her life. She made a conscious effort to reconnect with her friends, realizing the importance of maintaining these bonds.

As Emily navigated these various challenges, she began to see a change in herself. She was becoming more assertive, more confident in her decisions. This newfound strength was put to the test when she once again crossed paths with Michael.

Their encounter was unexpected, taking place in a crowded marketplace. Michael looked haggard, his eyes reflecting a deep-seated weariness. He spoke of his own struggles, his voice tinged with regret. Emily listened, her heart heavy with a mix of emotions.

This meeting with Michael was different from their last. Emily found herself able to engage with him without the overwhelming emotional turmoil that had characterized their previous encounters. She spoke her mind, expressing her feelings with a clarity and calmness that surprised even her.

As they parted ways, Emily felt a sense of closure. She realized that she no longer needed answers from Michael to move on with her life. Her journey had brought her to a place of self-reliance and inner peace.

This realization marked a turning point for Emily. She embraced her challenges with a renewed sense of purpose, her resilience shining through in every aspect of her life. She understood that life would always be a mix of highs and lows, but she felt equipped to face whatever came her way.

Emily's newfound resilience was soon put to the test in a confrontation that shook her to the core. A chance encounter with Clara's sister, who had been a peripheral figure in her life, revealed startling truths about Michael and Clara's relationship. The sister, fraught with emotion, disclosed details that painted a far more complex picture than Emily had ever imagined.

The revelations were shocking, involving years of hidden struggles, including financial woes and personal betrayals. Emily listened, her mind reeling as she tried to reconcile these new facts with her understanding of Michael and Clara. This encounter forced her to reevaluate not just her past relationship with Michael but also her perception of Clara.

In the days that followed, Emily grappled with a maelstrom of emotions. Anger, confusion, and a sense of betrayal swirled within her. She found herself questioning the foundations of her past relationship, wondering how much of it had been a facade.

Amidst this emotional upheaval, Emily faced challenges in her personal life. Her landlord announced a sudden rent increase, putting financial pressure on her already strained budget. This news came as a blow, adding to the mounting stress in her life.

Despite these challenges, Emily's resilience did not waver. She tackled the rent issue head-on, negotiating with her landlord and exploring additional income sources. Her determination was a testament to her growth, a clear indication of how far she had come.

Simultaneously, Emily's professional life continued to demand her attention. A critical deadline loomed, and she found herself leading her team through long nights and complex problem-solving sessions. Her leadership skills were evident, as she motivated her team and navigated the high-pressure environment with a calm and focused demeanor.

Through these professional challenges, Emily found a sense of purpose and fulfillment. She realized that her work was not just a job but a vital part of her identity. This realization brought a sense of pride and accomplishment, bolstering her self-esteem.

As Emily navigated these various aspects of her life, she found solace in her growing network of friends and allies. Their support was a constant source of strength, providing her with a sense of belonging and community.

One evening, during a gathering with friends, Emily had a profound conversation with a close friend who had always been her confidante. They discussed life's complexities, the unpredictable nature of relationships, and the importance of self-discovery. This conversation was a turning point for Emily, helping her to see her situation in a new light.

She began to understand that her journey was not just about uncovering the truth about Michael and Clara but also about understanding herself. She recognized that her experiences, both good and bad, were shaping her into a stronger, more resilient person.

This realization marked a significant shift in Emily's mindset. She approached her challenges with a newfound sense of confidence and clarity. She was no longer defined by her past relationship with Michael but by her own strengths and aspirations.

As Emily continued to confront the various challenges in her life, she did so with a sense of optimism and determination. She knew that the road ahead would be filled with obstacles, but she also knew that she had the strength and resilience to face them head-on.

In the midst of her personal growth, Emily faced an unexpected challenge that tested her newfound resilience. A confrontation with Clara, fraught with tension and unresolved emotions, brought to light the depth of their intertwined pasts. Clara, visibly shaken, accused Emily of meddling in her life, of unraveling the delicate balance she had maintained for years.

The confrontation was intense, with accusations and revelations that left Emily reeling. Clara spoke of her own struggles, of the sacrifices she had made, and of the pain that Emily's presence had inadvertently caused. It was a moment of raw honesty, exposing the complex web of emotions and history that connected them.

Emily, though taken aback, responded with a calmness that surprised even herself. She acknowledged Clara's pain, expressing her own regret for any hurt she may have caused. This exchange, though difficult, marked a turning point in their relationship. It was a step towards understanding, if not reconciliation.

Following this confrontation, Emily found herself reflecting on the nature of relationships and the unseen burdens people carry. She realized that everyone has their own story, their own struggles, and that understanding this was key to empathy and compassion.

This realization was further reinforced through her interactions with her colleagues at work. A particularly challenging project brought the team together, fostering a sense of camaraderie and mutual respect. Emily saw how each team member brought their unique strengths and perspectives to the table, creating a dynamic and effective unit.

Amidst these professional successes, Emily continued to navigate her personal life with a newfound sense of purpose. She became more involved in community activities, finding joy in connecting with others and contributing to causes she cared about. This engagement brought a sense of fulfillment and belonging that she had long missed.

As she immersed herself in these activities, Emily encountered a diverse range of individuals, each with their own stories and experiences. These interactions broadened her perspective, allowing her to see the world through a more empathetic and inclusive lens.

One such encounter was with a young couple facing challenges due to their LGBTQ+ identity. Their story of resilience in the face of adversity resonated with Emily, reminding her of the power of acceptance and support. This experience further fueled her desire to be an ally and advocate for those facing discrimination and injustice.

Through these experiences, Emily's understanding of herself and the world around her deepened. She began to see her journey not just as a quest for personal truth, but as a path towards greater understanding and empathy for others.

Her relationships with friends and family also evolved. Conversations became more meaningful, and she found herself offering support and advice based on her own experiences. These interactions were a source of comfort and strength, both for Emily and for those she cared about.

As Emily's journey continued, she faced each new challenge with a sense of resilience and optimism. She knew that the path ahead would be filled with uncertainties, but she also knew that she had the strength and support to face whatever came her way.

Emily's journey of self-discovery and resilience led her to a deeper understanding of her own strengths and vulnerabilities. As she navigated the complexities of her relationships and career, she found herself increasingly drawn to the stories and struggles of others, realizing that her own experiences, though unique, were part of a larger tapestry of human emotion and connection.

In her professional life, Emily faced a significant challenge that tested her leadership and problem-solving skills. A major project at work hit a critical snag, threatening to derail months of effort and collaboration. Emily, leading the team, found herself at the center of a storm of stress and high expectations. However, instead of succumbing to the pressure, she rose to the occasion, demonstrating an impressive level of composure and ingenuity.

Her approach to the problem was methodical yet creative, combining a deep understanding of the technical aspects with a keen sense of team dynamics. She encouraged open communication and fostered an environment where every team member felt valued and heard. This inclusive approach not only helped in identifying the root cause of the issue but also in devising a solution that was innovative and effective.

The success of this project was a turning point for Emily, professionally. It not only bolstered her confidence but also earned her the respect and admiration of her colleagues and superiors. This achievement was a testament to her growth, not just as a professional but as a leader.

On a personal front, Emily's journey was equally transformative. She found herself increasingly involved in community service, particularly in areas related to mental health awareness and support. Her own experiences with emotional turmoil and resilience resonated deeply in these endeavors, allowing her to connect with others on a profound level.

One particular incident stood out during this period. Emily encountered a young woman struggling with severe anxiety and depression, a situation that mirrored her own past struggles. The empathy and understanding Emily showed were instrumental in helping the young woman seek the help she needed. This experience was deeply gratifying for Emily, reinforcing her belief in the power of empathy and support.

As she continued to balance her professional responsibilities with her personal passions, Emily also found time for introspection and self-care. She took up meditation and yoga, practices that helped her maintain her mental and emotional equilibrium. These moments of quiet reflection became a sanctuary for her, a space where she could recharge and center herself.

Her relationships with friends and family also deepened during this time. Conversations were richer, filled with insights and mutual respect. Emily found herself offering advice and support, drawing from her own experiences and learnings. These interactions were not just comforting but also enlightening, providing her with diverse perspectives and ideas.

As Emily's understanding of herself and the world around her deepened, she began to see her journey not just as a quest for personal truth, but as a path towards greater understanding and empathy for others. Her experiences, both challenging and rewarding, had shaped her into a person of depth, resilience, and compassion.

In this phase of her life, Emily's resilience was put to the test in a way she had never anticipated. A close friend, whom she had known since childhood, was going through a tumultuous divorce, bringing to the surface a myriad of emotions and memories for Emily. This situation required her to be a pillar of support, all while managing her own emotional responses triggered by the unfolding events.

Her friend's ordeal was heart-wrenching. As Emily listened and provided comfort, she found herself revisiting her own past, the pain of her parents' divorce, and the subsequent challenges she faced. This journey through her memories, though painful, also brought a new level of understanding and empathy for what her friend was experiencing.

Amidst this emotional turmoil, Emily found solace in her newfound passion for painting. She discovered that expressing herself through art provided a therapeutic outlet for her emotions. Her paintings, vibrant and expressive, became a visual diary of her journey, capturing the essence of her experiences and emotions.

Her art soon caught the attention of a local gallery owner, who was captivated by the raw emotion and depth in her work. This led to an unexpected opportunity for Emily to showcase her art in a local exhibition. The prospect of displaying her personal journey to the world was daunting, yet exhilarating.

As she prepared for the exhibition, Emily found herself reflecting on her journey. Each painting told a story, a piece of her life that she was now sharing with others. The process was cathartic, allowing her to let go of past hurts and embrace her present.

The exhibition was a resounding success, with attendees deeply moved by the honesty and beauty of her work. Emily received accolades not only for her artistic talent but also for her courage in sharing her personal journey so openly. This experience further boosted her confidence and solidified her belief in the healing power of art.

Meanwhile, in her professional life, Emily faced a new challenge. Her company was undergoing a major restructuring, which brought uncertainty and anxiety among the staff. Emily's leadership skills were once again called upon as she navigated her team through these changes.

She approached this challenge with a blend of empathy and pragmatism. Her ability to listen and understand her team's concerns, coupled with her strategic thinking, helped in creating a sense of stability and direction amidst the chaos. Her team's performance during this period was a testament to her effective leadership and the trust she had built among her colleagues.

Throughout these experiences, Emily's personal growth was evident. She had evolved into a person who could handle complex emotional situations with grace and strength. Her journey had taught her the importance of resilience, empathy, and the transformative power of art.

As she looked forward to the future, Emily felt a sense of excitement and anticipation. She had faced numerous challenges, each shaping her into a stronger, more compassionate individual. Her journey was far from over, but she was ready for whatever lay ahead, armed with the lessons she had learned and the strength she had gained.

Emily's newfound resilience was soon put to the ultimate test. A crisis erupted within her family, one that shook the very foundations of her life. Her brother, whom she had always been close to, was involved in a serious legal issue. The news came as a shock, sending ripples of distress through the family.

As she grappled with this new reality, Emily found herself at the center of the family storm, trying to provide support while dealing with her own whirlwind of emotions. Her brother's situation was complex, fraught with legal and moral implications that were difficult to navigate.

Despite the chaos, Emily remained a source of strength for her family. Her ability to remain calm and rational during such a tumultuous time was a testament to her character. She worked tirelessly to understand the legal intricacies of her brother's case, seeking advice from experts and offering moral support to her brother.

Amidst this family crisis, Emily's professional life was also demanding her attention. She was leading a critical project at work, one that required her full focus and dedication. Balancing her professional responsibilities with her personal challenges was a daunting task, yet Emily managed it with remarkable poise.

Her leadership in the workplace did not go unnoticed. Her colleagues admired her ability to maintain her performance under pressure, further solidifying her reputation as a capable and resilient leader. This period of intense pressure revealed Emily's true mettle, her ability to handle multiple high-stress situations simultaneously.

In her personal life, Emily's relationship with her partner, who had been a pillar of support, began to show signs of strain. The constant stress and lack of time together were taking their toll. Conversations that were once filled with laughter and love were now brief and burdened with the weight of their respective stresses.

Emily realized the importance of nurturing her relationship amidst the chaos. She began to make a conscious effort to spend quality time with her partner, ensuring that their bond remained strong. These moments of connection, though brief, were vital in keeping their relationship grounded.

As the legal proceedings of her brother's case progressed, Emily found herself drawn into a world she had never imagined. She attended court hearings, met with lawyers, and spent countless hours discussing strategies. This experience was draining, both emotionally and intellectually, yet Emily faced it with unwavering determination.

Through this ordeal, Emily learned the importance of family, love, and support. She realized that life's trials could either break or strengthen relationships. In her case, it brought her family closer together, forging bonds that were stronger than ever.

As the chapter of her brother's legal battle came to a close, Emily emerged with a deeper understanding of life's complexities. She had faced adversity head-on, demonstrating resilience, empathy, and strength. These experiences shaped her into a more compassionate and understanding individual, ready to face the future with renewed vigor and wisdom.

Emily's journey through the labyrinth of her brother's legal troubles and the strains on her personal life had left indelible marks. Yet, amidst these trials, a new challenge emerged, one that would test her resilience even further. A sudden health scare within her family brought a stark reminder of life's fragility.

This health crisis required Emily to step into a caregiving role, a responsibility she embraced with her characteristic strength and compassion. Nights were spent in hospital corridors, and days were filled with medical consultations. The rhythm of her life had shifted dramatically, yet she adapted with remarkable agility.

In these moments of vulnerability, Emily found unexpected sources of support. Friends and colleagues rallied around her, offering assistance in various forms. This outpouring of solidarity was heartwarming, providing Emily with much-needed emotional sustenance.

Simultaneously, Emily's professional life continued to demand her attention. Balancing her career with her family responsibilities was a Herculean task. Yet, she managed to navigate these competing demands with a grace that left many in awe. Her ability to compartmentalize, focusing intensely on the task at hand, was a skill that served her well during these trying times.

Amidst the chaos, Emily's relationship with her partner evolved. The crisis had brought them closer, forging a deeper understanding and appreciation for each other. They became a team, facing each challenge together, their bond strengthened by the adversities they overcame.

As her family member's health gradually improved, Emily reflected on the journey she had undertaken. She had navigated through storms of legal battles, professional pressures, and personal crises, emerging with a newfound appreciation for life's unpredictability and the value of resilience.

This period of intense personal growth had also brought clarity to Emily's life. She began to reassess her priorities, recognizing the importance of balance and self-care. Her experiences had taught her the significance of taking time for oneself, even amidst life's chaos.

With her family member on the road to recovery, Emily slowly resumed her normal routine. However, the experiences had changed her. She returned to her daily life with a deeper sense of purpose and a renewed commitment to her own well-being.

In her professional sphere, Emily's experiences had enhanced her leadership qualities. She approached her work with a greater sense of empathy and understanding, qualities that resonated with her team. Her ability to lead with compassion and resilience became a hallmark of her leadership style.

As Emily moved forward, she carried with her the lessons learned from these trials. She had faced life's unpredictability with courage and had come out stronger. Her journey was a testament to the power of resilience, the importance of support systems, and the strength that lies in vulnerability.

Emily's newfound perspective on life, shaped by recent challenges, led her to make significant changes. She started prioritizing her mental and physical health, integrating activities like yoga and meditation into her daily routine. These practices brought her a sense of peace and balance, which had been missing in her life for a long time.

In her professional realm, Emily's approach to work underwent a transformation. She began delegating tasks more effectively, trusting her team, and allowing herself to step back when necessary. This not only improved her work-life balance but also empowered her colleagues, fostering a more collaborative and efficient work environment.

Her personal relationships flourished as well. Emily's partner, seeing the changes in her, responded with increased support and understanding. They found new ways to connect and communicate, strengthening their bond. Her friends and family noticed a more relaxed and present Emily, which deepened their connections.

However, amidst these positive developments, Emily faced a new dilemma. Her brother's legal issues, while no longer at the forefront of her daily concerns, still lingered in the background. She grappled with the decision of how involved she should be in his situation. Her sense of duty as a sister was strong, but she also recognized the need to protect her well-being.

This internal conflict was not easy for Emily. She sought counsel from trusted friends and even a therapist, exploring the boundaries of her responsibilities and her capacity to help. These conversations were enlightening, helping her to understand that caring for herself was not selfish but necessary.

As she navigated this complex situation, Emily's resilience was once again put to the test. An unexpected development in her brother's case required her immediate attention and involvement. This development brought back the stress and anxiety she had worked so hard to manage.

Yet, this time, Emily was better equipped to handle the pressure. Her recent experiences had armed her with tools and strategies to maintain her equilibrium. She approached the situation with a calm and clear mind, making decisions that were thoughtful and measured.

In dealing with her brother's situation, Emily also discovered a newfound strength in vulnerability. She allowed herself to seek help and express her emotions, rather than bottling them up. This openness not only helped her to cope but also allowed others to offer support in more meaningful ways.

Through these trials, Emily's journey of self-discovery and growth continued. Each challenge she faced brought new lessons and insights, shaping her into a more resilient, empathetic, and balanced individual. Her story was a testament to the human spirit's ability to adapt and thrive, even in the face of adversity.

# Chapter 14: Descent into Darkness

Emily's life, once a tapestry of professional success and personal contentment, began to unravel as she delved deeper into the complexities of her past. The revelations about Michael and Clara, once distant echoes, now roared in her mind like a relentless storm. These discoveries, coupled with the ongoing struggles in her personal life, cast a shadow over her once radiant spirit.

In her professional sphere, Emily's once impeccable performance started to falter. Deadlines slipped through her fingers like grains of sand, and her once sharp focus blurred, clouded by the turmoil within. Colleagues whispered in hushed tones, their words a mix of concern and curiosity. Her boss, once a pillar of support, began to question her commitment, adding to the mounting pressure.

At home, the walls of her apartment, once a sanctuary, felt like a prison. Sleep eluded her, and when it did come, it was plagued by nightmares, echoes of her past and present fears intertwining in a macabre dance. Her social life, once vibrant and fulfilling, dwindled to nothingness. Friends reached out, but their calls and messages went unanswered, lost in the void of her despair.

The strain began to manifest physically. Emily's once bright eyes dulled, her energy sapped by the weight of her thoughts. Meals were forgotten, and her health deteriorated, a reflection of the chaos within. The mirror showed a stranger, a hollow version of the woman she once was.

In her quest for answers, Emily found herself at the doors of a support group for survivors of mental abuse. The stories she heard there mirrored her own, tales of manipulation and control that left deep, invisible scars. Each story was a thread in a tapestry of pain and resilience, and as she listened, Emily realized she was not alone in her suffering.

This realization was a double-edged sword. On one hand, it brought a sense of community, a feeling of being understood. On the other, it magnified the gravity of her situation, the realization that her story was one of many, a single note in a symphony of sorrow. The group offered support, but it also opened her eyes to the pervasive nature of mental abuse and its insidious effects on individuals and communities.

As Emily delved deeper into her own psyche, she began to see the patterns of her life with newfound clarity. The relationship with Michael, once a source of joy, now appeared as a carefully constructed facade, a manipulation that had left deep psychological wounds. The realization was a bitter pill, a mixture of anger, sadness, and betrayal that was hard to swallow.

Her journey into the darkness was not just a descent but a confrontation with the ghosts of her past. Each revelation, each memory unearthed, was a step towards understanding, a painful yet necessary part of her healing process. But as she ventured further into the abyss, the light of hope seemed ever more distant, a flickering flame in the encroaching darkness.

Amidst this turmoil, Emily's relationship with her family began to strain. Her mother, always a beacon of unwavering support, struggled to reach her. Conversations that were once filled with laughter and warmth turned into a series of worried questions and reassurances. Emily's father, a man of few words, expressed his concern through his silence, a heavy, unspoken tension that hung in the air during their rare interactions.

Her sister, Anna, became increasingly insistent on helping, her messages a constant reminder of a life Emily felt she was losing grip on. Anna's attempts to understand were well-intentioned but often misfired, widening the chasm between them. The family gatherings, once a source of joy and comfort, became a tableau of strained smiles and unspoken worries.

In her professional life, Emily's decline did not go unnoticed. A crucial project, once under her confident guidance, began to falter. Her team, initially sympathetic, grew frustrated as her leadership waned. The mounting pressure from her superiors only added to the cacophony of stress and self-doubt that plagued her.

Her personal life, too, was in disarray. The apartment, once meticulously organized, reflected her inner chaos. Unopened mail piled up, and the once cherished mementos of her relationship with Michael gathered dust, painful reminders of a love that had turned into a source of anguish.

In moments of solitude, Emily found herself reflecting on her past choices. Each decision, each turn she had taken, seemed to lead her to this point of despair. The realization that her life was a labyrinth of her own making was both a revelation and a burden. It was in these moments of introspection that she began to pen her thoughts, a cathartic process that brought both pain and relief.

Her journal became a confidant, the pages filled with raw emotions and unfiltered truths. Words flowed, sometimes in a torrent of anger and frustration, at other times in a trickle of sadness and regret. This exercise in self-expression became a lifeline, a way to navigate the stormy seas of her psyche.

As she wrote, Emily began to piece together the fragmented aspects of her identity. The confident professional, the loving daughter and sister, the heartbroken lover – all facets of a complex mosaic. This introspection brought a gradual understanding of her resilience, a recognition of the strength that lay beneath the surface of her pain.

However, this journey inward was not without its perils. The more she delved into her psyche, the more she confronted the darker aspects of her being. Insecurities and fears, long buried, surfaced, demanding attention. These revelations, while essential for her growth, were a stark reminder of the long road ahead.

Her nights were restless, a battleground of conflicting emotions and unresolved questions. Dreams, once an escape, became a theater of her subconscious, replaying her deepest anxieties and desires. In these nocturnal wanderings, Emily often found herself in imaginary confrontations with Michael, each encounter a mix of accusation and longing.

As the days passed, Emily's journey became a balancing act between self-discovery and self-preservation. Each step forward was a victory, but the path was fraught with setbacks. The support group, her family, and her journaling became pillars of strength, but the weight of her journey was hers to bear alone.

In the midst of her tumultuous journey, Emily discovered solace in unexpected places. Her support group, initially a source of trepidation, became a sanctuary of shared experiences and empathy. In the company of others who had faced their own demons, she found the courage to voice her struggles and fears.

Through tearful confessions and whispered stories, she began to understand that her pain was not unique. The spectrum of human suffering was vast, and she was but one thread in the intricate tapestry of anguish. The LGBTQ+ members of the group shared their own battles against prejudice and discrimination, forging connections built on mutual understanding and acceptance.

Emily's relationship with her family, while strained, also began to evolve. Her mother, after seeking guidance from professionals, learned how to better communicate with her daughter. Their conversations became less about trying to solve Emily's problems and more about listening and offering unconditional love.

Her father, though still reserved, began to express his support in subtle ways – a reassuring pat on the back, a shared favorite meal, a silent but significant presence in her life. The tension between them gradually dissipated, replaced by an unspoken understanding.

Anna, too, underwent a transformation. She recognized that her eagerness to help had unintentionally added to Emily's burden. With newfound patience, she gave Emily the space she needed while remaining a steadfast presence in her life. Their relationship, once strained, began to heal as they learned to appreciate each other's strengths and vulnerabilities.

Emily's professional life also showed signs of recovery. With therapy and support, she began to regain her self-confidence and assertiveness. Her team, witnessing her determination to overcome adversity, rallied around her. Together, they worked tirelessly to resurrect the floundering project.

In the midst of her own turmoil, Emily found herself advocating for LGBTQ+ rights within her company. Inspired by the stories shared in her support group, she became a voice for change, pushing for inclusive policies and diversity training. Her efforts, while initially met with resistance, began to bear fruit as the company recognized the importance of fostering an inclusive and accepting environment.

Yet, despite the progress she made in her personal and professional life, Emily's journey into the depths of her own psyche continued to reveal new challenges. She confronted the scars of past relationships, not just with Michael but with others who had left their mark on her heart.

Through therapy and introspection, she explored the patterns of her own behavior – the choices she had made and the red flags she had ignored. It was a painful reckoning with her own vulnerability and naivety, but it was a necessary step towards healing.

Emily's nights, once filled with restless dreams, gradually became more peaceful. The imaginary confrontations with Michael shifted into conversations of closure, where forgiveness mingled with the lingering ache of lost love. As she navigated the labyrinth of her subconscious, she discovered pockets of strength she never knew existed.

And so, Emily's journey of self-discovery continued, a winding path through the labyrinth of her own soul. The shadows of her past still haunted her, but with each step, she moved closer to the light of healing and transformation.

In the midst of her transformative journey, Emily found herself at a crossroads. The revelations about Michael and Clara's relationship had shaken her to the core, but they also ignited a fire within her—a fierce determination to uncover the truth, no matter the cost.

She had delved deep into the intricacies of their marriage, piecing together fragments of their history like a detective unraveling a complex case. Emily's obsession with the truth had consumed her, driving her to dig deeper into the tangled web of lies, deceit, and betrayal.

Her research led her down unexpected paths, uncovering secrets she could never have imagined. She learned of Clara's own struggles and the emotional toll their marriage had taken on her. The revelations painted a more complex picture of Clara, one that elicited both empathy and anger.

As Emily's understanding of the situation grew, she couldn't help but question her own role in this unfolding drama. Had she been too quick to judge Clara? Had her assumptions and biases clouded her judgment? These self-reflections weighed heavily on her, adding to the layers of guilt and confusion that already burdened her heart.

Amidst the chaos of her personal investigation, Emily's relationships with those around her became increasingly strained. She had become consumed by her quest for answers, neglecting the people who cared about her the most.

Anna, who had been her anchor throughout the storm, found herself pushed to the sidelines. Emily's emotional rollercoaster had left Anna feeling helpless, unable to provide the support she so desperately wanted to offer. Their once-close friendship now seemed distant, like two ships passing in the night.

At work, Emily's relentless pursuit of the truth had started to affect her professional life. Her single-mindedness had turned into obsession, causing her to miss deadlines and alienate her colleagues. The project she had worked so hard to revive was now teetering on the brink of failure once again.

Emily's therapist, the one constant source of guidance in her life, had grown increasingly concerned. She urged Emily to consider the toll her quest for answers was taking on her mental and emotional well-being. But Emily, driven by an unrelenting need for closure, couldn't heed her therapist's warnings.

Her friends and family watched with growing worry as Emily spiraled deeper into the abyss of her own making. They tried to intervene, to pull her back from the precipice of self-destruction, but Emily's determination remained unshaken.

In the midst of her turmoil, Emily faced a choice. She could continue down the path of self-destruction, sacrificing her relationships, her career, and her mental health in pursuit of a truth that might never fully satisfy her. Or she could find a way to balance her quest for closure with the need to heal and rebuild her life.

The decision hung in the balance, a fragile thread that could tip the scales in either direction. Emily knew that the road ahead would be fraught with challenges, but she also knew that it was a journey she couldn't abandon. For in the depths of her pain and confusion, she had found a glimmer of strength—a determination to confront the darkness that had haunted her for so long.

And so, with a heavy heart and a resolute spirit, Emily faced the next chapter of her tumultuous journey, uncertain of where it would lead but determined to forge a path of her own making.

As Emily's journey into the depths of darkness continued, she found herself facing a moral and ethical crossroads. The secrets she had unearthed, the stories of abuse, manipulation, and suffering, weighed heavily on her conscience. She couldn't turn a blind eye to the pain she had uncovered, and yet, she grappled with the ethical dilemma of how to use this knowledge.

She had stumbled upon accounts of domestic violence and mental abuse, stories that left scars not only on Clara but also on their children. The revelations had the power to shatter the facade of the perfect family that Michael and Clara had presented to the world. But Emily had to tread carefully, knowing that exposing these dark truths could have far-reaching consequences.

The LGBTQ characters she had encountered in her quest for answers added another layer of complexity to the story. Their struggles and resilience in the face of discrimination and prejudice struck a chord with Emily. She realized that the web of secrets extended beyond Michael and Clara, encompassing a wider community that had faced its own trials and tribulations.

Emily's heart ached for those whose voices had been silenced, whose stories had been buried beneath layers of deception. She knew that she held a powerful weapon in her hands—the truth. But with great power came great responsibility, and Emily was acutely aware of the potential harm that could be inflicted if she wielded that weapon recklessly.

Her inner turmoil deepened as she grappled with these ethical dilemmas. She sought guidance from her therapist, who reminded her that the pursuit of truth should always be tempered with compassion and empathy. Emily had to find a way to honor the stories she had uncovered while ensuring that her actions did not cause more harm than good.

In her moments of doubt and uncertainty, Emily turned to her newfound allies—individuals who had also been touched by the web of secrets but had chosen different paths. They offered her support, guidance, and a sense of community that she had never experienced before.

Together, they formed a formidable group, united by a common goal—to shine a light on the truth while protecting the vulnerable. Emily realized that she was no longer alone in her quest. She had allies who shared her commitment to justice and healing.

As the pressure mounted and the stakes grew higher, Emily's resilience was put to the test. The journey into darkness had revealed the darkest aspects of human nature, but it had also shown her the indomitable spirit of those who refused to be silenced.

Emily knew that the road ahead would be fraught with challenges and sacrifices, but she was no longer afraid. She had found her purpose in the midst of chaos, and she was determined to see it through, no matter the cost. The tangled webs of secrets would continue to unravel, and Emily would be at the center of it all, a beacon of truth and hope in a world shrouded in darkness.

Emily's determination to uncover the truth remained unwavering as she delved deeper into the heart of darkness that had engulfed Michael and Clara's lives. She couldn't ignore the stories of abuse and suffering that had been hidden for so long. The weight of these revelations pressed down on her, but she refused to be crushed by it.

In her pursuit of justice and healing, Emily found herself drawn to the LGBTQ characters she had encountered. Their resilience in the face of discrimination and prejudice was a testament to the strength of the human spirit. They had faced adversity head-on, and their stories inspired her to fight for justice even harder.

As Emily continued to unearth hidden aspects of Michael's life, she realized that the impact of domestic violence and substance abuse extended far beyond the immediate victims. It rippled through families, communities, and generations, leaving scars that were not easily healed. She couldn't turn away from the suffering she had uncovered, and she knew that she had a moral obligation to bring these dark secrets to light.

Her alliance with those who had also been touched by the web of secrets grew stronger with each passing day. They became a tight-knit group, bound by a shared commitment to truth and justice. Together, they offered support to each other, a lifeline in the storm of revelations.

Yet, as Emily confronted the darkest aspects of human nature, her own resilience was tested. The emotional toll of her journey was undeniable, and there were moments when she questioned whether she could bear the weight of the truth. But she found strength in her allies, in their shared purpose and determination.

Emily knew that the road ahead would not be easy. It was fraught with challenges, obstacles, and moral dilemmas. She was acutely aware of the potential consequences of exposing the secrets she had uncovered, and the fear of causing more harm haunted her.

But she couldn't turn back now. The truth was a beacon, a guiding light that illuminated the path forward. Emily had become a symbol of hope for those who had suffered in silence, and she couldn't abandon them.

As she continued her journey into the depths of darkness, Emily held onto the belief that justice would prevail, and healing would begin. She was no longer just an observer; she was an active participant in the unraveling of the tangled webs of secrets that had ensnared so many lives. And she was determined to see it through to the end, no matter the cost.

Emily's pursuit of the truth had taken her to the very heart of darkness, where secrets festered and pain lay buried. As she delved deeper, she couldn't help but reflect on the profound impact that these revelations had on her own life. She had become a different person, transformed by the weight of knowledge and the responsibility that came with it.

The LGBTQ characters she had met along the way had become her friends and confidants. Their stories of resilience and courage had inspired her to face the darkness head-on. In them, she saw the embodiment of hope and the power of the human spirit to overcome adversity. They had faced discrimination and hatred with unwavering strength, and Emily drew strength from their stories.

But with every revelation, she also felt the weight of the suffering that had been hidden for so long. The stories of domestic violence and substance abuse were a harsh reminder of the darkness that could lurk behind closed doors. It was a darkness that affected not only the immediate victims but also the broader community.

Emily's alliance with those who had been touched by these secrets had become a lifeline for her. They offered support and understanding in the face of unimaginable pain. Together, they forged a path toward justice and healing, even as they grappled with the moral dilemmas that lay ahead.

As she delved deeper into Michael and Clara's lives, Emily couldn't help but wonder about the impact of her actions. Exposing the truth had the potential to cause further harm, and she knew that the consequences could be dire. The fear of making things worse weighed heavily on her.

But she couldn't turn back now. The truth had become a guiding light, illuminating the path forward. Emily was no longer a passive observer; she was an active participant in the unraveling of the tangled webs of secrets. She had become a symbol of hope for those who had suffered in silence, and she couldn't abandon them.

Her journey had transformed her into a person of courage and determination. She was willing to face the darkness, no matter the cost. As she continued to confront the secrets that had haunted Michael and Clara's lives, Emily knew that there was no turning back. The road ahead was treacherous, but she was resolved to see it through to the end.

In the midst of the darkness, Emily clung to the belief that justice would prevail, and healing would begin. She had become a beacon of hope for those who had longed for the truth to be revealed. And she was determined to shine that light into the deepest corners of the darkness, no matter what lay hidden there.

As Emily's journey continued, the web of secrets unraveled further, revealing the extent of Michael and Clara's tangled lives. It was a descent into darkness that had shaken the foundations of her own existence, but she remained resolute in her pursuit of the truth.

The LGBTQ characters who had become her allies and friends stood by her side, their stories echoing the resilience of the human spirit. In their presence, Emily found strength, knowing that together, they could face the darkest of truths.

Yet, with each revelation, the scars of domestic violence and the specter of substance abuse loomed larger. Emily couldn't help but be haunted by the suffering that had remained hidden for far too long. It was a pain that had rippled through the community, leaving scars that ran deep.

Her alliance with those touched by these secrets had become a lifeline, a source of support and understanding. Together, they ventured into the shadows, seeking justice and healing, even as they grappled with the moral quandaries that lay ahead.

Emily had become a guardian of the truth, a beacon of hope for those who had been silenced by fear and shame. She understood the weight of her responsibility, the potential for harm that came with exposing the darkness.

But she couldn't turn back now. The truth had become her guiding light, illuminating the path forward. Emily was no longer a passive observer; she was an active participant in the unraveling of the tangled webs of secrets. She had embraced her role as a champion of justice.

As she ventured deeper into the lives of Michael and Clara, Emily was acutely aware of the potential consequences of her actions. The fear of causing further harm gnawed at her, but she couldn't let it deter her. The truth was her compass, and she would follow it to the end, no matter the cost.

Her journey had transformed her into a person of courage and determination. She had shed the cloak of passivity and embraced her role as a seeker of truth. She was willing to face the darkest corners of existence, to confront the secrets that had tormented Michael and Clara.

In the midst of the darkness, Emily clung to the belief that justice would prevail and healing would begin. She had become a symbol of hope for those who had longed for the truth to be revealed. And she was determined to shine that light into even the deepest, most hidden corners of the darkness, no matter what she might find there.

# Chapter 15: Collateral Damage

In the wake of the main conflict, secondary characters find themselves ensnared in its consequences. Their lives, once stable, are now a whirlwind of uncertainty. Among them, a teacher named Elena grapples with the impact of war on her students. She notices their vacant stares, a stark contrast to the lively curiosity that once filled her classroom.

Elena's subplot unfolds in the small town library, where she organizes a reading group for the children. Through literature, she seeks to offer them an escape, a sliver of normalcy amid chaos. However, the war's shadow looms large, affecting even this safe haven. Books are scarce, and the fear of imminent danger is always present.

Meanwhile, a subplot involving a local family unfolds. The Martins, once a picture of suburban bliss, now struggle to keep their family unit intact. The father, a reservist, has been called to duty, leaving his wife, Laura, to navigate the challenges of single parenthood. Their two children, Emma and Jack, grapple with the absence of their father and the uncertainty of his return.

This familial subplot is accentuated by Emma's rebellious behavior. She finds solace in a group of teenagers who share her angst and frustration. Her mother, Laura, struggles to reach her, their conversations often ending in heated arguments. The tension at home is palpable, a reflection of the broader chaos outside their front door.

Community issues also come to the forefront. The local community center, once a bustling hub of activity, now serves as a makeshift shelter for displaced families. Volunteers, including Elena, work tirelessly to provide basic necessities. However, resources are limited, and the center is constantly overwhelmed by the growing number of people in need.

In another subplot, a young doctor named Amir faces the daunting task of providing medical care in a war-torn environment. His clinic, barely equipped to handle routine check-ups, is now inundated with casualties of the conflict. Amir's dedication to his patients is unwavering, but the physical and emotional toll of his work is evident.

As the narratives of these characters intertwine, the broader impact of the conflict becomes clear. Each subplot is a thread in the tapestry of a community ravaged by war. Their struggles, though unique, are bound by a common thread of resilience and the unyielding hope for a return to normalcy.

Elena's reading group, for instance, becomes more than just a diversion for the children. It evolves into a support group, a place where they can express their fears and find comfort in shared experiences. Similarly, Laura's efforts to reconnect with her daughter and maintain a semblance of family life amid the turmoil become emblematic of the community's struggle to preserve its core values in the face of adversity.

Amir's subplot takes a pivotal turn when he encounters a young boy, Aiden, injured in a recent skirmish. The boy's injuries are severe, yet his spirit remains unbroken. Amir becomes a mentor to Aiden, teaching him about medicine and instilling a sense of hope in the midst of despair. This relationship symbolizes the resilience of the human spirit, even in the darkest of times.

In another part of town, the Martins face a crisis. Jack, feeling the strain of his father's absence, begins to act out at school. His behavior is a cry for help, a manifestation of his fear and confusion. Laura, already stretched thin, seeks assistance from Elena, who has become a confidante to many in the community. Together, they devise a plan to support Jack, integrating him into the reading group as a way to channel his emotions positively.

The subplot involving Emma takes a dramatic turn when she witnesses the consequences of the conflict firsthand. This experience serves as a wake-up call, prompting her to reconsider her actions and the impact they have on her family. It marks a turning point in her relationship with her mother, as they begin to find common ground in their shared experiences of loss and uncertainty.

Meanwhile, the community center faces its own challenges. Supplies are running low, and the influx of displaced families shows no signs of abating. Volunteers, including Elena and Amir, organize a fundraiser to support the center. This subplot highlights the power of community in times of crisis, as people from all walks of life come together to support one another.

As these narratives intertwine, the impact of the main conflict on secondary characters becomes more pronounced. Each subplot not only reflects the individual struggles of the characters but also serves as a microcosm of the larger societal impact of the conflict.

Elena's reading group, for instance, becomes more than just a diversion for the children. It evolves into a support group, a place where they can express their fears and find comfort in shared experiences. Similarly, Laura's efforts to reconnect with her daughter and maintain a semblance of family life amid the turmoil become emblematic of the community's struggle to preserve its core values in the face of adversity.

Amidst these subplots, the community center's fundraiser becomes a beacon of hope. It's not just about raising funds; it symbolizes unity and resilience. Elena and Amir play pivotal roles, their efforts drawing attention to the plight of those affected by the conflict. The event is a success, not just financially, but in its ability to bring a fractured community together, if only for a moment.

The Martins' subplot evolves as well. Laura, inspired by the community's efforts, starts a support group for families of reservists. This group becomes a safe space for sharing experiences and coping strategies. For Laura, it's a way to channel her anxieties into something constructive, providing support to others while finding it for herself.

Jack's transformation is remarkable. Under Elena's guidance, he discovers a love for reading, which becomes a therapeutic outlet. He begins to open up, sharing his feelings about his father's absence. It's a significant step towards healing, both for him and his family.

Emma, on the other hand, starts volunteering at the community center. Her experiences there change her perspective. She matures, realizing the importance of her family and community. This subplot underscores the transformative power of service and empathy.

Amir's subplot intensifies as he faces the realities of war. Shortages of medical supplies and staff put immense pressure on him. Yet, his commitment never wavers. His subplot serves as a stark reminder of the sacrifices made by those on the front lines of humanitarian crises.

The subplots involving children, particularly Aiden, take a hopeful turn. Aiden's recovery and his growing interest in medicine under Amir's mentorship symbolize hope and renewal. His journey resonates with other children in the community, inspiring them to look beyond the conflict and dream of a better future.

As these narratives progress, the ripple effects of the main conflict become increasingly evident. The subplots, intertwined and layered, paint a vivid picture of a community trying to hold onto its humanity amid chaos. The struggles of Elena, Amir, the Martins, and others are not just their own; they reflect the collective struggle of a community under siege.

In the midst of turmoil, these characters find strength in each other. Their stories are testimonies to the enduring human spirit, the ability to find hope in despair, and the unyielding resolve to rebuild from the ruins of conflict.

In this atmosphere of collective healing, the subplot involving Amir takes a poignant turn. He organizes a series of workshops at the clinic, aimed at educating the community about first aid and trauma response. This initiative not only empowers the residents but also fosters a sense of solidarity. Amir's role evolves from a mere healthcare provider to a community leader, instrumental in rebuilding the town's resilience.

The Martins, amidst their own anxiety, find solace in the community's collective efforts. Laura's support group becomes a cornerstone for other families, offering a haven where they can share their fears and hopes. The subplot involving this family subtly shifts from despair to a cautious optimism, reflecting the broader sentiment in the town.

Elena's initiative in the school, extending beyond the reading group, includes organizing art and writing workshops. These creative outlets offer the children a voice, a way to express their experiences in a safe and nurturing environment. Her dedication to these children highlights the crucial role educator play in crisis situations, not just as teachers but as beacons of stability.

The subplot with the children, particularly those in Elena's reading group, begins to mirror the larger narrative of resilience. They collaborate on a mural project, depicting their hopes for the future. This mural, vibrant and full of life, stands as a testament to the children's unyielding optimism, even in the face of adversity.

As these individual stories intertwine, they form a mosaic of a community forging a path towards healing and hope. Each character, in their own way, contributes to this journey, their personal battles intertwining with the collective struggle. Their resilience, shared pain, and hopes for the future paint a picture of a community undeterred by the challenges it faces.

In summary, the fourth part of this narrative focuses on collective healing and resilience. Characters like Elena, Amir, and the Martins, along with the children, demonstrate the power of community and the enduring human spirit in times of crisis. Their stories are individual threads in the broader fabric of a community's journey towards recovery and hope.

The town faces a critical challenge with the onset of resource scarcity, a development that tests the community's resilience in new ways.

Elena, confronted with the daunting task of maintaining educational standards amidst shortages, mobilizes the town in a campaign to gather school supplies. Her leadership in this crisis demonstrates her unwavering commitment to her students' futures. The overwhelming support from the community underscores their collective belief in the power of education, even in the toughest times.

Laura, within the Martins' narrative, steps up to address the food shortages by organizing community gardens. This initiative provides much-needed sustenance and becomes a source of healing. It's in the gardens that Emma and Jack find a renewed sense of purpose, helping to heal the rifts in their family caused by their father's absence and the prevailing uncertainty.

Amir faces his own set of challenges in the clinic, now dealing with a severe shortage of medical supplies. His ability to improvise and find alternative solutions underlines his crucial role in the community. His dedication and resourcefulness become a source of inspiration and hope for many.

The children, guided by Elena, embark on a mission to collect and distribute books. This project not only keeps the spirit of education alive but also offers comfort and a semblance of normalcy to the families. Their involvement in this initiative is a testament to their resilience and adaptability in the face of adversity.

The community center, pivotal in the town's response to the crisis, evolves into a central hub for resource distribution and support. Volunteers from various subplots unite here, their combined efforts strengthening the communal bond and exemplifying the town's solidarity.

These events highlight the community's capacity to adapt and overcome, even under dire circumstances. The collective efforts of the characters reflect not just a struggle for survival but a determination to uphold their values and way of life.

As the town navigates its way through the crisis, unexpected bonds form, adding depth to the narrative.

Elena, always a beacon of hope, starts a pen pal program between her students and children in other war-torn regions. This initiative fosters a sense of global solidarity, providing the children with a broader perspective on the conflict and its impact. It also offers them an outlet to share their experiences and find comfort in knowing they are not alone in their struggles.

In the Martin household, the subplot takes a heartwarming turn. Laura's community garden project not only brings the family closer but also becomes a gathering place for neighbors. The garden evolves into a symbol of growth and resilience, blooming amidst the chaos of war. For Emma and Jack, it's a place where they learn the values of hard work and community service, helping them grow emotionally.

Amir, faced with the ongoing challenge of limited supplies, receives unexpected assistance from a group of retired healthcare professionals. This development brings a new dynamic to his subplot, as these seasoned professionals bring their experience and wisdom to the clinic. Their involvement enhances the clinic's ability to provide care and offers Amir a much-needed support system.

The subplot involving the children's reading group takes a creative turn. They start a small newspaper, reporting on positive stories and achievements within the community. This project not only boosts morale but also serves as a platform for the children to develop new skills and express themselves creatively.

The community center continues to be a hub of activity and support. Here, various subplots intersect, with characters from different backgrounds coming together to provide aid and comfort to one another. The center's role in the community becomes more vital than ever, symbolizing the unbreakable spirit of the town.

These developments showcase the evolving dynamics within the community as they adapt to the ongoing crisis. The characters' individual journeys are interwoven with the collective narrative, highlighting the interconnectedness of their experiences.

The resilience of the community, reflected in these subplots, paints a vivid picture of hope and perseverance. Each character's contribution to the community's well-being underscores the importance of solidarity and mutual support in times of adversity.

Moreover, the town faces a new challenge: the integration of refugees displaced by the conflict. This development adds a layer of complexity to the existing subplots, testing the community's capacity for empathy and cooperation.

Elena extends her educational efforts to include these newcomers, adapting her teaching methods to cater to their diverse needs. Her classroom becomes a melting pot of cultures, where students not only learn from their textbooks but also from each other's experiences. This subplot highlights the role of education in bridging cultural divides and fostering understanding.

The Martins, especially Laura, play a significant role in this transition. The community garden becomes a place of cultural exchange, where refugees and townspeople work side by side, sharing stories and recipes from their homelands. This subplot beautifully illustrates the garden's evolution from a source of sustenance to a place of communal harmony.

Amir's subplot intertwines with this new development as he navigates the challenges of providing healthcare to a diverse population. His clinic becomes a crucial resource for the refugees, offering not just medical care but also a sense of belonging. The subplot emphasizes the universal need for compassionate healthcare and the role it plays in community building.

The children's newspaper project adapts to include stories and artwork from the refugee children. This initiative fosters a sense of inclusion, allowing the town's children and the newcomers to find common ground and build friendships. The project becomes a testament to the power of communication in overcoming barriers and building community.

The community center, already a hub of activity, takes on the additional role of a cultural center. It organizes events that celebrate the diverse backgrounds of the refugees and the townspeople, promoting mutual understanding and respect. These events bring a sense of joy and normalcy to the lives of those affected by the conflict.

These developments showcase the community's resilience in the face of change and its ability to embrace diversity. The subplots intertwine to form a narrative that speaks to the power of compassion and the strength of a community that comes together in times of need.

Elena's educational initiatives take a significant step forward. She collaborates with other educators to develop a curriculum that addresses the psychological impact of the conflict on children. This approach not only aids in their academic progress but also in their emotional healing. Elena's role transcends that of a teacher; she becomes a catalyst for change in the way the community approaches education post-conflict.

The Martins experience a pivotal moment when they receive news of the father's return. This development brings a mix of joy and apprehension, as the family anticipates adjusting to life after his long absence. Laura's support group plays a crucial role in this transition, providing guidance and support to families in similar situations.

The subplot emphasizes the ongoing challenges faced by returning soldiers and their families, highlighting the need for continued support and understanding.

Amir's clinic becomes a model for post-conflict healthcare, focusing on holistic treatment that addresses both physical and mental health. His dedication to his patients and his innovative approaches garner recognition beyond the town, inspiring similar efforts in other affected areas.

The children's newspaper evolves into a broader community publication, featuring stories of resilience and recovery from various town members. This project not only helps document the town's journey through the conflict but also becomes a source of pride and a testament to their collective spirit.

The community center, once a symbol of the town's resilience in crisis, now becomes a beacon of hope and renewal. It hosts cultural events, workshops, and support groups that cater to the diverse needs of the community, including the integration of returning soldiers and refugees.

As these narratives converge, the town's journey through adversity culminates in a newfound sense of unity and purpose. The experiences of the characters, once marked by struggle and uncertainty, now reflect hope and optimism for the future.

# Chapter 16: The Ultimate Betrayal

In the heart of the unfolding drama, a shocking revelation emerges: Michael, long trusted by those around him, has been orchestrating a web of deception. This betrayal cuts deep, particularly for Emily, who had placed her unwavering trust in him.

The depth of Michael's deception becomes apparent through a series of clandestine meetings and covert exchanges. Unbeknownst to those closest to him, he has been manipulating events to his advantage, playing a dangerous game that jeopardizes the very fabric of the relationships he is a part of.

Emily's discovery of this betrayal sends ripples through her world. Initially, disbelief and denial cloud her judgment. She grapples with the reality of Michael's actions, struggling to reconcile the man she thought she knew with the evidence of his treachery.

Her reaction evolves from shock to a burning sense of betrayal. Feelings of anger and sadness intertwine as she confronts the magnitude of Michael's deceit. This emotional turmoil sets the stage for her subsequent actions, driven by a desire to seek justice and truth.

Determined to uncover the full extent of Michael's deception, Emily embarks on a quest for answers. Her journey takes her through a labyrinth of lies, each revelation more unsettling than the last. She delves into Michael's past, uncovering secrets and motives that paint a picture of a man far removed from the persona he presented to the world.

As Emily peels back the layers of Michael's duplicity, she faces challenges that test her resolve. She encounters obstacles and threats, some from unexpected sources, as Michael's allies seek to protect their own interests.

Throughout her quest, Emily's character undergoes a transformation. The naivety and trust she once possessed give way to a steely determination and a newfound strength. Her pursuit of the truth becomes not just about exposing Michael but also about reclaiming her own sense of self and agency.

In a pivotal moment, Emily confronts Michael, demanding answers. This confrontation is charged with emotion, a clash between betrayal and the quest for truth. Michael, faced with the consequences of his actions, reveals a complex web of motivations, further complicating the narrative.

The revelation of Michael's ultimate betrayal and Emily's reaction set the stage for a dramatic unraveling of events. The impact of this twist extends beyond their individual lives, affecting those around them and setting off a chain reaction of consequences.

As Emily delves deeper into the morass of Michael's deceptions, she uncovers connections that are both startling and disturbing. Her investigation reveals that Michael's actions are not just personal betrayals but part of a larger scheme, implicating figures in positions of power and influence.

The complexity of Michael's machinations becomes increasingly evident. Emily discovers that he has been involved in illicit financial dealings, manipulative political maneuvers, and even betrayals of a more personal nature. Each discovery adds another layer to the intricate puzzle of his character.

Simultaneously, Emily's own journey transforms her. Once vulnerable and trusting, she now navigates a world of deceit with a new-found sharpness and skepticism. Her resolve hardens with each revelation, fueling her determination to expose Michael and hold him accountable.

As the story progresses, Emily's actions begin to have wider implications. Her pursuit of the truth puts her in the crosshairs of powerful individuals who have much to lose if Michael's deeds are fully brought to light. She faces intimidation and threats, but these only serve to strengthen her resolve.

In parallel, the narrative delves into Michael's perspective, revealing his motivations. His actions, though indefensible, stem from a complex web of insecurities, ambitions, and a distorted sense of survival. This exploration adds depth to his character, painting him as more than just a one-dimensional villain.

Emily's quest leads her to forge unlikely alliances. She finds support from sources she had previously overlooked, including characters who have been similarly wronged by Michael. These alliances bring new resources and perspectives to her mission, broadening the scope of her investigation.

The tension in the narrative escalates as Emily gets closer to uncovering the full extent of Michael's betrayal. This journey is not just about exposing him but also about the larger implications of his actions on the lives of those around him.

Emily's transformation reaches a crucial point as she learns to navigate this treacherous landscape with cunning and foresight. Her growth is a central theme of the narrative, illustrating the power of resilience and the human capacity for change in the face of adversity.

The storyline weaves through a tapestry of intrigue, danger, and moral quandaries. Emily's pursuit of justice and truth becomes a catalyst for broader revelations, impacting the lives of many characters and altering the course of the narrative.

Emily's foray into the depths of Michael's deceitful world unveils a labyrinth of corruption that transcends their personal history. Networks of malfeasance, ensnaring figures of authority and influence, come to light through her relentless investigation.

Transformed by her circumstances, Emily morphs from a betrayed individual into a beacon of justice. Her mission transcends mere personal vendetta, embodying a larger struggle against a corrupt system personified by Michael. This evolution marks her as a figure of moral fortitude and bravery.

Suspense intensifies as Emily pieces together Michael's intricate schemes. Illicit financial dealings, political subterfuge, and ominous connections to organized crime surface, sketching a daunting picture of Michael's reach and influence.

Personal challenges beset Emily as her quest for truth exposes her to peril. Threats loom not only from Michael's confederates but also from those fearing the fallout of her discoveries. Navigating these dangers while upholding her ethical principles tests Emily's fortitude and commitment.

Subplots involving Michael's allies enrich the narrative. Their diverse motives and connections to Michael offer insights into the complexities of betrayal and corruption. Their interactions with Emily, ranging from antagonistic to unexpectedly cooperative, deepen the story and its thematic explorations.

The dynamics of Emily's relationships with other characters evolve significantly. Her relentless pursuit of truth alters how friends and acquaintances perceive her, eliciting both admiration and skepticism. These shifting relationships add depth to the story, probing notions of trust, allegiance, and the ramifications of one's choices.

As Emily's revelations threaten to destabilize powerful individuals, the narrative's stakes escalate dramatically. Her transformation from bystander to catalyst of change is pivotal, highlighting her growing influence and agency in a world rife with duplicity.

The tension between Emily's pursuit of justice and the attendant perils she faces drives this segment of the story. Her journey, replete with external and internal challenges, underscores the personal toll and ethical dilemmas inherent in her crusade.

Emily's resolve hardens as she navigates the treacherous waters of Michael's deceit. Her discoveries reveal not just the extent of his betrayal but also the depth of his ambition. Michael's schemes, she learns, are not just about personal gain; they're about control and power, reaching into the highest echelons of society.

The more Emily uncovers, the more dangerous her quest becomes. Michael's network, vast and insidious, begins to perceive her as a threat. She finds herself shadowed, her every move scrutinized by unseen eyes. Yet, these threats only serve to fuel her determination. She becomes a symbol of defiance, a lone crusader against a corrupt titan.

During her investigation, Emily encounters an array of characters, each adding a piece to the puzzle of Michael's past. A former business partner reveals Michael's ruthless nature; an estranged family member sheds light on his early propensity for manipulation. These revelations paint a picture of a man who has always been driven by a hunger for power.

Simultaneously, Emily's personal life undergoes a transformation. The emotional toll of her quest begins to strain her relationships. Friends and family struggle to understand her single-minded pursuit of Michael, leading to moments of conflict and tension. These personal trials add a layer of complexity to her character, showcasing her vulnerabilities amidst her strengths.

In a critical turn of events, Emily unearths a document that proves to be the linchpin of Michael's plans. This discovery, fraught with implications, sets the stage for a confrontation that has been brewing since the beginning of her journey. It's not just a clash of wills; it's a battle for justice and truth.

The document reveals a plan years in the making, implicating not only Michael but also a network of influential figures. This revelation positions Emily as a pivotal figure in a larger narrative of corruption and power. Her role in exposing this could change the course of many lives, including her own.

Emily prepares for the inevitable showdown with Michael, knowing that the stakes are higher than ever. Her journey from a betrayed partner to a champion of justice reaches its climax. She stands ready to confront Michael, armed with evidence and a resolve forged in the fires of her trials.

As the story builds towards this climax, the themes of betrayal, power, and resilience interweave to create a compelling tapestry. Emily's character, tested and tempered, emerges as a formidable force against the backdrop of Michael's machinations.

Emily's pursuit of truth and justice stands as a testament to the enduring human spirit, facing down corruption and deceit with unwavering courage.The anticipated confrontation between Emily and Michael brims with tension. Emily, armed with damning evidence, confronts Michael in a setting that once symbolized their shared past. The encounter, charged with emotion and history, marks a pivotal moment in their intertwined narratives.

Michael, faced with the revelations of his deceit, initially attempts to deflect and deny. His demeanor, a blend of arrogance and charm, falters as Emily methodically lays out the evidence of his betrayals. The dynamic between them shifts; the hunter becomes the hunted, the power balance irrevocably altered.

In this confrontation, Emily's transformation is fully realized. She stands not just as an aggrieved party seeking retribution but as a representative of justice. Her journey, fraught with challenges, has honed her into a figure of authority and resilience. She navigates the confrontation with a composed ferocity, a stark contrast to the Michael who now appears cornered and desperate.

The dialogue between Emily and Michael unveils layers of their relationship and Michael's character. His motivations, a complex tapestry of ambition, insecurity, and a distorted perception of loyalty, come to light. This exchange adds depth to the narrative, offering insights into the nuances of betrayal and the complexities of human relationships.

As the confrontation reaches its climax, Emily presents the final piece of evidence, irrefutable and damning. Michael's facade crumbles; the realization of his defeat is palpable. This moment, a culmination of Emily's quest, signifies not just the downfall of a betrayer but also the triumph of truth over deceit.

The aftermath of this confrontation ripples through the narrative. The exposure of Michael's schemes leads to legal and social repercussions for him and his network. Emily's role in bringing this to light earns her a mixture of admiration, gratitude, and awe from those affected by Michael's actions.

In the wake of these events, Emily reflects on her journey. The experience has left indelible marks on her character and life. She grapples with the aftermath of her actions, the sacrifices made, and the personal costs of her crusade. This introspection adds a poignant layer to the narrative, exploring the theme of what it truly means to seek and achieve justice.

In the aftermath of the confrontation, Emily grapples with the new reality she has helped to create. The downfall of Michael and his network has left a void, one that various players in the story scramble to fill. This shift in power dynamics introduces new challenges and opportunities within the narrative.

Emily finds herself at the center of this transition. Her actions have not only toppled Michael but also disrupted the status quo, making her a figure of significant influence. This newfound status brings with it a set of responsibilities and decisions that test her character further.

One of the key themes that emerges in this part of the narrative is the nature of power and its impact on individuals. Emily, who once sought justice, now faces the challenge of wielding influence responsibly. Her interactions with other characters, who seek her guidance or partnership, reflect the complexities of her new role.

Amidst these developments, Emily starts to rebuild her personal life. The quest against Michael left little room for personal connections, and she now seeks to mend and foster relationships that were strained or neglected. This subplot adds a dimension of emotional depth to the story, highlighting the human aspect of Emily's journey.

In the aftermath of the confrontation, Emily finds herself navigating a new reality. The revelation of Michael's true nature and the extent of his machinations send shockwaves through her life and the lives of those around her.

The impact of Emily's revelations is far-reaching. Legal proceedings are initiated against Michael and his associates, unraveling the vast web of corruption he had woven. This subplot adds a layer of legal drama to the narrative, highlighting the complexities and intricacies of bringing powerful individuals to justice.

Emily's personal journey continues to evolve in this new landscape. She grapples with the consequences of her actions, both the positive outcomes and the unforeseen repercussions. Her relationships undergo a transformation, as those around her adjust to the changes brought about by her quest for truth.

In a poignant turn, Emily begins to reconnect with parts of her life that had been neglected in her pursuit of justice. She seeks solace in simple pleasures and rekindles relationships that had suffered under the strain of her mission. This subplot explores the theme of personal healing and the importance of balance in the aftermath of conflict.

Meanwhile, the narrative also delves into the fallout for Michael. His downfall is not just legal but also personal, as he confronts the consequences of his actions. His character is further explored, offering a glimpse into his psyche as he faces the unraveling of his carefully constructed world.

As the legal proceedings against Michael progress, Emily is called upon to testify. This moment is crucial, not just for the case but for her own journey. She stands as a key witness, her testimony a powerful amalgamation of evidence and personal narrative. Her role in the courtroom is a stark contrast to the woman who had once been deceived and betrayed.

The resolution of the legal battle brings a sense of closure to the narrative. Justice is served, though not without its complexities and moral questions. The outcome of the trial and its implications for the characters involved provide a satisfying conclusion to the legal subplot.

# Chapter 17: Edge of the Abyss

In the depths of despair, Emily found herself teetering on the precipice of an abyss, a chasm of darkness that threatened to consume her. Her descent into this shadowy realm was both literal and metaphorical, mirroring the profound transformation that had taken hold of her.

The weight of betrayal bore down on her with an almost physical force. It was a burden she had carried for far too long, the pain of deception etched into her very being. The wounds inflicted by those she had trusted ran deep, leaving scars that would forever mark her soul.

As Emily navigated this treacherous terrain, the world around her seemed to unravel. The once familiar landscape had become unrecognizable, obscured by the fog of deception. She had ventured into the heart of darkness in search of the truth, and now she grappled with the consequences of her relentless pursuit.

The narrative painted a vivid picture of Emily's inner turmoil. Her thoughts were a whirlwind of confusion and anger, emotions that threatened to overwhelm her. The weight of her mission bore down on her shoulders, a constant reminder of the responsibilities she had shouldered.

Every step she took into the abyss felt like a descent into the unknown. The shadows that loomed around her seemed to whisper secrets and half-truths, further blurring the line between reality and illusion. Emily's journey had become a labyrinth of uncertainty, and she was its solitary traveler.

The narrative's depiction of Emily's descent was a masterful exploration of the human psyche. It delved into the complexities of betrayal and the toll it took on her mental and emotional well-being. Her character, once defined by her innocence and trust, had evolved into a figure of resilience and determination.

In this part of the story, the reader was invited to witness Emily's inner struggle as she grappled with the darkness that threatened to engulf her. The weight of betrayal and the descent into the abyss were central themes, and the narrative painted a vivid and harrowing portrait of her journey.

As the story progressed, Emily's transformation would continue, and the narrative would explore the depths of her resilience in the face of overwhelming odds. The descent into darkness was only the beginning of her odyssey, and the reader would accompany her on every step of this harrowing journey.

In the wake of betrayal's heavy blow, Emily found herself in a world that seemed to unravel before her very eyes. The revelations she had uncovered had torn away the veneer of trust and security, leaving behind a landscape marred by deception and uncertainty.

Secrets, once carefully concealed, were now exposed to the harsh light of truth. The narrative masterfully portrayed the aftermath of these revelations, capturing the raw emotions that coursed through Emily's veins. The world she had known had crumbled, replaced by a harsh reality where trust was a rare and fragile commodity.

The weight of betrayal lingered in every interaction, casting a shadow over even the most mundane of moments. Emily's relationships had become strained, their foundations shaken by the knowledge of deception. The sense of isolation that had crept into her life was palpable, and she felt adrift in a sea of uncertainty.

As the narrative delved deeper into this unraveling world, it highlighted the theme of trust, or rather, the lack thereof. Emily found herself questioning the motives of those around her, unable to fully trust even those who had once been her closest allies. The sense of paranoia and suspicion added layers of complexity to the story.

The web of deceit, intricately woven by her adversaries, continued to ensnare Emily. The labyrinth of lies and half-truths left her navigating a treacherous path, where every step held the potential for danger. The narrative's portrayal of this web of intrigue was a testament to its ability to maintain suspense and intrigue.

In this part of the story, the reader was invited to witness the consequences of betrayal on a personal and emotional level. The narrative explored the themes of trust and mistrust, highlighting the toll that deception takes on both individuals and relationships.

As Emily grappled with the fallout of her discoveries, her character continued to evolve. The once innocent and trusting protagonist had transformed into a figure of resilience and determination. Her journey through this unraveling world was a testament to the enduring human spirit in the face of adversity.

The narrative promised more twists and turns as it hurtled towards its climax, where Emily would confront her ultimate adversary. The world may have unraveled around her, but she remained resolute in her quest for justice.

Amidst the chaos of an unraveling world, Emily found herself navigating a labyrinth of deceit, where hidden truths and half-truths intertwined in a web of complexity. The narrative's exploration of this labyrinth delved into the heart of the conspiracy, unraveling the threads of deception that bound together the narrative's central mystery.

Uncovering hidden truths became a relentless pursuit for Emily, an odyssey that led her deeper into the heart of the conspiracy. Each revelation was a double-edged sword, shedding light on the darkness that had plagued her, yet simultaneously plunging her into greater danger. The narrative skillfully portrayed the tension between knowledge and danger, emphasizing the high stakes of Emily's mission.

The web of intrigue that had ensnared her was intricate and far-reaching. The narrative expertly wove together the various elements of the conspiracy, creating a tapestry of deception that spanned across multiple layers of society. Emily's journey through this labyrinth was a testament to her resourcefulness and determination.

The narrative's depiction of the labyrinth of deceit was a masterclass in suspense and intrigue. It introduced a cast of enigmatic characters, each with their own motivations and secrets. The reader was left to decipher the puzzle alongside Emily, piecing together the fragments of information in a quest for truth.

Trust remained a rare commodity in this complex world. Emily had to navigate the treacherous waters of shifting allegiances and hidden agendas. The moral dilemmas she faced were as intricate as the conspiracy itself, challenging her principles and forcing her to make choices that would define her character.

As Emily ventured further into the labyrinth, she discovered connections that hinted at a conspiracy much larger and more dangerous than she had anticipated. The narrative's ability to maintain suspense and intrigue was showcased in every twist and turn of the plot. Each revelation brought her closer to the heart of the mystery, yet also deeper into the abyss of danger.

In this part of the story, the reader was invited to delve into the complexities of the conspiracy alongside Emily. The narrative painted a vivid picture of a world where deception and betrayal ran deep, and trust was a fragile commodity. The labyrinth of deceit was a central theme, driving the story's tension and suspense.

As the narrative hurtled towards its climax, the reader could only anticipate more revelations and twists in the labyrinth of deceit. Emily's journey was far from over, and the web of intrigue continued to tighten around her. The narrative promised a resolution that would bring the intricacies of the conspiracy to light.

In the heart of the labyrinth of deceit, Emily found herself facing her ultimate adversary. The confrontation was a culmination of the narrative's suspense and tension, a battle of wills that would determine the course of her journey.

Emily's final showdown was a high-stakes moment, a clash of ideologies and determination. Her character had evolved from a victim of betrayal to a relentless seeker of justice, and this confrontation would define her legacy. The narrative's portrayal of this pivotal moment was a testament to its ability to maintain suspense and intrigue.

The adversary she faced was a figure shrouded in mystery, their motives and machinations carefully concealed. The narrative expertly built the tension, leaving the reader on the edge of their seat as Emily squared off against this formidable foe. It was a battle that would test her resilience and resourcefulness.

The weight of the revelations that had come before hung heavy in the air, adding complexity to the confrontation. Emily's pursuit of truth had uncovered a conspiracy of staggering proportions, and the ultimate adversary held the key to unraveling it all. The narrative's ability to intertwine personal and global stakes added depth to the showdown.

As the narrative reached its zenith, Emily's character was pushed to its limits. She grappled with the moral dilemmas of her mission, forced to make choices that carried high personal costs. The narrative explored the ethical complexities of justice and the sacrifices made in its pursuit.

The suspense in this part of the story was palpable, as Emily and her adversary engaged in a battle of wits. Each move was calculated, each word laden with meaning. The narrative's ability to maintain intrigue and tension was showcased in every interaction.

In this part of the narrative, the reader was immersed in the high-stakes confrontation between Emily and her ultimate adversary. The battle of wills, the weight of revelations, and the moral dilemmas added layers of complexity to the story. It was a moment that would reshape the narrative's trajectory.

As the story hurtled towards its resolution, Emily found herself at a crossroads. The choices she made in the aftermath of this showdown would determine not only her fate but also the fate of those around her. The narrative promised a conclusion that would be both satisfying and thought-provoking.

In the wake of the intense confrontation, a revelation loomed on the horizon, poised to transform everything Emily had known. The narrative's portrayal of this pivotal moment was a testament to its ability to maintain suspense and deliver shocking twists.

The truth that emerged was both shocking and transformative. It peeled back the layers of deception that had shrouded Emily's world, exposing the core of the conspiracy. The narrative masterfully built up to this revelation, keeping the reader in a state of anticipation.

As the truth unfurled, Emily's character was tested in ways she could never have imagined. The weight of the revelations bore down on her, and the choices she had made in pursuit of justice took on new significance. The narrative explored the profound impact of truth and the power it held to reshape her world.

The revelation also had far-reaching implications beyond Emily's personal journey. It cast a spotlight on the larger narrative's themes of corruption and deception, illuminating the depths to which those in power would go to protect their secrets. The narrative skillfully wove together the personal and the political, creating a tapestry of intrigue.

The atmosphere in this part of the story was charged with a sense of urgency. The reader was drawn into the narrative's web of suspense, eagerly awaiting the next twist in the plot. The narrative's ability to maintain tension and intrigue was on full display.

Emily's character continued to evolve in the aftermath of the revelation. She was faced with choices that carried immense consequences, and her decisions added depth to her character. The narrative explored the ethical complexities of justice and the sacrifices made in its pursuit.

In this part of the narrative, the reader was invited to witness the transformative power of truth. The revelation reshaped the narrative's trajectory, setting the stage for the story's resolution. It was a moment that carried both emotional weight and narrative significance.

As the story hurtled towards its conclusion, Emily found herself at a crossroads once again. The choices she made in the wake of the revelation would determine the course of her journey and the legacy she left behind. The narrative promised a conclusion that would be both satisfying and thought-provoking.

At the crossroads of her journey, Emily stood on the precipice of decisions that would shape her destiny. The choices she faced were fraught with complexity, and the consequences of her actions would resonate far beyond her personal quest for justice.

Emily's character had undergone a profound transformation, evolving from a victim of betrayal into a figure of resilience and determination. The narrative's exploration of her choices in this critical moment added depth to her character and highlighted the moral dilemmas she grappled with.

The legacy of justice loomed large as Emily weighed her options. The narrative delved into themes of redemption and the enduring quest for justice in a world filled with deception. Her choices carried the weight of moral responsibility, and the narrative portrayed the ethical complexities of her decisions.

The atmosphere in this part of the story was charged with anticipation. The reader was drawn into Emily's inner turmoil, sharing in the emotional weight of her choices. The narrative's ability to maintain tension and suspense was a testament to its storytelling prowess.

The choices Emily made would not only define her character but also set the narrative's course towards its resolution. The narrative promised a conclusion that would be both satisfying and thought-provoking, inviting the reader to reflect on the themes of trust, justice, and resilience.

As Emily stood at the crossroads, the reader was left in suspense, eagerly awaiting the narrative's final revelation. The story had taken them on a journey filled with suspense, intrigue, and transformation, and the resolution promised to be a fitting culmination of Emily's odyssey.

In this part of the narrative, the reader witnessed the culmination of Emily's character arc and the choices that would shape her legacy. It was a moment of reflection and decision, where the narrative's themes of trust, justice, and resilience came to the forefront.

In the wake of Emily's momentous choices at the crossroads, the narrative continued to unfold, carrying with it the weight of her decisions. The reader followed Emily on her journey, where trust, justice, and resilience were put to the ultimate test.

As the narrative progressed, Emily's character continued to evolve, shaped by the consequences of her choices. The themes of betrayal and redemption played a central role in the story, creating a tapestry of emotions and conflicts that resonated with the reader.

The story had reached a point of no return, where the intricacies of the conspiracy had been laid bare, and the battle for justice had reached its climax. Emily's unwavering determination and resilience had brought her to this pivotal moment, and the reader was left in suspense, eagerly awaiting the story's resolution.

The narrative's ability to maintain tension and suspense was a testament to its storytelling prowess. It had kept the reader engaged, weaving a complex tapestry of intrigue and emotion that had left a lasting impression.

As the story hurtled towards its conclusion, Emily's legacy was still uncertain. The choices she had made had set her on a path that would forever change her life and the lives of those around her. The narrative promised a resolution that would be both satisfying and thought-provoking, inviting the reader to reflect on the complexities of trust, justice, and resilience.

Emily's journey continued to unfold, each step bringing her closer to a resolution that had eluded her for so long. The weight of her choices and the consequences of her actions hung heavy in the air as she forged ahead, determined to see justice served.

The world around her had shifted, transformed by the revelations that had come to light. The once-hidden truths had sent shockwaves through society, exposing corruption and deceit at the highest levels. Emily's relentless pursuit of justice had exposed the underbelly of power and privilege, and the narrative explored the ripple effects of her actions.

As Emily delved deeper into the heart of the conspiracy, she encountered unexpected allies and formidable adversaries. The alliances she forged and the conflicts she faced added layers of complexity to the story. The narrative skillfully portrayed the interplay of trust and betrayal, highlighting the blurred lines between friend and foe.

The suspense in this part of the story was palpable, as Emily navigated treacherous waters where danger lurked at every turn. The narrative's ability to maintain tension and intrigue was on full display, keeping the reader captivated by the unfolding events.

Emily's character continued to evolve, shaped by the challenges she faced and the choices she made. The narrative explored her inner journey, delving into the depths of her resilience and determination. It was a testament to the enduring human spirit in the face of adversity.

The legacy of justice remained at the forefront of Emily's mission, a beacon guiding her through the darkest moments of her journey. The narrative delved into the complexities of justice and the sacrifices made in its pursuit. It was a theme that resonated with the reader, prompting reflection on the moral dilemmas at the heart of the story.

# Chapter 18: Calm before the Storm

In the aftermath of the earth-shattering revelations that had unfolded in the previous chapter, the narrative plunged headlong into the emotional fallout that gripped the characters. The truth had been unveiled, its weight bearing down on them like an insurmountable burden.

Emotions ran high in the wake of the revelations. Shock, anger, and disbelief painted a vivid mosaic of human reactions. The reader was drawn into the tumultuous sea of feelings that surged through the characters, each grappling with the profound implications of the truth.

Relationships, once steadfast and unshakeable, now stood on fragile ground. Trust, the foundation upon which alliances had been built, was in short supply. The bonds that had once held the characters together were strained to the breaking point. The narrative masterfully portrayed the intricacies of human connection unraveling in the face of betrayal.

Amidst this emotional turmoil, Emily found herself at the epicenter of the storm. She bore the weight of her choices like a heavy mantle, reflecting on the decisions that had led to this moment. The narrative provided a window into her inner thoughts, inviting the reader to witness her journey of self-examination and introspection.

As Emily contemplated the choices she had made, the reader was given insight into the depths of her character. Her resilience and determination remained unwavering, but the toll of her mission was evident in the lines etched upon her face. The narrative explored the moral complexities of her quest for justice, offering a nuanced portrayal of her internal struggles.

The aftermath of revelations served as a pivotal moment in the narrative, where the characters confronted the truth and its consequences. The tension that had been meticulously built throughout the story now found its release in the raw and unfiltered emotions of the characters.

In this part of the narrative, the reader was immersed in the complexities of human emotion, as relationships were tested and trust was shattered. Emily's introspection added depth to her character, showcasing the internal battles that mirrored the external conflicts of the story.

In the aftermath of the revelations that had sent shockwaves through their lives, the characters found themselves in a state of collective disbelief. It was as though the ground had shifted beneath their feet, and they were struggling to find their footing amidst the chaos. The truth, once concealed in the shadows, now loomed large, casting a stark and unforgiving light on their world.

Emily, the relentless seeker of justice, bore the brunt of the revelations. As she grappled with the enormity of what had been exposed, she couldn't help but reflect on the choices she had made along her arduous journey. The weight of her decisions pressed upon her like a heavy yoke, and the lines of determination etched into her face were now accompanied by furrows of introspection.

The emotions that coursed through Emily were a tempest of conflicting feelings. Anger, directed both inward and outward, simmered beneath the surface. She questioned herself, wondering if her pursuit of truth had come at too high a cost. The collateral damage of her quest weighed heavily on her conscience, and the narrative allowed the reader to delve into the depths of her inner turmoil.

But Emily was not alone in her struggle. The web of relationships that had once defined her world had been strained to the breaking point. Trust, once freely given, had been shattered, and suspicion lingered in the air like a bitter taste. The narrative skillfully portrayed the fraying bonds between characters who had stood side by side, now finding themselves on opposing sides of a moral divide.

Amidst the emotional turbulence, moments of vulnerability and raw authenticity emerged. Characters who had been defined by their stoicism now revealed their humanity. Tears were shed, harsh words exchanged, and the facade of invulnerability crumbled. The narrative captured these intimate moments with a poignant and empathetic lens, showcasing the complexity of human emotion.

The revelations had unveiled not only the truth but also the complexities of human nature. The narrative did not shy away from the moral ambiguities of the characters' choices. It posed challenging questions about the pursuit of justice and the collateral damage it could inflict. There were no easy answers, and the characters grappled with the shades of gray that colored their world.

As the narrative unfolded this intricate tapestry of emotions, it set the stage for what lay ahead. The reader was left in suspense, knowing that the final confrontation loomed on the horizon. The characters, battered and bruised by the revelations, would soon be called upon to make choices that would determine the course of their destinies.

In the midst of turmoil and chaos, a brief interlude of respite emerged in the narrative, offering a temporary refuge from the storm that had engulfed the characters. Subheading 2, "A Moment of Respite," invited the reader to step back from the edge of suspense and tension and breathe in scenes of normalcy and connection.

Scenes of everyday life punctuated the narrative, providing a stark contrast to the high-stakes drama that had defined the story thus far. It was as though time had slowed, allowing the characters and the reader alike to catch their breath. The mundane became a sanctuary, a place where the characters could briefly shed the weight of their burdens.

Emily, the indomitable force at the heart of the narrative, sought solace in these moments of respite. She gathered her allies, forming a circle of trust and camaraderie. The narrative painted a vivid picture of their interactions, showcasing the bonds that had been forged through trials and tribulations.

As Emily and her allies gathered to regroup and strategize, the reader was invited to witness the intricate dance of planning and preparation. The narrative skillfully wove together moments of tactical discussion with glimpses of vulnerability. Emily, despite her unwavering determination, revealed moments of doubt and uncertainty, adding depth to her character.

Amid the strategic discussions and preparations, the characters found moments of connection that were both heartwarming and poignant. Laughter and shared stories punctuated the narrative, reminding the reader of the humanity that resided within these complex individuals. The bonds of friendship and camaraderie remained unbroken, even in the face of adversity.

These moments of respite served as a reminder that life, with all its complexities, continued to unfold. It was a testament to the resilience of the human spirit, the ability to find solace and connection even in the darkest of times. The narrative celebrated these moments as a testament to the indomitable nature of the characters.

The atmosphere in this part of the story was marked by a sense of quiet determination. The characters, though weary, remained resolute in their quest for justice. The narrative hinted at the challenges that lay ahead, foreshadowing the final confrontation that loomed on the horizon. The moments of respite were not a departure from the central narrative but a necessary pause in the relentless pursuit of truth.

In these scenes of normalcy and connection, the reader was given a glimpse into the characters' lives beyond their roles in the larger narrative. It humanized them, allowing the reader to relate to their struggles and triumphs on a personal level.

Amidst the relentless storm of suspense and tension, a rare oasis of calm emerged in the narrative. It was a moment of respite, a pause in the unending chaos that had gripped the characters' lives. In this brief interlude, scenes of normalcy became a sanctuary, offering solace and reprieve.

Emily, the steadfast protagonist, stood at the center of this respite. She had been the driving force behind the relentless pursuit of truth and justice, but even she needed moments of respite. The narrative portrayed her as more than just a determined seeker of justice; she was a human being with vulnerabilities and moments of doubt.

Gathering her allies around her, Emily created a circle of trust and camaraderie. It was a poignant reminder that even in the darkest of times, bonds of friendship and loyalty remained unbroken. The characters shared stories, laughter, and the simple pleasure of each other's company. These moments of connection were a testament to the enduring power of human relationships.

As Emily and her allies regrouped, the narrative shifted its focus to the intricacies of planning and preparation. The tactical discussions were juxtaposed with glimpses of vulnerability. Emily, while resolute in her determination, revealed moments of uncertainty. These instances of self-doubt humanized her character, making her relatable to the reader.

The atmosphere during this respite was marked by a quiet determination. The characters, though weary, were unwavering in their commitment to the cause. The narrative subtly hinted at the challenges that lay ahead, foreshadowing the final confrontation that loomed on the horizon. The moments of respite were not a departure from the central narrative but a necessary pause in the relentless pursuit of truth.

In the midst of the strategic discussions and preparations, the characters found solace in each other's presence. These moments of connection were both heartwarming and poignant. They served as a reminder that life, with all its complexities, continued to unfold. It was a testament to the resilience of the human spirit, the ability to find solace and connection even in the darkest of times.

In the wake of the revelations and the moments of respite that had provided a brief oasis of calm, the characters found themselves standing on the precipice of the ultimate climax. It was a juncture where the narrative's focus shifted decisively towards the preparations for the impending final showdown, and the stakes had reached unprecedented heights.

With meticulous precision, plans were set into motion. Every detail, no matter how minute, was scrutinized with a keen eye for perfection. There was simply no room for error in the elaborate web of strategy that the characters, under Emily's steadfast leadership, were weaving. Their adversary, lurking in the shadows, was a formidable force that demanded nothing less than perfection.

Emily, the unwavering pillar of their mission, stood resolute in the face of mounting tension. Her determination, like a burning ember, had only grown brighter with each trial and tribulation they had faced. The weight of responsibility, borne on her shoulders, was a burden she accepted with unwavering resolve. Her unwavering commitment to the pursuit of justice served as both a guiding light and a source of strength for the group.

As the characters refined their strategy, the atmosphere crackled with an intensity that was almost palpable. The gravity of the situation hung heavily in the air, casting a shadow of unease over their interactions. Every decision made, every word spoken, carried profound implications. The moral complexities of their choices weighed heavily on their minds, for they were acutely aware that the final confrontation loomed ever closer.

The sense of urgency and anticipation was electrifying. The characters were acutely aware that they were hurtling towards a moment of reckoning, where the choices they made in the crucible of conflict would define the trajectory of their destinies. It was a precipice of uncertainty and high-stakes drama, where the narrative's tension reached its zenith.

The reader, too, was drawn into this maelstrom of anticipation, eagerly awaiting the resolution that lay just beyond the horizon. The narrative skillfully crafted an atmosphere that left the reader on the edge of their seat, fully immersed in the characters' world. The impending final showdown held the promise of answers and revelations, and the characters were prepared to confront their adversary head-on, whatever the cost.

In this atmosphere charged with urgency and mounting tension, the characters' unwavering determination and meticulous preparations set the stage for the climactic confrontation that loomed on the horizon. The narrative's deft handling of these elements left the reader captivated and eager to uncover the resolution that awaited.

In the relentless pursuit of justice, the characters found themselves on the cusp of the ultimate climax. The narrative continued to unfold as plans were set in motion for the impending final showdown. The tension reached its zenith, and the characters' determination remained unwavering.

Every aspect of their strategy was refined with meticulous attention to detail. The characters understood the magnitude of the task before them, and there was no room for error. Victory hinged on their ability to outwit and outmaneuver their formidable adversary.

Emily, the unwavering leader of their mission, epitomized determination. Her resilience in the face of mounting tension was a source of inspiration for the group. She shouldered the weight of responsibility with grace, embodying the spirit of their quest for justice.

As the characters honed their strategy, tensions continued to rise. The narrative captured the essence of their unease, highlighting the moral dilemmas that accompanied their choices. Each decision carried profound consequences, and the characters grappled with the ethical complexities of their mission.

The atmosphere was electric with anticipation, and the reader could sense that the narrative was hurtling towards its climactic resolution. The final confrontation, the culmination of their journey, awaited on the horizon. The reader was drawn deeper into the characters' world, captivated by the unfolding drama and eagerly anticipating the resolution that loomed.

In the midst of Alderidge's bustling streets, Emily Carter, a dedicated art teacher, found solace in her daily routine. Her world brimmed with vibrant colors and the creative energy of her students, providing a comforting cocoon of simplicity.

One crisp October evening, Emily's path intersected with Michael Harrison, a graphic designer capturing life's moments through his lens. Fate wove their meeting into destiny, sparking a connection that would redefine their lives.

In the days that followed, Emily and Michael's inexplicable attraction grew. Their bond was a blend of intellectual harmony and emotional resonance, drawing them closer with each passing moment.

Emily's transformation was evident to her friends, a newfound radiance illuminating her life. Michael, in turn, found in Emily a soothing presence, a balm for his restless creativity. As winter arrived, they navigated challenges together, their love growing stronger. They spoke of future dreams, unaware of the impending storm. Their relationship deepened as winter enveloped Alderidge. Michael introduced Emily to photography, while she shared her passion for art.

Weekends were filled with adventures, exploring hidden gems and art galleries, their love blossoming further with the arrival of spring. They celebrated Valentine's Day intimately, surrounded by candlelight and music. Their love flourished, symbolized by a balcony garden and cycling through the countryside. Family and friends embraced them, and plans for a coastal road trip brought excitement.

Yet, beneath their idyllic love story, subtle undercurrents emerged. Michael's restlessness grew, unnoticed by Emily. As they prepared for their road trip, Emily's unease lingered. Little did she know, their journey would test their bond in unforeseen ways.

For now, they stood on the precipice of a promising summer, their hearts entwined, oblivious to the shadows lurking ahead.

Amidst the tapestry of their love, a gathering storm loomed, casting an ominous shadow over Emily and Michael's idyllic world. The serene melody of their romance now carried an undertone of discord, as if the very air held its breath in anticipation of what was to come.

As spring unfurled its petals, the couple's plans for a coastal road trip neared fruition. Excitement coursed through them, a sense of adventure that had drawn them together in the first place. Yet, there was an unspoken tension, a subtle disquiet that had settled in the depths of their hearts.

Emily, ever perceptive, had noticed the restlessness in Michael's eyes growing more pronounced. Moments of distraction had transformed into lengthy silences, and the warmth of his smile seemed to wane. She couldn't help but wonder about the source of his inner turmoil, a gnawing doubt that refused to be silenced.

In the quiet hours of the evening, as they discussed the final details of their journey, a heavy question hung in the air like a storm cloud waiting to unleash its fury. Emily ventured into the treacherous territory of honesty, her voice trembling slightly as she broached the subject.

"Michael," she began, her eyes searching his for answers, "Is everything alright? You've seemed... distant lately." Michael's gaze shifted, avoiding her penetrating scrutiny. His voice, when it finally emerged, carried a weight that seemed to resonate with the impending tempest. "I've been wrestling with some decisions, Emily. Choices I need to make, and I'm not sure how they'll impact us."

The words hung in the air like an unresolved chord, and Emily felt a knot of unease tighten in her chest. The implications of Michael's cryptic confession reverberated through the room, casting a pall over their plans. As the days passed and the date of their departure drew near, the atmosphere between them grew increasingly charged. Each moment carried the weight of unspoken words, a tension that threatened to unravel the delicate fabric of their love.

Emily found herself grappling with her own set of emotions. She was torn between her love for Michael and the growing sense of foreboding that surrounded him. Doubts crept in, whispering their insidious tales of uncertainty.

The coastal road trip, once a symbol of their shared dreams, now felt like a journey into the unknown, a path fraught with hidden obstacles. The gathering storm, both literal and metaphorical, cast its shadow over their once-bright horizon.

The night before their departure, as they lay side by side under a star-studded sky, Emily broke the silence that had become their constant companion. Her voice was soft, almost lost amidst the symphony of the night.

"Michael, whatever challenges lie ahead, we'll face them together, won't we?" He turned to her, his eyes reflecting a mixture of longing and uncertainty. "I hope so, Emily. I truly do."

The words hung in the air, a fragile promise in the face of the gathering storm. In that moment, their love stood at a crossroads, poised on the brink of a climactic showdown that would test the very foundations of their relationship.

As the first light of dawn broke over the horizon, Emily and Michael stood on the precipice of uncertainty, the narrative of their love poised for its final act, where choices made and secrets kept would converge in a tumultuous climax.

# Chapter 19: Confrontation

As the sun dipped below the horizon, casting long shadows across the landscape, the world seemed to hold its breath. In the quietude of the evening, the stage was set for the climactic confrontation that had been building since the story's inception. It was a moment that had been foreshadowed, a reckoning that could no longer be delayed.

To fully grasp the significance of this impending clash, a recap of the key events leading up to this chapter is essential. The story had unfolded with a complexity that mirrored the intricacies of human nature itself.

From the very beginning, the narrative had been a tapestry woven with threads of ambition, betrayal, and unfulfilled desires. Characters had navigated a treacherous maze of secrets and hidden agendas, their paths intersecting and diverging in a dance of intrigue and deception.

Emily, the once-contented art teacher, had found herself at the center of a web of deceit, drawn into a world of conflicting loyalties and unforeseen consequences. Michael, the enigmatic photographer, had harbored his own secrets, his lens capturing not only moments of beauty but also the shadows that lurked beneath the surface.

Their love story, initially marked by serendipity and warmth, had taken unexpected turns. Beneath the facade of blissful romance, doubts had festered, trust had eroded, and alliances had shifted. It was a journey that had led them to this pivotal moment, where all the threads would converge.

The tension that hung in the air was palpable. It was not merely the clash of personalities but a confrontation of the very choices that had defined these characters. Each decision, each action, had been a stepping stone on the path to this inevitable showdown.

Emily's heart, once filled with the simplicity of her passions, now beat with a mixture of anticipation and fear. Her journey had been one of self-discovery, a realization that the world could be as deceptive as the art she cherished. She had come to understand that even the most beautiful canvases could hide hidden motives.

Michael, too, had evolved from a carefree wanderer capturing life's moments to a man burdened by the weight of his own decisions. His restless spirit had led him down a path strewn with uncertainties, and the choices he had made would now come under scrutiny.

As the narrative had unfolded, it had become increasingly clear that the world in which these characters existed was far from black and white. Motivations had blurred, alliances had shifted, and the lines between right and wrong had become indistinct.

The anticipation that filled the air was not confined to the protagonists alone. Readers, who had followed this intricate interplay of characters and events, were on the edge of their seats. They, too, were eager to see how the web of deceit would unravel, how the conflicts would be resolved, and what revelations would come to light.

In the moments leading up to the climactic confrontation, the narrative had taken on an extra layer of complexity. It was a delicate dance of emotions and motivations, where the past collided with the present, and the consequences of choices made were laid bare.

The air was thick with tension as the characters prepared for the impending confrontation. It was a moment they had all seen coming, a reckoning that had been lurking on the horizon, growing like a gathering storm. As they readied themselves, the suspense in the narrative intensified, each heartbeat echoing the uncertainty that lay ahead.

Emily's apartment, once a haven of warmth and love, now felt like a battleground. The flickering candlelight that had once illuminated their intimate moments now cast eerie shadows on the walls. Emily herself stood by the window, gazing out at the city's twinkling lights, her thoughts a whirlwind of emotions.

She couldn't help but reflect on the journey that had brought her to this point. Her encounter with Michael had been serendipitous, a chance meeting that had sparked a love story she had never expected. But as the layers of their relationship had peeled away, revealing hidden agendas and buried secrets, she had been forced to confront a reality she had never imagined.

Emily grappled with conflicting emotions. Her love for Michael was undeniable, but so was the growing doubt that had crept into her heart. She questioned the choices she had made, the trust she had placed in him, and the implications of his actions. It was a tormenting inner struggle, and it cast a shadow over her as she prepared for what lay ahead.

Michael, on the other hand, found himself torn between the past and the present. He had always been a wanderer, capturing life's fleeting moments through his lens. But his journey with Emily had brought him face to face with a side of himself he had long suppressed. The weight of his own secrets bore down on him, and he knew that the time for reckoning had come.

As he stood in Emily's living room, his fingers absently tracing the vintage camera she had gifted him, he couldn't escape the turmoil within. His emotions were a tempest, a storm of conflicting desires and loyalties. He was drawn to Emily's warmth and simplicity, but his past held him in a vice grip, threatening to unravel the fragile bond they had built.

The foreshadowing of the impending clash was evident in every gesture, every unspoken word. The characters moved through their preparations with a sense of purpose, but also with a heaviness that hung in the air like a shroud. It was a clash of worlds, of ideals, and of the choices that had brought them to this crossroads.

Outside, the city's bustling streets carried on, oblivious to the turmoil within Emily's apartment. But within those walls, a battle of emotions raged. The anticipation of the confrontation weighed on everyone, a gnawing uncertainty that refused to be ignored.

Friends and allies of both Emily and Michael had their roles to play in this narrative of suspense. They had witnessed the evolution of the relationship, the highs and lows, and the cracks that had begun to form. Their loyalties were divided, torn between the two central figures, and they, too, grappled with their own motivations.

Some were determined to see the truth come to light, to unravel the mysteries that had shrouded their friends' lives. Others, however, were torn by their own agendas, their own secrets that they feared would be exposed in the impending clash.

In the days leading up to the confrontation, alliances shifted and fractured. Trust was a fragile commodity, and as the characters delved deeper into their own motivations, they realized that the battle ahead was not only about love and loyalty but also about the fundamental truths that underpinned their lives.

As the clock ticked relentlessly towards the appointed hour, the narrative braced itself for the inevitable clash that had been brewing beneath the surface. The moment had arrived, and with it, the beginning of the confrontation that would define the characters' fates.

The scene unfolded in Emily's apartment, a space that had witnessed the most intimate moments of her relationship with Michael. But now, it was transformed into a battleground, a place where hidden truths and unspoken words would come to light.

Emily stood at the center of the room, her gaze steady and resolute, though her heart raced with a mix of anxiety and determination. She had known this moment was coming, had felt it in the shifting winds of their relationship. And now, there was no turning back.

Michael entered the room, his presence commanding attention. His eyes held a storm of emotions, a mixture of regret and defiance.

It was a dramatic entrance, a collision of two worlds that had once been intertwined but now stood on opposing sides.

Their eyes locked, and in that charged moment, the confrontation began. It was a silence pregnant with unspoken words, a palpable tension that hung heavy in the air. The room seemed to hold its breath, as if it, too, recognized the gravity of the situation.

Emily's voice, when it finally broke the silence, was steady but laced with a hint of sorrow. "Michael, we need to talk. There are things we can't ignore any longer."

He nodded, his jaw set with a determination that mirrored hers. "I know, Emily. It's time."

The confrontation was not just about their personal dynamics, but also about the revelations that had the power to shatter the world they had built together. The stakes were high, and as the characters began to speak, emotions ran wild.

Words spilled forth like a torrent, a deluge of long-suppressed feelings and hidden truths. The confrontation was a clash of perspectives, a battle of narratives that had evolved independently, each character grappling with their own version of events.

Emily, her voice tinged with frustration and hurt, confronted Michael about his hidden agendas and the secrets he had kept. Her accusations were like arrows aimed at his heart, piercing through the defenses he had built.

Michael, in turn, revealed his own vulnerabilities, the struggles that had led him down this path of deception. His voice cracked with the weight of his admissions, and it was clear that he, too, had been carrying a burden of guilt and remorse.

As the confrontation unfolded, the emotional intensity reached its zenith. It was a raw, unfiltered exchange that laid bare the cracks in their relationship. The room echoed with their words, each sentence a testament to the complexity of human emotions.

Their friends and allies, who had been waiting in the wings, could only watch in silence as the confrontation played out. They, too, were emotionally invested, torn between their loyalties and the painful truths that were being exposed.

The room itself seemed to absorb the emotions, the walls echoing with the echoes of their voices. It was a pivotal moment, a turning point in the narrative, where the characters confronted not only each other but also themselves.

The stakes were laid bare, and the consequences of their choices loomed large. The confrontation was a crucible in which their true selves were revealed, stripped of pretenses and facades. It was a moment of reckoning, a test of their resilience and the depth of their love.

As the confrontation continued, it became evident that there were no easy answers, no quick resolutions. The emotions ran high, but so did the complexities of their shared history. It was a clash of hearts and minds, a battle of wills that would shape the narrative's final act.

The beginning of the confrontation marked the point of no return. The characters had crossed a threshold, and there was no going back. The emotional turmoil was a tempest that raged within them, and the narrative held its breath, waiting to see how it would all unfold.

In the charged atmosphere of the confrontation, the narrative took a deep dive into the heart of the characters' hidden truths. Major plot points were unveiled, secrets were laid bare, and the characters were forced to confront the consequences of their past actions and decisions.

Emily's voice quivered with a mix of anger and hurt as she confronted Michael about the secrets he had kept. Her accusations were relentless, a torrent of questions that had simmered beneath the surface for far too long.

"Michael, how could you?" Emily's words pierced the air, accusing him of betraying the trust they had built. "All this time, you kept these secrets from me. You hid your true intentions, and I had no idea."

Michael, his eyes filled with remorse, finally confessed to the hidden agendas that had driven his actions. It was a painful admission, and his voice trembled as he spoke of the choices he had made and the consequences they had wrought.

"I never meant for things to turn out this way, Emily," he admitted, his shoulders slumping under the weight of his admissions. "I thought I was protecting you, but I see now that I only hurt you."

As the characters confronted their past actions and decisions, the narrative peeled away the layers of their personalities, revealing the vulnerabilities and insecurities that had driven them. It was a moment of reckoning, a catharsis that allowed them to confront their own flaws and shortcomings.

Emily, too, had her own secrets to unveil. As the confrontation continued, she spoke of her own choices and the decisions she had made in the face of betrayal. Her voice wavered as she revealed the depths of her pain and the sacrifices she had made for the sake of their relationship.

The unveiling of secrets was not limited to Emily and Michael alone. Their friends and allies, who had been drawn into the web of deception, also had their own confessions to make. As the characters' narratives intertwined, the true extent of the interplay of hidden agendas became apparent.

Amidst the revelations, emotions ran high. The characters' voices cracked with raw intensity, their words a torrent of pent-up feelings. It was a moment of emotional release, a cathartic unburdening that laid bare the complexities of their relationships.

The narrative navigated through the maze of conflicting emotions, allowing the characters to confront their past actions and decisions without judgment. It was a process of self-discovery, a journey into the depths of their own motivations and desires.

The room seemed to hold its breath as the characters bared their souls. The unveiling of secrets was not just a plot device but a moment of profound transformation. It was a turning point in the narrative, where the characters confronted not only each other but also themselves.

In the midst of the revelations, alliances shifted and fractured. Loyalties were tested as the characters grappled with the weight of their choices. The narrative captured the intricacies of human relationships, the ebb and flow of trust, and the fragile nature of love.

As the characters continued to unveil their secrets, the narrative wove a tapestry of emotions and motivations. It was a delicate dance of vulnerability and resilience, a testament to the complexities of human nature.

The unveiling of secrets was a pivotal moment in the confrontation, a climax that laid bare the true nature of the characters and the tangled web of their relationships. It was a reckoning that would shape the narrative's final act, where the characters would have to confront not only the consequences of their past actions but also the choices they would make in the face of the truths that had been exposed.

As the confrontation continued, the narrative held the reader in suspense, eager to see how the characters would navigate the revelations and whether they would find a way to reconcile their conflicting desires and motivations. The unveiling of secrets was not just a plot twist but a profound exploration of the human psyche, a testament to the power of storytelling to delve into the depths of the human soul.

As the confrontation raged on, the narrative delved deeper into the escalating conflict that had seized the characters in its relentless grip. It was a clash of wills, a tumultuous exchange of words and emotions that left no one untouched.

The room, once a sanctuary of love and warmth, had become a battleground. Verbal salvos were exchanged, each word a cutting blade that left wounds that ran deeper than the surface. The characters clashed, not just verbally, but emotionally, as the weight of their choices bore down upon them.

Emily's voice, which had initially trembled with hurt and anger, grew steadier as the confrontation escalated. Her accusations were precise, her words a reflection of the betrayal she had felt. She had trusted Michael with her heart, and now, that trust lay shattered.

"Michael, you can't just explain this away," Emily's tone was unyielding as she confronted him. "Your actions have consequences, and we have to face them."

Michael, though remorseful, was not without his own defenses. He argued passionately, his voice rising in desperation. "Emily, you have to understand. I never wanted to hurt you. I did what I thought was best."

Their verbal clash was like a storm, thunder and lightning flashing in the confined space of the room. Resolutions seemed distant, impossible to grasp as tempers flared. It was a battle of ideals, a clash of perspectives that left no room for compromise.

The supporting characters, who had been drawn into the confrontation, added their own voices to the fray. Friendships were tested as loyalties wavered. The narrative captured the complex interplay of emotions, the struggle to reconcile conflicting allegiances.

Emily's closest friends, who had watched her transformation with concern, voiced their own frustrations. They had seen the toll the relationship had taken on her, and they were determined to protect her, even if it meant confronting the man she loved.

Michael's allies, too, rallied to his defense. They believed in his intentions, even if they questioned his methods. The conflict was not just a battle of individuals but a clash of alliances, each side determined to defend their own.

Amidst the escalating conflict, the weight of choices and consequences pressed heavily on everyone. The characters grappled with the realization that there were no easy answers, no simple resolutions. The narrative explored the moral complexities of their decisions, the shades of gray that blurred the lines between right and wrong.

Emily's heart ached as she faced the reality of her choices. She had loved Michael with a depth she had never known, but that love had come at a cost. The consequences of her decisions weighed heavily on her, and she questioned whether the relationship had been worth the pain it had caused.

Michael, too, confronted the consequences of his actions. He had made choices driven by his own sense of duty and protection, but those choices had led to a rift that now seemed impossible to bridge. The narrative delved into his internal turmoil, the inner conflict that mirrored the external confrontation.

The room crackled with emotional intensity as the characters grappled with their own vulnerabilities and insecurities. It was a moment of reckoning, a test of their resilience in the face of the conflict that threatened to tear them apart.

The escalating conflict was not just a plot device but a reflection of the human condition. It captured the essence of relationships, the complexities of love, and the choices that define our lives. The characters were trapped in a storm of their own making, and the narrative held them in its grip, eager to see how they would navigate the turbulent waters.

As the confrontation continued, the narrative kept the reader on edge, immersed in the emotional turmoil of the characters. The weight of choices and consequences loomed large, casting a shadow over the room, and the resolution seemed distant, elusive, like a mirage on the horizon. The narrative had set the stage for a climactic showdown, and the conflict would shape the story's final act, where the characters would have to confront not only each other but also the truths they had uncovered and the choices they had made.

In the midst of the escalating conflict, the narrative shifted its focus to explore the pivotal turning points that shaped the characters' development and growth. As they grappled with their roles in the conflict, the story delved into the complex interplay of emotions and motivations that led some characters to reconsider their allegiances, ultimately altering the dynamics of the confrontation.

Emily, who had once led a life marked by comforting routines as an art teacher, found herself at a profound turning point. The confrontation had forced her to confront not only her love for Michael but also the sacrifices she had made for the relationship. It was a moment of self-discovery, and her character development became marked by newfound strength and determination.

"I can't keep sacrificing my own happiness for the sake of this relationship," Emily declared, her voice filled with a resolve that had been absent before. "I deserve better, and I won't let anyone hold me back any longer."

Her words were a testament to her growth, a transformation from a woman defined by her love for Michael to one who was determined to define her own path. The narrative captured her journey from passivity to assertiveness, a compelling evolution that resonated with readers.

Michael, too, experienced a profound transformation as he grappled with the consequences of his actions. Once a carefree wanderer, he now confronted the weight of his choices, realizing that he could no longer run from the past. His character development was marked by a growing sense of accountability and self-reflection.

"I have to face the truth," Michael admitted, his voice tinged with remorse. "I can't keep running from the consequences of my actions. It's time to take responsibility."

His words signaled a shift in his character, a willingness to confront his own vulnerabilities and shortcomings. The narrative delved into his internal struggle, the battle to reconcile the conflicting desires that had driven him and the difficult path of self-redemption.

As the characters faced their turning points, some began to reconsider their allegiances. Friendships were tested as loyalties wavered, and the dynamics of the confrontation shifted in unexpected ways.

Emily's closest friends, who had initially rallied to her defense, found themselves questioning whether they had been too hasty in their judgments. They had witnessed her newfound strength and determination, and they began to reevaluate their roles in the conflict.

"I want what's best for Emily," one of her friends admitted, her voice filled with uncertainty. "But maybe we should give Michael a chance to explain himself. People can change."

The narrative explored the complexity of human relationships, the fluidity of allegiances, and the evolving dynamics of the confrontation. It revealed that turning points were not merely moments of revelation but catalysts for character development and growth.

Michael's allies, too, experienced their own turning points. They grappled with the realization that their unwavering support might not be enough to shield him from the consequences of his actions.

Their loyalty was tested, and some began to question whether their allegiances were misplaced.

The narrative captured the intricate interplay of emotions and motivations as characters navigated their turning points. It was a delicate dance of growth and transformation, a reflection of the fluid nature of human relationships.

Amidst the turmoil, new alliances began to form, further changing the dynamics of the confrontation. Characters who had once been allies found themselves on opposite sides, and unexpected bonds began to emerge.

The narrative revealed that turning points were not static events but catalysts for evolution. They propelled the characters forward on their journeys of self-discovery and transformation. The shifting allegiances and evolving dynamics added layers of complexity to the story, keeping the reader engaged and eager to see how the characters would navigate their turning points.

In this world of unexpected twists and turns, transformation was inevitable, and the turning points were the crucibles in which the characters forged their destinies. The narrative had set the stage for a climactic showdown, and the character development and growth would be central to the resolution of the conflict. The turning points were not just moments of revelation but opportunities for characters to redefine themselves and their roles in the unfolding narrative.

The room crackled with tension, the air heavy with anticipation, as the confrontation reached its climactic moment. It was the highest point of tension in their conflict, a pivotal moment that would ultimately decide the outcome for all involved. Emotions ran high, and difficult decisions loomed on the horizon.

Emily and Michael stood face to face, their eyes locked in a fierce battle of wills. The room seemed to shrink around them, the walls bearing witness to the emotional turmoil that raged within. Each word spoken was a weapon, each accusation a wound that cut deep.

"Emily, you have to understand," Michael's voice was tinged with desperation, his eyes pleading for understanding. "I never wanted to hurt you. I did what I thought was best."

Emily's resolve remained unshaken as she countered, her voice unwavering. "Michael, you can't just explain this away. Your actions have consequences, and we have to face them."

Their voices clashed like thunder and lightning, the words echoing in the confined space of the room. It was a battle of ideals, a clash of perspectives that left no room for compromise. The climactic moment had arrived, and the narrative captured the raw intensity of their emotions.

Supporting characters, who had been drawn into the confrontation, added their voices to the fray. Friendships were tested, and loyalties wavered as they too grappled with the weight of their choices.

Emily's closest friends, who had watched her transformation with concern, voiced their own frustrations. They had seen the toll the relationship had taken on her, and they were determined to protect her, even if it meant confronting the man she loved.

"Emily, we're here for you," one of her friends said, her voice filled with empathy. "But we also need to hear Michael out. Maybe there's more to this than we know."

Michael's allies, equally passionate in their support, rallied to his defense. They believed in his intentions, even if they questioned his methods. The climactic moment had pushed their allegiances to the breaking point, and the narrative captured the complexity of their emotions.

The room had become a battleground not only of individuals but of alliances. The characters grappled with the realization that their loyalties were not easily defined, that the lines between right and wrong were blurred by their own desires and motivations.

Amidst the emotional turmoil, the weight of choices and consequences pressed heavily on everyone. Emily, who had once been cautious with her heart, questioned whether the relationship had been worth the pain it had caused. She loved Michael deeply, but the narrative delved into the difficult decision she faced.

"I thought we had something special," Emily admitted, her voice trembling with vulnerability. "But at what cost? Can we ever trust each other again?"

Michael, too, confronted the consequences of his actions. He had made choices driven by his own sense of duty and protection, but those choices had led to a rift that now seemed impossible to bridge.

"I never wanted to hurt you," Michael confessed, his voice filled with remorse. "But I understand if you can't forgive me."

The climactic moment had brought their relationship to a breaking point, and the narrative explored the fragility of their love. It was a moment of reckoning, a test of their resilience in the face of the conflict that threatened to tear them apart.

As the confrontation continued, the narrative kept the reader on edge, immersed in the emotional turmoil of the characters. The climactic moment was not just a plot device but a reflection of the human condition, capturing the essence of relationships, the complexities of love, and the choices that define our lives.

The room crackled with emotional intensity as the characters grappled with their vulnerabilities and insecurities. Resolutions seemed distant, elusive, like a mirage on the horizon. The climactic moment had set the stage for a final act, where the characters would have to confront not only each other but also the truths they had uncovered and the choices they had made.

As the tension in the room began to subside, there was a palpable shift in the atmosphere. The climactic confrontation had taken its toll, and now, as the dust settled, the characters started to find common ground. It was a moment of reconciliation and resolution, where major plot points were either resolved or set on a new path.

Emily and Michael, who had been locked in a fierce battle of words, now stood before each other with a newfound sense of clarity. The weight of their choices and the consequences of their actions hung heavy in the air. It was time to come to terms with their past and forge a path toward a different future.

"I never wanted us to end up like this," Michael admitted, his voice filled with regret. "I wish I had handled things differently."

Emily nodded, her eyes filled with a mixture of pain and understanding. "I do too, Michael. But we can't change the past. What matters now is where we go from here."

Their words marked a turning point in their relationship. It was a moment of vulnerability, a recognition of their shared mistakes, and a commitment to moving forward. The narrative captured the complexity of their emotions, the bittersweet realization that love could endure even in the face of adversity.

Supporting characters, who had been entangled in the conflict, also began to find common ground. Friendships that had been strained by allegiances now started to heal. Major plot points that had driven a wedge between characters were addressed, and resolutions were set in motion.

Emily's closest friends, who had voiced their concerns and rallied to her defense, now extended an olive branch to Michael. They saw the remorse in his eyes and recognized that he, too, had suffered as a result of his choices.

"We want what's best for Emily," one of her friends said, her voice filled with empathy. "But we also believe in second chances. If you're willing to change, we're willing to give you that chance."

Michael's allies, equally relieved that the conflict was subsiding, welcomed the opportunity for reconciliation. They had stood by his side out of loyalty and belief in his intentions, and now, they saw a path to rebuilding trust.

The room, once filled with acrimony, was now a space where characters extended forgiveness and sought understanding. It was a testament to the resilience of human relationships, the capacity for growth, and the power of empathy.

As the conflict continued to resolve, the narrative touched upon major plot points that had been central to the story. Secrets and hidden agendas were exposed, and characters confronted their past actions and decisions. It was a moment of reckoning, where the truth was laid bare, and the characters faced the consequences of their choices.

Some secrets led to painful revelations, while others paved the way for redemption. The narrative explored the intricacies of forgiveness and the healing power of honesty.

Characters who had once been adversaries now found common cause. They recognized that their differences had been driven by misunderstandings and miscommunications. The conflict had forced them to confront their biases and prejudices, and they were determined to move beyond them.

Amidst the resolution of the conflict, the narrative touched upon the complex interplay of emotions and motivations. It was a delicate balance of remorse, forgiveness, and the desire for a fresh start. The characters had come to terms with the consequences of their actions, and they were ready to embark on a new path.

The room, once filled with tension, was now a place of reflection and reconciliation. The characters had weathered the storm of conflict, and they emerged stronger, their relationships deepened by the trials they had faced.

As the narrative drew to a close, it left readers with a sense of closure and the understanding that conflict, while painful, could also be a catalyst for growth and transformation. The characters had found common ground, and the resolution of the conflict marked the beginning of a new chapter in their lives.

In the aftermath of the intense confrontation, a somber stillness hung in the air. The characters gathered their thoughts and began to reflect on the events that had unfolded. It was a moment of introspection, a time to consider how the confrontation had changed them and the direction of the story.

Emily sat by the window, her gaze fixed on the cityscape outside. Her mind was a whirlwind of emotions as she replayed the words and actions of the confrontation in her mind. It had been a turning point, a moment that had tested the limits of her love and resilience.

"I never thought it would come to this," she whispered to herself, her voice tinged with a mixture of sadness and relief. "But maybe it needed to. Maybe we all needed to confront our demons."

Michael, too, was deep in thought. He had never imagined that his choices would lead to such a dramatic showdown. The confrontation had forced him to confront his own shortcomings and acknowledge the pain he had caused.

"I can't change the past," he muttered to himself, a heavy sigh escaping his lips. "But I can change the future. I owe it to Emily and to myself."

Supporting characters gathered in small groups, their conversations filled with a sense of resolution. Friendships had been tested, alliances had shifted, and now, they faced the challenge of rebuilding trust.

One of Emily's friends spoke up, her voice filled with hope. "Maybe this was a wake-up call for all of us. We can't take our relationships for granted. We have to nurture them and be honest with ourselves."

Michael's allies nodded in agreement, recognizing that the conflict had exposed the flaws in their assumptions and beliefs. It was a moment of growth and self-awareness.

As the characters reflected on the confrontation, loose ends began to tie up. Secrets and hidden agendas had been exposed, and resolutions were set in motion. It was a moment of clarity, where the truth had come to light, and the characters faced the consequences of their choices.

# Chapter 20: Aftermath

The aftermath of the climactic confrontation was a landscape littered with emotional debris, and the characters found themselves navigating through the wreckage of their choices. The immediate aftermath was marked by a palpable tension that hung in the air, as raw emotions threatened to engulf them.

Emily and Michael, who had been at the center of the storm, faced each other with a mixture of regret and determination. Their love had been tested to its limits, and the wounds of the confrontation were still fresh. They knew that the decisions made in the heat of the moment could not be ignored; they needed to be addressed.

"I never wanted it to come to this," Emily whispered, her voice trembling as she met Michael's gaze. "But we can't just pretend it didn't happen."

Michael nodded, his eyes filled with a profound sadness. "You're right, Emily. We need to face the fallout of our choices, no matter how painful."

Supporting characters who had been entangled in the conflict also grappled with the immediate aftermath. Friendships had been strained, and alliances had been tested. The tension persisted as they tried to make sense of what had transpired.

Emily's closest friends, who had voiced their concerns and rallied to her defense, now watched her with a mix of worry and empathy. They knew that healing would take time and that forgiveness might be a distant goal.

Michael's allies, equally concerned for his well-being, stood by his side but understood that their loyalties had been tested. The immediate fallout had forced them to confront the consequences of their actions and allegiances.

As the characters faced the fallout, they acknowledged that the road ahead would be fraught with challenges. The decisions made in the heat of the moment had left scars, and the wounds needed time to heal. It was a moment of reckoning, where the characters understood that they could no longer avoid the consequences of their actions.

The immediate aftermath was a time of reflection and introspection, as the characters grappled with the emotional toll of the confrontation. The tension in the air was a constant reminder of the choices they had made, and the path to resolution seemed uncertain.

But they were determined to face the fallout head-on, to confront the emotions and tensions that persisted, and to find a way to address the decisions that had brought them to this point. The immediate aftermath was only the beginning of their journey toward understanding and healing.

In the wake of the climactic confrontation, the characters embarked on a challenging journey of rebuilding trust with one another. The wounds were deep, and the scars of the conflict still lingered, but they were determined to find a way back to the bonds that had once united them.

Apologies were offered, and forgiveness became a sought-after treasure. It was a time for humility and reflection, as characters acknowledged their mistakes and the pain they had caused. The process of rebuilding trust was marked by sincerity and a genuine desire for reconciliation.

Emily and Michael, who had borne the brunt of the conflict, were among the first to extend olive branches. They knew that their love had been tested but remained resilient. Apologies flowed freely from their lips, and forgiveness was sought with a sense of urgency.

"I'm sorry for the hurt I caused," Michael admitted, his voice filled with remorse. "I never meant for things to spiral out of control."

Emily, her eyes filled with tears, nodded in understanding. "I'm sorry too, for not trusting you enough. We both made mistakes, Michael."

Their efforts to mend their fractured relationship were marked by open communication and a commitment to rebuilding the trust that had been shaken. It was a slow and delicate process, but they were determined to heal the wounds that had threatened to tear them apart.

Supporting characters, who had been drawn into the conflict, also played their part in rebuilding trust. Friendships that had been strained were rekindled, and bridges that had been burned were rebuilt. Apologies and forgiveness were exchanged, and the characters understood that the bonds of their relationships were worth preserving.

One of Emily's friends, who had been among the most vocal critics of Michael, offered a heartfelt apology. "I judged him too harshly, and I'm sorry for that. I want to support you and see you happy, Emily."

Michael's allies, too, extended their hands in reconciliation. They recognized that their loyalty to him had been tested, but they believed in his capacity for change and growth.

Efforts to mend fractured relationships extended beyond the immediate circle of characters. Families, who had watched the conflict with concern, also played a role in the process of rebuilding trust. Parental love and support became pillars of strength, and the characters found solace in the understanding and forgiveness of their loved ones.

As the characters worked on rebuilding trust, they knew that the path to healing would be long and challenging. It required patience, understanding, and a willingness to let go of past grievances. The process was a testament to the resilience of human relationships and the power of forgiveness.

Slowly but surely, the bonds that had been strained began to mend. Apologies and forgiveness were the bridges that led the characters back to one another, and the process of rebuilding trust became a symbol of hope and renewal.

The scars of the confrontation would always remain, but they were now woven into the fabric of their relationships as a reminder of the strength and resilience that had carried them through the storm. The characters were on a journey of healing, and as they rebuilt trust, they discovered the enduring power of forgiveness and reconciliation.

As the characters grappled with the aftermath of the climactic confrontation, they found themselves navigating a landscape forever altered by the events that had unfolded. The confrontation had ushered in a new reality, one that demanded they come to terms with profound changes and adapt to unforeseen circumstances.

For Emily and Michael, the realization that their love had been tested to its limits marked a fundamental shift in their relationship. They had once lived in a world where their connection was unshakable, but now, they had to come to terms with the scars that adorned their love story.

"It's not going to be the same, is it?" Emily whispered to Michael, her voice tinged with both sadness and acceptance.

Michael, his gaze fixed on the uncertain horizon, replied, "No, it won't be the same. But maybe that's not a bad thing. We have the chance to build something stronger."

Their love had evolved, transformed by the trials they had faced. They understood that they had to adapt to this new reality, where their relationship was marked by resilience and a deeper understanding of each other.

Supporting characters also grappled with their own shifting realities. Friendships that had once been carefree were now tinged with the knowledge of the challenges they had faced. Some had to adapt to the changing dynamics of their relationships and adjust their expectations.

One of Emily's friends, who had been her staunchest supporter, admitted, "I thought I knew what was best for you, but I was wrong. I have to adapt to the fact that you can make your own choices, even if they're not what I expected."

Michael's allies, too, found themselves in a new reality where their loyalties had been tested. They had to adapt to a world where their trust in him was intertwined with the changes he was willing to make in his life.

Outside of their personal relationships, the characters had to come to terms with the broader consequences of the confrontation. Some faced professional challenges as a result of their actions, while others had to adjust to new circumstances brought about by the conflict.

The realization that life would never be the same began to sink in, and the characters understood that they had entered uncharted territory. It was a world where the past was forever marked by the confrontation, and the future held the promise of growth and transformation.

Yet, amid the challenges and uncertainties, there was a sense of resilience that permeated their journeys. The characters were determined to navigate these new realities, to adapt to the changes, and to find a way to move forward.

As they looked toward the horizon, they knew that the path ahead would not be easy, but it was one they were willing to tread. The confrontation had altered their lives in ways they could never have anticipated, but it had also revealed the strength of their spirits and their capacity for growth.

In the face of this new reality, the characters discovered that they had the power to shape their own destinies and embrace the changes that had come their way. Life would never be the same, but it held the promise of new beginnings and opportunities for those willing to embrace them.

In the aftermath of the climactic confrontation, the characters embarked on deeply personal journeys of self-discovery and healing. It was a time for them to confront the loose ends from the past, address unresolved issues, and seek the elusive sense of closure that had eluded them for so long.

For Emily and Michael, closure meant facing the demons that had haunted them. They both recognized that their past actions and choices had led them to this point, and they needed to come to terms with the consequences.

Emily, with a determination born of introspection, sought closure by revisiting her past traumas and addressing the insecurities that had held her back. She embarked on a journey of self-discovery, determined to find the inner strength to move forward.

Michael, too, delved into his past, confronting the patterns of behavior that had led to the confrontation. He sought closure by acknowledging his flaws and working on personal growth and change.

Their individual journeys toward closure were intertwined with their efforts to heal their relationship. Apologies and forgiveness played a crucial role in addressing the unresolved issues that had festered between them.

Supporting characters also embarked on their own quests for closure. Friendships that had been strained by the confrontation were now mended through open and honest conversations. Loose ends from the past were addressed, and resolutions were sought in interpersonal aspects of their lives.

One of Emily's friends, who had harbored lingering doubts and resentments, found closure by expressing her feelings and allowing herself to let go of the anger that had held her captive. It was a moment of catharsis that allowed her to move forward with renewed understanding.

Michael's allies, too, confronted their own roles in the conflict and sought closure by reevaluating their allegiances. They recognized that the confrontation had exposed the complexities of human relationships and the need for growth and change.

Beyond the interpersonal aspects of their lives, the characters also sought closure in personal endeavors. Professional challenges and unfulfilled dreams were addressed, and new paths were explored.

The quest for closure was marked by moments of vulnerability and introspection. It required the characters to confront uncomfortable truths and make peace with their past actions. It was a journey of healing and growth that allowed them to move forward with a sense of clarity and purpose.

As they sought closure, the characters discovered that it was not an endpoint but rather a continuous process of self-discovery and healing. It was a testament to their resilience and capacity for change, a reminder that the past could be acknowledged and integrated into their journeys toward a brighter future.

In the end, closure was not just about tying up loose ends; it was about finding a sense of peace and understanding within themselves and in their relationships with others. It was a powerful reminder that even in the face of adversity, the human spirit had the capacity to heal and grow.

In the wake of the climactic confrontation and their individual quests for closure, the characters found themselves standing on the threshold of uncharted territory. New beginnings and opportunities emerged, beckoning them to venture into the unknown, where change and growth awaited.

For Emily and Michael, the confrontation had transformed their relationship in unexpected ways. As they worked on rebuilding trust and seeking closure, they realized that their love story was not confined to the past but had the potential to evolve into something deeper and more profound.

They decided to take a leap of faith and embrace the uncharted territory of their relationship. It was a world where the scars of the confrontation were woven into the fabric of their love, a reminder of their resilience and capacity for growth.

Supporting characters also found themselves at crossroads, where new beginnings beckoned. Friendships that had been tested were now infused with a sense of renewal and the promise of unexpected alliances.

One of Emily's friends, who had undergone a personal transformation during the aftermath of the confrontation, decided to explore uncharted territory in her career. She pursued a passion she had long neglected, seizing the opportunity to embrace change and growth.

Michael's allies, too, ventured into new directions, forging unexpected alliances as they recognized the need for adaptation and evolution. The uncharted territory became a canvas for them to paint their own destinies, unburdened by the constraints of the past.

Outside of their personal relationships, the characters encountered new opportunities and challenges in their professional lives. Some decided to embark on entrepreneurial endeavors, while others embraced career changes that had once seemed daunting.

As they explored uncharted territory, the characters learned that change was not to be feared but embraced. It was a world where the past served as a foundation for growth, and the future held the promise of unexpected alliances and directions.

The uncharted territory was marked by moments of uncertainty and vulnerability, but it was also a place where the characters discovered the resilience of the human spirit. They embraced change as a catalyst for personal and interpersonal growth, finding strength in the unexplored possibilities that lay ahead.

Unexpected alliances formed, bringing together characters who had once been on opposing sides of the confrontation. The realization that they shared common goals and aspirations allowed them to set aside their differences and work together toward a brighter future.

As the characters ventured further into uncharted territory, they embraced the power of transformation and the capacity for change. It was a journey that tested their resolve and challenged their preconceived notions, but it was also a testament to their resilience and the endless possibilities that awaited them.

In the end, the uncharted territory became a symbol of hope and renewal, a reminder that even in the face of adversity, the characters had the power to shape their own destinies and create a future filled with promise and unexpected alliances.

As the characters ventured deeper into uncharted territory, they took moments to reflect on the profound transformations that had shaped their journeys. Each character had undergone a metamorphosis, and as they paused to look back, they acknowledged the lessons learned, the personal growth achieved, and the impact of the climactic confrontation on their identities.

Emily and Michael, at the heart of the story's transformation, found themselves profoundly changed by their experiences. Their love had weathered the storm, and in its wake, they had discovered new facets of themselves and each other.

Emily, once cautious and guarded, had learned the power of vulnerability and trust. She reflected on how the confrontation had forced her to confront her insecurities and fears, and in doing so, she had discovered a reservoir of inner strength.

"I used to be so afraid of getting hurt," Emily admitted to Michael, her voice tinged with gratitude. "But now, I realize that love is worth the risk."

Michael, too, had undergone a personal transformation, recognizing the need for self-improvement and growth. He reflected on how the confrontation had challenged his assumptions and propelled him toward a path of change.

"I thought I had it all figured out," Michael confessed. "But I've learned that growth and self-awareness are ongoing processes."

Supporting characters shared in this process of reflection and acknowledged their own lessons learned and personal growth. Friendships that had been strained were now infused with newfound depth and understanding.

One of Emily's friends, who had once been quick to judge, reflected on her own transformation. "I've learned to be more open-minded and accepting," she mused. "The confrontation showed me the importance of empathy."

Michael's allies also considered the impact of the confrontation on their identities. They reflected on how their loyalties had been tested and how the experience had shaped their beliefs and values.

The characters understood that transformation was an ongoing journey, and the climactic confrontation had been a catalyst for their growth. They acknowledged that they were not the same individuals who had embarked on this story's journey, and they embraced the evolution of their identities.

Beyond personal growth, the characters also reflected on the impact of the confrontation on their relationships and the broader narrative. They considered how the events had shaped their interactions and the alliances that had formed.

Emily and Michael recognized that their love story had been forever marked by the confrontation, but they saw it as a testament to their resilience and commitment. They understood that their relationship was a reflection of the transformations they had undergone as individuals.

Supporting characters also reflected on the impact of the confrontation on their relationships, acknowledging that the bonds they shared had deepened through adversity. They realized that the lessons learned and personal growth achieved were valuable assets in their journeys toward a brighter future.

As they looked back on their transformations, the characters understood that the climactic confrontation had been a pivotal moment in their lives. It had challenged them, tested their resolve, and ultimately propelled them toward growth and change.

The reflections on transformation served as a reminder that the journey was far from over. They looked toward the future with a sense of optimism, knowing that they had the capacity to shape their own destinies and create a narrative filled with growth, understanding, and resilience.

In the aftermath of personal transformations and reflections on the impact of the confrontation, the characters found themselves reconnecting with each other on a deeper level. Old friendships were rekindled, and new bonds were formed, celebrating the enduring power of human connection.

Emily and Michael, at the heart of the story's relationships, rediscovered the depth of their connection. Their love story had been tested, but it had also emerged stronger, and they cherished the opportunity to reconnect on a deeper level.

They spent hours talking, sharing their dreams, fears, and aspirations. The vulnerability they had shown during the confrontation had laid the foundation for a deeper emotional intimacy, and they reveled in the joy of rediscovering each other.

Supporting characters also found themselves reconnecting with old friends in meaningful ways. Friendships that had been strained by the conflict were now infused with renewed understanding and empathy.

One of Emily's friends, who had once been distant, reached out with a heartfelt apology. "I'm sorry for the way I treated you during the confrontation," she confessed. "I want to reconnect and rebuild our friendship."

Michael's allies, too, reconnected with old friends who had been affected by the conflict. They understood the value of human connection and the need to mend strained relationships.

Beyond rekindling old friendships, the characters also celebrated the formation of new bonds. The confrontation had brought them together in unexpected ways, forging alliances that transcended the past.

Emily and Michael's relationship deepened further as they realized that their love story had the potential to evolve into something even more profound. They celebrated the strength of their emotional connection and the resilience of their love.

Supporting characters also formed new bonds as they recognized the power of unity and shared purpose. They celebrated the strength of their alliances and the understanding that had emerged from their collective experiences.

The characters understood that human connection was a powerful force that could heal wounds, bridge divides, and bring people together in times of adversity. They celebrated the beauty of friendships rekindled and new bonds forged, finding solace in the knowledge that they were not alone on their journeys.

As they reconnected with each other on a deeper level, the characters felt a profound sense of gratitude for the human connections that had sustained them through the storm. They understood that relationships were a source of strength and support, and they celebrated the enduring power of these connections.

In the end, the characters recognized that the climactic confrontation had not only tested their relationships but had also revealed the depth of their bonds. They looked toward the future with a renewed appreciation for the beauty of human connection, knowing that it would continue to guide them on their journeys of growth, understanding, and resilience.

In the wake of personal transformations, reconnections, and reflections on their journey, the characters felt the need to revisit the resolutions and decisions made during the climactic confrontation. They recognized that the choices they had made in the heat of the moment might need reassessment to ensure they remained aligned with their newfound understanding and growth.

For Emily and Michael, revisiting their resolutions meant reevaluating the boundaries and expectations they had set for their relationship. The confrontation had challenged them, and they needed to ensure that their decisions were still in harmony with their current selves.

They engaged in candid conversations, discussing their relationship dynamics, commitments, and goals. They were open to the idea that some resolutions might need adjustment to accommodate their evolving love story.

Supporting characters also revisited the resolutions they had made during the confrontation. Friendships that had been strained were now given a second chance, and characters assessed whether the decisions they had made were still relevant in light of their personal growth and reflections.

One of Emily's friends, who had distanced herself from certain individuals during the confrontation, reconsidered her choices. She recognized that the judgments she had made were based on a limited perspective and decided to revisit her resolutions with an open heart.

Michael's allies, too, examined their decisions and alliances in the aftermath of personal growth and reconnections. They acknowledged that the confrontation had revealed complexities that required adjustments and course corrections.

Beyond personal relationships, the characters also revisited resolutions related to their careers and aspirations. Some decided to modify their professional goals, recognizing that their priorities had shifted in the wake of the confrontation.

As they engaged in this process of revisiting resolutions, the characters understood that growth and self-awareness demanded flexibility and adaptability. They were willing to make adjustments to align their decisions with their current selves and their deeper understanding of the world.

Emily and Michael realized that their love story was a dynamic narrative, and the resolutions they made during the confrontation were not set in stone. They were open to the idea that their relationship could evolve in unexpected ways, and they embraced the need for flexibility in their journey.

Supporting characters also recognized that resolutions made during moments of conflict might not always serve their best interests. They understood the importance of reassessing decisions to ensure they were aligned with their newfound clarity and personal growth.

In the end, revisiting resolutions became a symbol of the characters' commitment to growth, understanding, and resilience. It was a process that allowed them to make course corrections when needed and to adapt to the ever-changing landscape of their lives.

As they moved forward with this newfound flexibility, the characters felt a renewed sense of purpose and direction. They understood that their journey was marked by growth and evolution, and they celebrated the capacity to make adjustments and course corrections as they continued to navigate the complexities of their narratives.

With the weight of the climactic confrontation, personal transformations, reconnections, and the revisiting of resolutions behind them, the characters found themselves at a crossroads, ready to embrace the opportunities for fresh starts in their lives. They let go of past regrets and looked forward to the future with a renewed sense of optimism and hope.

For Emily and Michael, the prospect of fresh beginnings in their relationship filled them with excitement and anticipation. They had learned from their past and were ready to embark on a new chapter together, unburdened by the baggage of the confrontation.

They decided to celebrate their love by planning new adventures and creating cherished memories. The sense of optimism they felt was palpable, a testament to their resilience and commitment to each other.

Supporting characters also embraced the opportunities for fresh starts in their lives. Friendships that had been strained were now infused with newfound understanding and forgiveness, allowing for the possibility of deeper connections.

One of Emily's friends, who had previously held onto regrets from the confrontation, decided to let go of the past and embrace a fresh beginning. She understood that holding onto regrets only weighed her down and prevented her from moving forward.

Michael's allies, too, seized the chance to embrace fresh starts in their personal and professional lives. They recognized that the confrontation had revealed new paths and opportunities that were worth exploring.

Beyond their personal relationships, the characters welcomed fresh beginnings in their careers and aspirations. Some pursued new passions, while others made bold career moves, fueled by the sense of optimism that had been rekindled.

As they embraced these fresh starts, the characters felt a renewed sense of purpose and direction. The past no longer held them captive, and they looked forward to the future with hearts full of hope.

Emily and Michael understood that fresh beginnings required courage and a willingness to leave the past behind. They were ready to create a narrative that celebrated growth, understanding, and resilience.

Supporting characters also recognized that embracing new beginnings meant acknowledging the potential for change and growth. They celebrated the opportunities that lay ahead and looked forward to the possibilities of deeper connections and personal fulfillment.

# Chapter 21: Rebuilding

Emily Carter, once a figure contentedly woven into the fabric of Alderidge's mundane rhythms, has traversed a path marked by unforeseen upheavals and heartwarming revelations. Her narrative, initially painted in hues of routine and simplicity, gradually evolved into a canvas rich with the complexities of life, love, and self-discovery.

As an art teacher, Emily's life was a harmonious blend of colors and creativity, her days infused with the vibrant energy of her students. Her existence, though not expansive, brimmed with the quiet contentment of one who found joy in the small, beautiful details of everyday life. Yet, beneath this tranquil surface, there lingered a yearning, a subtle whisper of a life yet to be fully explored and experienced.

This yearning was unexpectedly awakened the day Michael Harrison entered her world. Their encounter, seemingly a stroke of serendipity, marked the beginning of a transformative journey for Emily. Michael, with his artistic soul and a keen eye for life's fleeting moments, brought with him a tide of new experiences, emotions, and revelations. Their burgeoning romance, tender and profound, unfolded against the backdrop of Alderidge's autumnal charm, adding a new dimension of depth and vibrancy to Emily's life.

However, with the sweet stirrings of love came the inevitable complexities of human relationships. As their story progressed, it became evident that love, in all its beauty, was also a crucible for personal growth and self-reflection. Emily, whose heart had cautiously treaded the waters of vulnerability, found herself navigating the ebb and flow of emotions, her relationship with Michael serving as both a mirror and a catalyst for inner exploration.

Through their shared moments – from the tranquil warmth of coffee shop conversations to the intimate stillness of nights under the starlit sky – Emily embarked on a journey not just of the heart, but of the soul. With Michael, she ventured beyond the familiar boundaries of her world, each step forward a testament to the resilience and strength that lay dormant within her.

Yet, as is often the case in the labyrinth of life, their path was not devoid of obstacles. Misunderstandings and differences cast shadows on their relationship, each challenge an opportunity for Emily to confront her fears, insecurities, and deepest desires. These trials, though harrowing, served as the forge in which Emily's character was further tempered, revealing a resilience and depth hitherto unacknowledged.

The journey toward healing is often a labyrinthine path, filled with introspection, realizations, and gradual acceptance. For Emily, this journey began in the quiet aftermath of her relationship with Michael. It was a time of deep soul-searching, where the echoes of her past mingled with the aspirations of her future. This segment of her story, spanning 3,000 words, delves into the intricate process of Emily's emotional and psychological healing.

As autumn's vibrant leaves faded and the city of Alderidge wrapped itself in the chilly embrace of winter, Emily found herself at a crossroads. The dissolution of her relationship with Michael, while painful, served as a catalyst for profound self-discovery. It was as if the end of their love story marked the beginning of Emily's personal odyssey, a journey not towards another but towards herself.

In the initial days of this journey, Emily grappled with a maelstrom of emotions. The solitude that once felt comforting now echoed with the remnants of her relationship. Each corner of her apartment, each street in Alderidge, whispered memories of moments shared with Michael. It was during these moments of acute loneliness that Emily first confronted the shadows of her past traumas – the fears, insecurities, and unhealed wounds that had subtly shaped her perceptions and reactions.

The process of healing, however, is seldom a solitary endeavor. Emily's support system – a tapestry of friends, family, and colleagues – played a pivotal role in her journey. Her friends, who had witnessed the transformation brought about by her relationship, now became the pillars of strength in her time of vulnerability. Long evenings were spent in the company of these steadfast companions, their conversations a blend of consolation, encouragement, and sometimes, much-needed distraction.

Among these friends was Sophia, a fellow art teacher, whose wisdom and empathy provided Emily with a safe space to unravel her tangled thoughts. Then there was Alex, her childhood friend, whose humor and lightheartedness often pierced the somber veil of her thoughts, reminding Emily of the joys still abundant in life. These friendships, each unique in its way, offered Emily varying perspectives and insights, aiding her in the process of understanding and healing.

Emily's family, too, emerged as a cornerstone of her support system. Her parents, though living a few hours away, were a constant presence in her life through daily calls and frequent visits. Their unconditional love and understanding provided Emily with a sense of security and belonging, reminding her that she was not alone in her journey.

In addition to the support of her loved ones, Emily sought solace in her passion for art. Her classroom, once a space of mere professional pursuit, transformed into a sanctuary where she could express and process her emotions. The act of creating art became a form of therapy, each stroke of the brush a step towards healing. The vibrant colors on her canvas were not just a manifestation of her artistic talent but also a reflection of her inner journey – from the somber tones of loss to the bright hues of newfound hope and strength.

As the weeks turned into months, Emily's journey of healing saw her delving into various forms of self-care and introspection. She took up yoga, finding in its disciplined postures and mindful breathing a way to center her thoughts and calm her tumultuous emotions. Books became her companions in solitude, offering her insights into the experiences of others and perspectives on her own.

Yet, the most transformative aspect of Emily's healing was her engagement in therapy. Initially hesitant, she found in her sessions a safe haven to unpack the layers of her past and present. Her therapist, a kind and insightful woman, guided Emily through the intricate corridors of her psyche, helping her to confront and understand the deep-seated patterns and beliefs that had influenced her life choices.

Through these therapeutic sessions, Emily began to unravel the complex tapestry of her identity. She explored the impact of her childhood experiences, her relationship with her parents, and the subtle ways in which these dynamics had played out in her adult life. She learned to identify and articulate her feelings, to recognize the triggers that evoked fear and anxiety, and to develop healthier coping mechanisms.

This journey of healing was neither linear nor devoid of setbacks. There were days when Emily felt overwhelmed by her emotions, moments when the progress seemed insubstantial compared to the depth of her pain. Yet, with each passing day, she gathered strength, her resilience fortified by each small victory over her inner demons.

As spring heralded new beginnings, Emily found herself emerging from the cocoon of her healing process. The world around her, bursting with life and color, mirrored the transformation within her. She began to view her experiences not as a series of losses but as lessons that had shaped her into a stronger, more self-aware individual.

Her relationship with Michael, once a source of deep pain, gradually transformed in the light of her healing. Emily learned to cherish the memories, to appreciate the growth it had catalyzed, and to let go of any lingering bitterness or regret. She realized that their story, though brief, was an integral chapter in the book of her life – one that had led her to a deeper understanding of herself.

In this newfound space of healing and self-discovery, Emily began to redefine her relationship with herself and the world around her. She engaged more deeply with her community, volunteering at local art programs and participating in initiatives that brought art to underprivileged children. These activities not only provided her with a sense of purpose but also connected her with people who shared her passion, expanding her world in meaningful ways.

Emily's journey of healing was a testament to the power of resilience and the human capacity for growth. It was a journey marked by pain, but more importantly, by triumph – the triumph of a woman who, through the crucible of her experiences, discovered her strength, her worth, and the boundless potential of her spirit.

Emily's path to empowerment unfolded like a beautifully intricate tapestry, each thread representing a step towards her newfound confidence, independence, and self-love. This journey, deeply personal and transformative, was marked by moments of significant self-discovery, particularly through her art and introspection.

At the heart of Emily's empowerment was her burgeoning independence. She embraced activities that had once piqued her interest but had been set aside. Photography became a new passion, teaching her to see the world through different perspectives, capturing fleeting moments of beauty and significance. Outdoor activities like hiking and cycling reconnected her with nature, instilling a sense of freedom and joy in exploration.

These hobbies were more than mere pastimes; they became conduits for self-exploration and growth. Emily's engagement with photography and nature was not just about learning new skills but about discovering hidden facets of her personality and preferences.

Central to her journey was the evolution of her self-love and acceptance. Her art became a powerful tool in this process. In her classroom, she encouraged her students to express their innermost thoughts and feelings through art. As she guided them, she embarked on her own journey of self-expression, using her canvas to explore her emotions, fears, and aspirations.

Each artwork she created during this period was a reflection of her inner state. She experimented with various styles and mediums, allowing her emotions to guide her creations. The evolving colors and textures on her canvas mirrored her journey – from confusion and chaos to clarity and harmony.

Professionally, Emily took on new challenges that furthered her growth. She spearheaded initiatives integrating art therapy into the curriculum, affirming her belief in art's therapeutic power and establishing herself as a leader in her field. Her success in these projects not only brought professional satisfaction but also bolstered her self-confidence.

In her personal life, Emily's transformation was evident in the new relationships she formed. These connections, based on mutual respect and shared interests, were reflective of her new self – confident, open, and adventurous. Her friendship with Laura, a fellow artist, was particularly influential. Laura's boldness and fearless approach to life inspired Emily to take risks and embrace new experiences.

Emily also devoted time to self-care practices that nurtured her mind and body. Meditation, mindfulness, journaling, and reading became integral parts of her routine, helping her cultivate inner peace and resilience. These practices offered her stability and a sense of control over her emotions and reactions.

As she grew more empowered, Emily began to challenge societal norms and expectations. She became more assertive in her decisions and expressive of her individuality. This newfound assertiveness extended into her professional life, where she advocated for progressive art education and mental health awareness.

The Emily that emerged from this journey of empowerment was a stark contrast to her former self. No longer just a survivor of heartbreak and challenges, she was a flourishing individual, rich in experiences and insights. She carried a quiet confidence, a sense of purpose, and a profound appreciation for the journey that had shaped her.

In her moments of self-discovery through art and introspection, Emily uncovered layers of her being that were previously unexplored. These revelations not only contributed to her personal empowerment but also painted a picture of a woman who had come into her own, ready to face the world with a renewed sense of self and an unshakeable belief in her capabilities. Emily's story thus stands as a testament to the transformative power of self-reflection, resilience, and the enduring quest for personal growth.

In the tapestry of Emily's journey, the resolution of her relationship with Michael was a crucial thread, bringing closure and clarity to a chapter filled with deep emotions and transformative experiences. This resolution, unfolding over time, addressed the unresolved issues, communication gaps, and the need for mutual understanding that had characterized their relationship.

As spring blossomed in Alderidge, bringing with it renewal and new beginnings, Emily found herself reflecting on her relationship with Michael with a perspective tempered by time and introspection. The distance that had grown between them since their separation had allowed her to view their past with a more objective lens, acknowledging both the beauty of their connection and the flaws that ultimately led to their parting.

In this period of reflection, Emily recognized the fundamental differences in their life paths and aspirations that had been overshadowed by the initial rush of their romance. She understood that while their love was genuine, it was not enough to bridge the gaps created by their individual needs and dreams. This realization, though painful, was also liberating, as it allowed Emily to let go of any lingering guilt or regret.

As fate would have it, a chance encounter brought Emily and Michael face to face once again. It was an unexpected meeting, in a familiar café where they had spent many afternoons engrossed in conversation. Seeing Michael after all this time, Emily felt a rush of emotions, but predominant among them was a sense of peace – an indication of the healing and growth she had undergone.

Their conversation, initially tentative, gradually delved into the heart of their past relationship. They spoke openly about their feelings, the misunderstandings that had created rifts, and the external pressures that had compounded their issues. This dialogue was not just a retrospective analysis of what went wrong; it was also an acknowledgment of their mutual respect and affection, untarnished by the passage of time.

Michael, like Emily, had spent the intervening time reflecting and growing. He expressed his admiration for the way Emily had handled the aftermath of their separation, her strength and grace in moving forward. For his part, Michael shared his journey, the realizations he had come to about his own needs, fears, and desires.

In this exchange, there was a profound sense of mutual understanding and empathy. Both Emily and Michael had come to appreciate the lessons their relationship had taught them, the ways in which it had contributed to their personal growth. They acknowledged that while their love story had ended, it had left them with invaluable experiences and memories.

The question of reconciliation arose, a possibility tinged with the nostalgia of their past. However, as they delved deeper into their current lives and aspirations, it became clear that their paths had diverged significantly. Emily, empowered and self-assured, was exploring new horizons, both personally and professionally. Michael, on his part, had embarked on a journey that was taking him in a different direction, one that was not compatible with Emily's life.

With this understanding, they arrived at a mutual decision – to cherish the time they had spent together but to continue their journeys separately. This decision was not made with bitterness or sorrow but with a deep sense of respect and love for what they had shared. It was an amicable separation, a conscious uncoupling that honored their past while acknowledging their individual futures.

In the days following their meeting, Emily found herself reflecting on the closure they had achieved. She felt a sense of completion, a closing of a chapter that was essential for her to move forward unencumbered. Her relationship with Michael had been a significant part of her life, but it was now a part of her past, a stepping stone to her future.

This resolution brought with it a new level of freedom and clarity for Emily. She was able to appreciate the beauty of their connection without the weight of unresolved emotions. She could look back at their time together with fondness and forward to her future with excitement and hope.

The resolution of Emily and Michael's relationship thus marked a significant milestone in Emily's journey. It was a testament to the power of honest communication, mutual respect, and the courage to face and embrace change. Their story, though concluded, remained a beautiful and integral part of their lives, a reminder of the transformative power of love, even when it does not last forever.

As Emily stepped into the next phase of her life, she did so with a heart full of gratitude for the experiences she had shared with

Michael and a soul enriched by the lessons learned. The resolution of their relationship was not just an end but also a beginning – a new chapter in Emily's story, filled with endless possibilities and the promise of continued growth and discovery.

The resolution of secondary subplots in Emily's story, much like the intricate details in a masterpiece painting, adds depth and richness to the overarching narrative. These subplots, involving key secondary characters and events, play a crucial role in complementing and reinforcing the central themes of healing and empowerment in Emily's journey.

One significant subplot involves Sophia, Emily's colleague and confidante. Sophia's own journey, paralleling Emily's in many ways, serves as a mirror to Emily's experiences. Throughout the story, Sophia grapples with professional challenges, facing obstacles in her career as an art teacher. Her struggles with the school administration over her innovative teaching methods create tension and uncertainty in her professional life.

As the story progresses towards its conclusion, Sophia finds resolution in her career conflicts. With Emily's support and inspiration, she successfully advocates for her creative teaching techniques, earning recognition and respect from her peers and the school board. This victory for Sophia is not just a personal triumph but also a testament to the power of perseverance and the importance of fighting for one's beliefs. For Emily, witnessing Sophia's journey serves as a source of encouragement, reinforcing her own beliefs in the transformative power of art and education.

Another subplot revolves around Alex, Emily's childhood friend, whose light-heartedness and humor have provided solace and relief in Emily's moments of distress. Alex's subplot introduces a romantic element, as he navigates the complexities of his relationship with his long-term partner. This storyline, marked by ups and downs, reflects the universal themes of love, compromise, and personal growth.

As Alex's relationship reaches a pivotal moment, he and his partner choose to embark on a journey of mutual understanding and growth, deciding to attend couples therapy. This resolution impacts Emily by showcasing the value of communication and effort in relationships, reminding her of the lessons learned from her own experience with Michael.

Additionally, the story includes a subplot involving Emily's involvement in community art projects. Throughout her journey, Emily becomes increasingly engaged in initiatives that bring art to underprivileged communities and schools. This subplot culminates in the successful establishment of a community art center, a dream that Emily had nurtured since the beginning of her story.

The establishment of the art center marks a significant achievement in Emily's life. It signifies not only her professional success but also her commitment to making art accessible to all. This accomplishment is a powerful reminder of the impact one individual can have on their community, further empowering Emily in her personal and professional pursuits.

Moreover, the narrative includes the evolving dynamics within Emily's family. Her parents, who have been a constant source of support, undergo their own journey of acceptance and understanding as they come to terms with Emily's choices and independence. The resolution of this subplot, characterized by a deeper bond and mutual respect between Emily and her parents, underscores the importance of family support in personal growth and healing.

Lastly, the story addresses the development of Emily's students, who have been influenced by her teaching and mentorship. As the school year concludes, several of her students showcase remarkable growth and talent in an end-of-year art exhibition. This event serves as a poignant reminder of Emily's impact as a teacher and mentor, reinforcing her sense of purpose and fulfillment in her chosen profession.

Each of these secondary subplots, as they reach their resolution, interweaves with the central narrative, enriching Emily's journey. They highlight different aspects of healing, empowerment, and personal growth, reflecting the multifaceted nature of human experiences. As Emily observes and participates in the resolutions of these subplots, she gains further insights into her own life, drawing strength and inspiration from the experiences of those around her.

In the wake of her profound journey of healing and empowerment, Emily Carter stands at the threshold of a new chapter, her spirit imbued with a sense of renewal and hope. This segment of her story, encapsulating her life post-healing, paints a vivid picture of her transformed outlook on life, relationships, and her own self.

As the narrative unfolds, we find Emily in a state of harmonious balance, her life a reflection of the inner growth she has experienced. The once familiar streets of Alderidge now hold new promises and possibilities. Her days, while maintaining the structure of routine, are imbued with an undercurrent of excitement for the unknown and the yet-to-be-discovered.

Professionally, Emily has ascended to new heights. Her role as an art teacher, once confined to the four walls of a classroom, now extends beyond into the community. The establishment of the community art center stands as a testament to her vision and dedication. Here, she not only teaches but also learns from the diverse experiences of those she mentors. The art center has become a hub of creativity and healing, much like Emily herself, who has grown into a beacon of inspiration for her students and peers.

In her personal life, Emily's relationships have evolved to reflect her newfound understanding and self-assurance. Her friendships, deeper and more meaningful, are sources of joy and mutual growth.

The bond with her family, strengthened by trials and time, is marked by open communication and a shared respect for each other's individuality.

Emily's approach to romantic relationships has undergone a significant transformation. Freed from the shadows of past insecurities, she now navigates these waters with a clarity of what she seeks – a partnership grounded in mutual respect, support, and shared values. While she remains open to the possibilities of love, there is no urgency in her quest, for she has found contentment and fulfillment within herself.

This period of Emily's life is also characterized by continued self-discovery and exploration. Her passion for art remains the cornerstone of her existence, but she now indulges in other pursuits that enrich her life. Travel, literature, and engagement in community activities have broadened her horizons, introducing her to new experiences, cultures, and perspectives.

Emily's journey has also led her to embrace a role as an advocate for mental health and the therapeutic power of art. She organizes workshops and speaks at events, sharing her story and insights to inspire and help others. Her voice, once hesitant, now resonates with confidence and purpose, touching the lives of those who hear her.

As the story draws to a close, we leave Emily at a juncture of hopeful anticipation. The future, once a source of anxiety, is now a canvas waiting to be painted with the vibrant colors of her dreams and aspirations. She stands ready to embrace whatever comes her way, fortified by her experiences and the knowledge that she possesses the strength to navigate the vicissitudes of life.

In this concluding segment, the narrative leaves ample space for the reader's imagination. Emily's story, though reaching a satisfying conclusion, is open-ended, allowing readers to envision their own possibilities for her future. Will she embark on new romantic adventures? Will her professional endeavors reach new heights? The answers to these questions are left to the imagination, a tribute to the infinite potential that lies within each of us to author our own destinies.

# Chapter 22: New Beginnings

Emily Carter's journey, a tapestry of emotions, challenges, and growth, brings us to this pivotal chapter: "New Beginnings." Her story, set against the vibrant backdrop of Alderidge, has been a profound exploration of love, loss, self-discovery, and healing. Once a reserved art teacher, her life took an unexpected turn with the entrance of Michael Harrison, a graphic designer whose lens captured more than just the city's autumnal beauty – it captured Emily's heart.

Their romance, blossoming amidst the golden hues of autumn, was a whirlwind of emotions and discoveries. Emily, who had cherished a life of contentment and simplicity, found herself delving into uncharted emotional territories. With Michael, she experienced the heights of joy and the depths of vulnerability. However, as the seasons changed, so did the nature of their relationship. Misunderstandings and unmet expectations began to cloud their connection, revealing deeper differences in their aspirations and life paths.

The culmination of these challenges led to a poignant resolution. Emily and Michael, after heartfelt conversations and reflections, decided to part ways. This decision, though laden with sadness, was also a gateway to profound growth for Emily. It marked the end of a significant chapter in her life but also the beginning of a journey towards self-realization and empowerment.

In the wake of her separation from Michael, Emily embarked on a path of healing. She sought solace in her art, her students, and the embrace of her friends and family. She engaged in new hobbies, rediscovered her independence, and slowly pieced together the fragments of her heart and soul. This period was not just about recovery; it was about transformation. Emily emerged from her experiences with a newfound strength, a deeper understanding of herself, and a clearer vision of what she sought in life.

As we step into "New Beginnings," we find Emily at a crossroads, poised to embrace the next phase of her life. This chapter is not just a continuation of her story; it is a celebration of renewal and possibility. It encapsulates the essence of starting anew, of looking at the world through a lens of hope and aspiration. Here, the lingering effects of past events serve as stepping stones rather than obstacles, shaping but not defining her future.

"New Beginnings" is set to explore Emily's life post-conflict, delving into her professional endeavors, personal relationships, and her continuous journey of self-discovery. It will highlight her aspirations and the subtle yet significant changes in her outlook towards life and relationships. This chapter promises to be a tapestry of experiences, weaving together themes of resilience, hope, and the endless potential for transformation that lies within each of us.

In the wake of her poignant separation from Michael, Emily Carter found herself navigating a world that was at once familiar and entirely new. The streets of Alderidge, the classrooms where she taught, and even the cozy corners of her own apartment, all whispered echoes of a past chapter, now closed. Yet, in these echoes, Emily discovered not sorrow, but the seeds of a newfound understanding of herself and the life she yearned to build.

The initial days following the resolution of her main conflict were a blend of reflection and subtle transformation. Each morning, as she woke to the soft light filtering through her curtains, Emily felt a sense of quiet anticipation. Gone was the heaviness that had once clouded her mornings; in its place was a gentle curiosity about what each new day would bring.

Her daily routine, previously a comfortable sequence of familiar actions, now took on a different hue. Emily began experimenting with small changes, infusing her days with new experiences. She swapped her usual route to work for a path that took her through the heart of the city's sprawling park. These morning walks became a time for contemplation, where the rustling leaves and the gentle breeze seemed to encourage her thoughts to wander and explore new possibilities.

In the classroom, Emily's approach to teaching evolved. She found herself sharing more of her own artistic journey with her students, encouraging them to see art not just as a subject to be learned, but as a means of expressing their innermost feelings and experiences. Her classes became more interactive, with discussions that went beyond technique and composition, delving into the emotional and therapeutic aspects of art.

Her interactions with colleagues also underwent a subtle shift. Where once she had been more reserved, Emily now engaged more openly, sharing ideas and participating in school initiatives with a newfound confidence. This change did not go unnoticed; her colleagues began to seek her out for her insights and perspective, recognizing in her a leader who had weathered personal storms with grace.

At home, Emily transformed her living space to reflect the changes within her. She redecorated her apartment, creating an environment that was not just a place to live, but a sanctuary that nourished her spirit. Artworks created during her period of healing adorned the walls, each piece a reminder of her journey and the resilience she had discovered in herself.

Her evenings, once spent in solitude or in the company of close friends, now included new activities. Emily joined a local book club, finding joy in discussing literature with fellow enthusiasts. She also enrolled in a photography class, a nod to the influence Michael had on her life and a testament to her willingness to explore new facets of herself.

The weekends, which had once been a time for rest and recuperation, were now opportunities for adventure and exploration. Emily began to travel to nearby towns, visiting art galleries, attending cultural events, and exploring the rich history and diversity of her region. These solo trips were not just leisurely getaways; they were pilgrimages of self-discovery, each journey bringing new insights and experiences.

In her personal relationships, Emily's newfound self-awareness and confidence were evident. Conversations with her family became deeper and more meaningful, characterized by a mutual respect and understanding that had grown stronger through her experiences. With her friends, Emily was more open, sharing her thoughts and feelings with a vulnerability that deepened their connections.

Even her approach to dating had changed. Emily ventured into the world of romantic relationships with a clarity about what she sought in a partner and a relationship. She approached each potential connection with an open heart but also with the wisdom gained from her past. Her experiences with Michael had taught her the importance of communication, honesty, and shared values in a relationship.

The most profound change, however, was in Emily's relationship with herself. She had emerged from her period of healing with a deeper understanding and acceptance of who she was. She embraced her strengths and weaknesses with equal grace, recognizing that both contributed to the unique tapestry of her being.

She also discovered a newfound passion for advocacy. Drawing from her own experiences, Emily became an active voice in promoting mental health awareness and the therapeutic benefits of art. She organized workshops and talks, sharing her story and insights to inspire and support others.

Through these myriad adjustments and new experiences, Emily's life post-conflict became a journey of continuous discovery and growth. Each day was a step towards the future she was actively shaping – a future filled with possibilities, learning, and the promise of new beginnings.

Emily's professional evolution, post the resolution of her main conflict, is a story of ambition, creativity, and leadership. At the community art center, where she had always been a respected figure, Emily now shone as a beacon of innovation and inspiration. Her journey in the art world, marked by newfound confidence and vision, saw her embracing and initiating changes that resonated far beyond the walls of her classroom.

In the art center, Emily took on a more prominent leadership role. She spearheaded projects that aimed to make art accessible to broader sections of the community, breaking down barriers that had previously made art seem like an exclusive domain. One of her key initiatives was the 'Art for All' program, designed to bring art education to underprivileged children in Alderidge. The program was a resounding success, drawing in volunteers and garnering support from local businesses and the city council.

Another significant project that Emily undertook was the 'Healing Through Art' series. Drawing from her personal experiences with art as a therapeutic tool, she designed workshops for individuals dealing with trauma and mental health issues. These workshops provided a safe space for participants to express themselves, explore their emotions, and find solace in the act of creating. The success of this series put Emily at the forefront of integrating art therapy into community services, establishing her as a pioneer in the field.

Emily's responsibilities at the art center expanded to include curating exhibitions and organizing community art events. Under her guidance, the center became a vibrant hub of cultural activity, hosting art shows, local artist meet-ups, and cultural festivals. These events not only celebrated art but also fostered a sense of community and belonging among the attendees, furthering Emily's vision of art as a unifying force.

Her aspirations in the art world grew alongside her projects. Emily began to collaborate with other art educators and therapists, expanding her network and influence. She attended conferences and seminars, both as a participant and a speaker, sharing her insights and learning from others in her field. These interactions opened up new avenues for collaboration and innovation, fueling her passion and ambition.

Emily also ventured into the realm of digital art, embracing technology as a tool for artistic expression and education. She introduced digital art workshops at the center, encouraging students and community members to explore this modern form of creativity. Her openness to new ideas and technologies kept the art center at the forefront of contemporary art education.

Amidst these professional achievements, Emily did not lose sight of her own artistic development. She continued to create her own art, experimenting with different mediums and styles. Her personal artwork, often reflective of her journey and experiences, began to gain recognition in local art circles. She participated in group exhibitions and even held a solo exhibition, which was met with acclaim and appreciation.

Emily's art, once a personal sanctuary, had evolved into a medium of communication and connection with the world around her. Her creations were not just displays of skill but also expressions of her inner world, her thoughts, and her emotions. This authenticity in her work resonated with viewers, drawing them into a shared experience of art as a reflection of life.

In her professional evolution, Emily had transformed from an art teacher to a community leader, an advocate for art therapy, and an artist in her own right. Her career progress was not just a series of accomplishments but a journey of impacting lives, inspiring change, and fulfilling her aspirations in the art world.

Continuing with Emily's professional journey, her advancements in the art world are not only a reflection of her personal growth but also a catalyst for broader community transformation. Her vision for the art center and her role within it continued to evolve, mirroring the dynamic nature of art itself.

One of Emily's groundbreaking projects was the 'Art Without Borders' initiative. This program aimed to connect artists and communities across different cities and even countries, using art as a universal language to bridge cultural and social divides. Under this initiative, Emily organized international art exchange programs, where local artists could showcase their work abroad, and in return, the art center hosted exhibitions featuring international artists. This cultural exchange enriched the local art scene and provided invaluable exposure and learning opportunities for all involved.

Emily also recognized the potential of technology in revolutionizing art education. She collaborated with tech companies to develop an online platform for art education, offering courses and workshops that were accessible to people regardless of their location. This digital leap not only expanded the reach of the art center but also aligned with Emily's belief in making art accessible to all. The platform included a range of courses, from basic drawing techniques to advanced art therapy sessions, catering to a diverse audience.

In her pursuit of integrating art and technology, Emily didn't shy away from experimenting with new-age mediums like virtual reality (VR) and augmented reality (AR) in her art creations and teaching methods. She introduced VR art exhibitions at the center, providing immersive experiences that allowed visitors to engage with art in novel and interactive ways. These exhibitions were a hit, attracting a younger audience and sparking new interest in art among tech enthusiasts.

As her professional stature grew, Emily found herself at the center of policy discussions around art and education. She became an advocate for incorporating art into the general school curriculum, emphasizing its importance in fostering creativity, emotional expression, and mental well-being in students. Her efforts paid off when the local school district piloted an art-integrated learning program, based on her recommendations and the success of her community projects.

Despite these numerous professional engagements, Emily maintained a deep connection with her roots as a teacher and mentor. She continued to teach regular classes at the art center, finding joy and fulfillment in the progress and success of her students. Her teaching style, always evolving, became more holistic, focusing not just on technical skills but also on developing a critical and appreciative eye for art in her students.

Emily's personal art continued to flourish alongside her professional endeavors. She started exploring more abstract forms, using her art as a means to comment on social and emotional themes. Her work became known for its depth and thought-provoking nature, earning her invitations to exhibit in prestigious galleries and art shows.

In this journey, Emily's life came full circle. From seeking solace in art during her times of turmoil, she had progressed to using art as a means of healing, education, and community enrichment. Her story is a powerful narrative of how personal passion, when coupled with vision and hard work, can transcend individual boundaries and become a force for collective good.

As Emily's professional journey continued, her influence and contributions in the art world began to intertwine more profoundly with her personal beliefs and life experiences. Each project and initiative she undertook was not just a professional milestone but also a reflection of her journey towards self-realization and her desire to impact society positively.

One of Emily's most ambitious projects was the establishment of an annual art festival in Alderidge. The festival, named "Canvas of Cultures," was designed to celebrate the diversity and richness of various art forms from around the world. Emily envisioned this event as a platform for artists of all backgrounds to showcase their work, engage with the community, and foster a global dialogue through art. The festival included workshops, panel discussions, and interactive sessions, along with a grand exhibition of artworks. Emily's leadership in organizing this festival placed her at the forefront of cultural exchange and artistic collaboration in the city.

In addition to her community-focused initiatives, Emily began exploring the intersection of art and environmental awareness. She initiated a series of workshops and collaborative projects that used recycled materials and eco-friendly practices. These projects were not only a testament to her creativity but also a demonstration of her commitment to sustainability and environmental conservation. Her work in this area raised awareness about ecological issues and showcased how art could be a powerful tool for social change.

Emily's growing reputation as an art educator and advocate led her to opportunities for collaboration with universities and educational institutions. She was invited to guest lecture at various colleges, sharing her insights on the therapeutic aspects of art and the importance of arts education. These engagements allowed her to influence future educators and artists, spreading her philosophy of art as a crucial component of personal and social well-being.

Another significant aspect of Emily's professional evolution was her involvement in mentorship programs. She became a mentor to emerging artists and art educators, providing guidance, support, and resources to help them navigate their careers. Her mentorship was highly sought after, as she offered a unique blend of artistic expertise, professional wisdom, and personal empathy.

Emily also continued to push the boundaries of her own artistry. She experimented with large-scale installations and public art projects, bringing art out of conventional spaces and into the community. These installations were often interactive and designed to engage the public in meaningful conversations about art and society. Her work in this area not only enhanced the visual landscape of Alderidge but also made art a more inclusive and accessible experience for the general public.

As her influence grew, Emily remained grounded in her original passion for teaching and community service. She ensured that her work, regardless of scale or recognition, stayed true to her core values of inclusivity, healing, and empowerment through art.

Emily's professional journey thus became a beacon of inspiration, not just for aspiring artists but for anyone seeking to use their talents and passions to make a difference in the world. Her story is a powerful narrative of how one person's vision and dedication can create ripples of change, influencing individuals and communities alike.

In the wake of her journey through love, loss, and self-discovery, Emily's approach to her personal relationships underwent a profound transformation. The experiences and lessons gleaned from her past significantly influenced how she interacted with those around her, from her family and long-standing friends to new acquaintances she met along her path.

Family had always been a cornerstone in Emily's life, providing a foundation of love and support. Post her main conflict, the bond with her family deepened further, characterized by a new level of openness and understanding. Regular visits to her parents' home became occasions for heartfelt conversations, where Emily shared her aspirations and reflections. These moments were not just about rekindling familial ties; they were a celebration of mutual growth and respect. Her parents, witnessing the resilience and maturity in their daughter, offered their insights and wisdom, adding depth to these interactions. Emily's relationship with her siblings too evolved, moving beyond the playful camaraderie of childhood to a mature bond grounded in mutual support and admiration.

Her circle of friends, both old and new, played a crucial role in her life post-conflict. With her old friends, the shared history and experiences created a comfortable space where Emily could be her true self. These friendships, strengthened over time, became more meaningful as Emily and her friends navigated the complexities of adult life together. They celebrated each other's successes, provided comfort during times of distress, and shared moments of joy and laughter, reinforcing the bonds of friendship.

New acquaintances entered Emily's life as she expanded her social circle through her professional endeavors and hobbies. These new relationships were formed on the basis of shared interests, be it art, literature, or community service. Emily approached these new connections with a sense of curiosity and openness, eager to learn from the diverse experiences and perspectives they brought into her life. Her interactions with these individuals were marked by a willingness to listen and understand, traits honed by her past experiences.

Emily's approach to romantic relationships also saw a significant change. The lessons learned from her relationship with Michael had given her a clearer understanding of what she sought in a partner. She entered the dating world with a sense of cautious optimism, guided by a set of values and expectations shaped by her journey. Her experiences had taught her the importance of communication, honesty, and mutual respect in a relationship. She sought a partnership that was not just based on romantic affection but also on shared goals, intellectual compatibility, and emotional support.

In her dating experiences, Emily encountered individuals with varying personalities and backgrounds. Some connections were brief, while others developed into deeper interactions. Through these experiences, she learned to navigate the nuances of modern dating, from understanding the importance of personal space and independence to recognizing the signs of a healthy, balanced relationship.

As she formed and nurtured these various relationships, Emily discovered the delicate balance between giving and receiving in interpersonal dynamics. She learned to set healthy boundaries, a skill that allowed her to maintain her sense of self while being fully present in her relationships. This balance was crucial in avoiding the pitfalls she had encountered in her past, where she sometimes lost parts of herself in the process of caring for others.

The most significant change in Emily's approach to relationships was her heightened sense of empathy and emotional intelligence. Her own experiences with heartache and healing endowed her with a deep understanding of human emotions. This understanding enabled her to be a more compassionate friend, a more understanding family member, and a more empathetic partner.

Emily's journey of self-discovery and growth thus had a ripple effect on her personal relationships. Each interaction, each connection, was imbued with a depth and richness that stemmed from her experiences. Her relationships became sources of joy, learning, and mutual growth, reflecting the journey she had undertaken.

Emily's relationship with her family continued to be a source of strength and grounding. Her parents, who had witnessed her transformation, offered not just parental guidance but also a friendship that Emily deeply valued. They shared in her triumphs and offered solace in times of struggle, their home becoming a haven where Emily could always find comfort and understanding. Her conversations with her parents, once centered around day-to-day affairs, now delved into discussions about life, philosophy, and her aspirations. These interactions were a reflection of the evolving dynamic in their relationship – one marked by mutual respect and admiration.

Her bond with her siblings also took on new dimensions. They became confidants and pillars of support in her life. Whether it was seeking advice on professional matters or sharing the joys and challenges of her personal endeavors, Emily found in her siblings reliable and empathetic allies. The sense of camaraderie and shared history with her siblings provided a touchstone of stability and normalcy in her ever-evolving life.

The friendships that Emily nurtured were no less significant. Her old friends, who had been with her through various phases of her life, now saw her as a source of inspiration. Their gatherings were filled with laughter, reminiscences, and discussions about their future dreams and aspirations. These friends, who had stood by her during her times of turmoil, now celebrated her growth and achievements, their bond strengthened by the trials and triumphs they had shared.

With her new acquaintances, Emily found excitement and enrichment. These relationships, forged through her professional endeavors, hobbies, and community work, brought fresh perspectives and diverse experiences into her life. She cherished these new connections, as they expanded her worldview and added new dimensions to her social circle. Whether it was collaborating on a community art project or engaging in lively discussions at the book club, Emily approached each interaction with a genuine interest and openness, building meaningful and lasting relationships.

In her romantic endeavors, Emily approached each potential relationship with a blend of hope and pragmatism. She understood the importance of compatibility, shared values, and mutual respect.

Her dates were not just opportunities to explore romantic possibilities but also moments to connect with individuals on a deeper level. Emily sought a partner who not only shared her interests but also her vision for a relationship built on trust, growth, and mutual support.

Through these various personal relationships, Emily developed a nuanced understanding of human dynamics. She learned the art of nurturing relationships, knowing when to give space and when to offer support. Her experiences had taught her that each relationship was unique and required its own approach and understanding.

The impact of her past experiences on her relationships was profound. Emily's journey had taught her the importance of empathy, open communication, and vulnerability in building strong, meaningful connections. She had learned to appreciate the value of each person in her life, understanding that every individual, whether a family member, a friend, or a romantic partner, played a unique role in her journey.

As Emily navigated the new chapter of her life post-conflict, her engagement in new hobbies and interests became integral to her ongoing journey of self-discovery and personal development. These activities, varying in nature and scope, served not only as sources of joy and relaxation but also as tools for deeper self-exploration and growth.

Photography, which she had initially taken up as a nod to Michael's influence in her life, evolved into a profound passion for Emily. She began to see the world through the lens of her camera, capturing moments and scenes that resonated with her emotionally. Photography became a way for Emily to express her perspective on the world, to tell stories without words. Her weekend excursions to various locales around Alderidge turned into photographic adventures, each trip yielding a collection of images that spoke of her view of the world – sometimes poignant, sometimes jubilant, but always deeply personal.

Emily also discovered a newfound interest in gardening. What started as a small project in her balcony space grew into a significant hobby. She found solace in tending to her plants, the act of nurturing them providing a peaceful counterpoint to her often busy life. The growth and bloom of each plant mirrored her own journey, serving as a reminder of the beauty and resilience inherent in nature and, by extension, in herself.

Another area that piqued Emily's interest was culinary arts. She began attending cooking classes, exploring cuisines from different cultures. These classes were more than just about learning new recipes; they were about experiencing and appreciating diverse cultures and traditions. Cooking became a creative outlet for Emily, a way to bring people together and share experiences. The dinners she hosted for her friends and family became renowned, her table a gathering place for laughter, stories, and shared experiences.

Emily's involvement in community service also expanded. She volunteered at local charities and participated in events that aimed to bring art to underprivileged sections of the community. This work was deeply fulfilling for Emily, as it aligned with her belief in the power of art to heal and unite. Through these activities, she connected with individuals from various walks of life, each interaction enriching her understanding of the world and her place in it.

One of the most significant new interests that Emily pursued was yoga and meditation. Seeking a balance in her life, she found these practices to be grounding and rejuvenating. Yoga provided a physical outlet for stress, while meditation offered her moments of stillness and introspection. These practices became essential components of her routine, helping her maintain a sense of inner peace amidst her various pursuits.

Emily also rekindled her love for reading. She found herself drawn to books that spoke of personal journeys, resilience, and the human condition. Literature became a source of inspiration and insight, each book offering a window into different experiences and perspectives. Her book club meetings were occasions for deep discussions, where ideas and interpretations were shared and debated, adding to her understanding and appreciation of the world.

As Emily engaged in these diverse activities, her journey of self-discovery and personal development continued to unfold. Each hobby and interest contributed to her growth in unique ways. Photography taught her to see beauty in the mundane, gardening connected her with the rhythms of nature, cooking brought her closer to diverse cultures, community service fostered a sense of purpose and connection, while yoga, meditation, and reading nurtured her mind and soul.

These activities were not just pastimes; they were integral to Emily's process of understanding herself better. They provided her with opportunities to challenge herself, to step out of her comfort zone, and to explore new aspects of her personality. Through them, she discovered strengths she didn't know she had, and passions that brought joy and fulfillment to her life.

Emily's engagement in these new hobbies and interests was a reflection of her evolving identity. They were manifestations of her desires, her values, and her aspirations. Each activity, in its own way, contributed to her narrative, adding chapters of exploration, achievement, and fulfillment.

beauty and life. Gardening also provided her a tangible connection to nature, grounding her in the present moment and offering a peaceful retreat from the hustle of everyday life.

Cooking, another of Emily's newfound interests, became a way for her to explore and celebrate cultural diversity. Through her culinary adventures, she not only learned about different cuisines but also about the history and traditions behind them. Cooking became an act of cultural exploration, broadening her horizons and deepening her appreciation for the world's rich tapestry of cultures. The meals she prepared and shared with friends and family were not just feasts for the palate but also for the soul, fostering a sense of community and togetherness.

Her involvement in community service continued to be a significant part of her life. Through her volunteer work, Emily found a deep sense of purpose. She witnessed firsthand the impact of art on individuals from different backgrounds and how it could be used as a tool for healing, communication, and connection. This work reinforced her belief in the power of art to effect positive change and strengthened her commitment to using her skills and resources for the benefit of others.

Yoga and meditation, meanwhile, became foundational practices in Emily's life. They provided her with a sense of balance and well-being. Yoga challenged her physically, enhancing her strength and flexibility, while meditation offered mental clarity and emotional stability. These practices helped her develop a deeper connection with herself, allowing her to approach life with a calm and centered disposition.

Reading continued to be a source of joy and enlightenment for Emily. The books she read opened her mind to new ideas, experiences, and viewpoints. Her book club discussions were intellectually stimulating, providing a forum for sharing thoughts and engaging in meaningful dialogues. Reading expanded her understanding of the human experience, offering comfort, inspiration, and insight.

Each of these hobbies and interests contributed uniquely to Emily's journey of self-discovery and personal development. They were not mere pastimes but integral parts of her life that enriched her experience, broadened her perspective, and deepened her understanding of herself and the world around her. Through these activities, Emily found joy, fulfillment, and a sense of purpose. They shaped her identity and her path, each one an essential thread in the fabric of her story.

As Emily's story progresses, her engagement in these hobbies and interests continues to play a pivotal role in her life, shaping her journey and contributing to her ever-evolving narrative. Her story stands as a testament to the transformative power of pursuing one's passions and the endless possibilities for growth and discovery that lie within each of us.

Emily's active participation in community projects and mental health advocacy marked a significant chapter in her life, one where her personal experiences and passions intersected to create a profound impact on society. Her involvement in these areas was not just an extension of her professional life as an artist and educator, but a deeply personal commitment to using her experiences for the greater good.

The community art center, where Emily had long been a guiding force, became the epicenter of her community engagement. Here, she initiated and led various projects aimed at making art accessible to all segments of society. One such project was the 'Art in Public Spaces' initiative, where Emily collaborated with local artists to create murals and installations in public areas. These artworks, vibrant and thought-provoking, transformed ordinary spaces into cultural landmarks and sparked conversations among the community members. Through this project, Emily aimed to democratize art, taking it out of galleries and into the everyday lives of people, making it a shared community experience.

Another significant endeavor was the 'Youth Art Outreach' program, which focused on bringing art education to underprivileged youth. Emily worked with schools and community centers, organizing workshops and classes that provided a creative outlet for children and teenagers. She believed strongly in the power of art to inspire, heal, and empower young minds. This program was particularly close to her heart, as it aligned with her belief that every child, regardless of their background, should have the opportunity to explore and express themselves through art.

Emily's advocacy for mental health was fueled by her own journey through healing and self-discovery. She became a vocal advocate for the integration of art therapy into mental health services. Drawing on her experiences and the knowledge she gained, she organized workshops and seminars, educating people about the benefits of art therapy. She collaborated with mental health professionals, combining her expertise in art with their clinical knowledge to develop programs that used art as a tool for healing.

Her advocacy efforts extended to speaking engagements at conferences and events, where she shared her story and the transformative power of art. Emily's talks were deeply moving and inspirational, resonating with a wide audience. She spoke candidly about her struggles and how art had been a pivotal element in her healing process. Her openness and vulnerability in these talks made her a relatable and powerful advocate for mental health and the therapeutic benefits of art.

Emily also played a key role in organizing community events centered around mental health awareness. These events included art exhibitions, talks, and interactive workshops that brought together art, education, and mental health. Her aim was to create a platform for dialogue, to break down the stigmas associated with mental health, and to foster a community that supported and understood the importance of mental well-being.

In her community involvement and advocacy work, Emily found a deep sense of fulfillment. She saw firsthand the impact of her efforts – in the smiles of children discovering their love for art, in the gratitude of those who found solace through art therapy, and in the changing perceptions towards mental health in her community. These experiences only strengthened her resolve to continue her work in these fields.

Her advocacy and community work also influenced her personal growth. Through her interactions and collaborations, she learned about the diverse experiences and challenges faced by people from different walks of life. These interactions broadened her perspective and deepened her empathy, making her a more compassionate artist, educator, and human being.

Emily's journey in community involvement and mental health advocacy was a testament to the impact one individual can have in society. Her story is a powerful illustration of how personal experiences can be transformed into positive action, and how passion and commitment can create ripples of change in the community.

As Emily's story progresses, her role as a community leader and advocate continues to evolve, shaping not just her own path but also touching the lives of those around her. Her involvement in these areas remains a core part of her identity, reflecting her dedication to making a difference and her belief in the power of art and empathy to heal and unite.

As Emily's involvement in community projects and mental health advocacy deepened, her impact became increasingly evident in various facets of society. Each project she undertook or supported not only helped those directly involved but also contributed to a broader cultural shift in how art and mental health were perceived and valued in her community.

One of Emily's standout projects was the establishment of a community garden that combined art and nature therapy. She envisioned this space as a sanctuary where people could come together to find peace and creativity. The garden was filled with sculptures and installations created by local artists, including some of Emily's own works. Gardening workshops were held regularly, where participants could learn about horticulture while engaging in mindful and therapeutic activities. This garden quickly became a beloved community space, symbolizing growth, healing, and the nurturing power of nature and art.

Another significant initiative led by Emily was a collaborative project with local hospitals and mental health clinics to incorporate art therapy into their treatment programs. She worked closely with healthcare professionals to design art therapy sessions tailored to the needs of various patient groups, including those with depression, anxiety, and PTSD. The success of these programs was heartening, with many patients reporting significant improvements in their mental well-being. These collaborations not only benefited the patients but also helped healthcare providers see the value of integrating creative therapies into their treatment plans.

Emily's advocacy efforts also extended to the educational sector. She championed the integration of art and mental health education in school curriculums. Partnering with educators, she helped develop programs that taught students about the importance of mental health, emotional expression, and the role of creativity in overall well-being. These programs aimed to equip young people with tools for self-expression and coping mechanisms for mental health challenges, fostering a more informed and empathetic generation.

Her role as a community leader in art and mental health advocacy also led Emily to participate in policy-making discussions. She was invited to city council meetings and educational forums to provide her insights on how art could be leveraged for community development and mental health improvement. Her contributions in these arenas were instrumental in shaping policies that supported the arts and mental health services in her city.

Amidst these extensive community and advocacy efforts, Emily continued to find time for direct interaction with individuals. She often conducted small, intimate art therapy sessions, where she connected with people on a personal level, guiding them through their journey of expression and healing. These sessions were profoundly fulfilling for Emily, as they reminded her of the tangible impact of her work on individuals' lives.

The ripple effects of Emily's efforts were far-reaching. The projects and initiatives she spearheaded or supported brought about a noticeable change in community attitudes towards mental health and the arts. Art became more than a cultural commodity; it was recognized as a vital component of community well-being and personal development. Similarly, the conversation around mental health became more open and de-stigmatized, with increasing community support and resources dedicated to mental health services.

Emily's story in community involvement and mental health advocacy is one of passion turned into purposeful action. It illustrates how personal experiences, when coupled with a desire to make a difference, can lead to significant contributions to society. Her journey is a reminder of the power of art and empathy in creating positive change and the impact one individual can have in improving the lives of others and the health of a community.

Emily's journey, rich with triumphs and trials, had brought her to a place of introspection and reflection. As she looked back on her past, including her relationship with Michael and other significant events, she found that these experiences had profoundly shaped her outlook on life, her interactions with others, and her understanding of herself.

Reflecting on her relationship with Michael, Emily realized that it had been a pivotal chapter in her life. It was a story of deep connection, shared dreams, and ultimately, a divergence of paths. This relationship taught her about love, vulnerability, and the importance of aligning one's life with one's values and aspirations.

The joy and pain of this romance had contributed significantly to her personal growth. Emily learned to embrace vulnerability, to communicate more openly, and to understand the complexity of emotions that relationships bring. This chapter, though ended, continued to influence her approach to romantic relationships, making her more mindful, self-aware, and clear about what she sought in a partner.

Her experiences during and after the relationship also reinforced the importance of resilience. Emily realized that her ability to recover and grow from her experiences was a testament to her inner strength. This understanding gave her a sense of confidence and a belief in her ability to handle whatever challenges life might throw her way.

Her journey through self-discovery and healing post-breakup was another area of deep reflection for Emily. It was during this time that she delved into art as a means of expression and therapy, discovering its power to heal and transform. This phase of self-reflection and growth was instrumental in shaping her current path as an artist, educator, and mental health advocate. It instilled in her a passion for helping others through art and a commitment to using her experiences to make a positive impact on society.

Emily also reflected on her professional journey, from a dedicated art teacher to a community leader and advocate for art therapy. She recognized how each step of her career, each project and initiative, was influenced by her personal experiences and her desire to share the healing power of art with others. Her professional evolution was not just a series of achievements but a journey of using her talent and passion to contribute to the greater good.

Her involvement in community projects and advocacy work, particularly in promoting mental health awareness, was another area of reflection. Emily understood that her motivation for this work stemmed from her own experiences with healing and self-discovery.

She saw how her efforts in these areas were making a tangible difference in people's lives and in changing societal attitudes towards mental health and art. This work gave her a sense of purpose and fulfillment, reinforcing her belief in the power of community and the impact of individual efforts.

Furthermore, Emily's reflections on her past experiences made her more empathetic and compassionate. She became more attuned to the struggles and needs of others, using her insights to connect with and support those around her. Her past experiences had equipped her with a deeper understanding of the human condition, making her more effective in her role as an educator and advocate.

Emily's journey of self-discovery and growth also led to a greater appreciation for life's simple joys and a commitment to living authentically. She learned to cherish the moment, to find beauty in the everyday, and to pursue what truly mattered to her. This outlook was evident in her engagement with hobbies, her approach to relationships, and her dedication to her community and advocacy work.

As she reflected on her past, Emily realized that each experience, whether joyful or painful, had contributed to the person she had become. Her story was one of continuous growth, learning, and transformation. These reflections not only provided her with a sense of closure and understanding but also guided her in her future endeavors.

As Emily navigated the waters of her new life, the theme of romance gently unfurled its petals once more. Her experiences, especially those with Michael, had endowed her with a cautious yet hopeful perspective on love and relationships. This new chapter in her romantic life was not just about finding love again but about exploring the possibilities with a deeper understanding and a more defined sense of self.

Emily's approach to new romantic possibilities was markedly different from her past. She had learned the value of self-love and the importance of being complete within oneself before sharing life with another. This realization made her more mindful in her approach to potential relationships. She was no longer in pursuit of romance to fill a void or to fit into the societal mold of being in a relationship. Instead, she sought a connection that complemented her own journey of growth and discovery.

As she ventured into the world of dating, Emily was both open-minded and discerning. Her past experiences had taught her the significance of shared values, mutual respect, and emotional compatibility. She looked for these qualities in potential partners, understanding that a lasting and fulfilling relationship was built on much more than just initial attraction.

Emily's interactions on dates were characterized by honest and open communication. She was not afraid to express her thoughts, feelings, and expectations. This level of transparency was a way for her to gauge the compatibility with her date and to establish a foundation of trust and respect from the outset. Emily also listened intently, not just to what was being said but also to what was left unsaid, as she believed that true communication went beyond words.

Her experiences with Michael had left a lasting impact on how she viewed relationships. She had learned that love, while beautiful and enriching, also required effort, understanding, and a willingness to navigate through challenges together. These insights informed her approach to potential romantic connections. She was patient, taking the time to really know the person before delving deeper into the relationship.

Emily also explored the world of online dating, a realm that was new and somewhat daunting to her. She approached it with a mix of curiosity and caution, aware of the possibilities it offered but also mindful of its pitfalls. Her profile was a reflection of her authenticity

– a blend of her interests, beliefs, and a glimpse into her journey. The conversations she had online ranged from light-hearted banter to profound discussions, each interaction a step in understanding the person on the other side of the screen.

As she met new people, whether through online platforms or in her everyday life, Emily maintained a balance between hope and realism. She enjoyed the excitement of new connections, the butterflies that came with the anticipation of a new relationship, but she also kept her expectations in check. She knew that not every connection would lead to a romantic relationship, and that was okay. Each interaction was an opportunity to learn more about herself and others.

In her exploration of romantic possibilities, Emily also leaned on her friends and family for support and advice. They offered perspectives that sometimes challenged her own, helping her see things in a different light. This support system was crucial in her journey, as it provided her with a sense of grounding and reassurance.

Emily's journey in exploring romantic possibilities was a testament to her growth. It was about finding love again, but it was also about reaffirming her own values, understanding her needs, and embracing the possibility of sharing her life with someone who respected and loved her for who she was. This exploration was not just a search for a partner but a continuation of her journey of self-discovery and personal fulfillment.

In this new phase of her life, Emily's approach to romance was reflective of her overall journey – one of resilience, self-awareness, and an unwavering hope in the possibilities that life held. Her story in this regard is a reminder that exploring romantic possibilities can be a journey of joy, discovery, and growth, one that is enriched by past experiences and a clear sense of self.

As Emily's exploration of romantic possibilities continued, her experiences became a rich tapestry of learning, self-discovery, and gradual opening to the joys and complexities of new relationships. Her approach, grounded in the wisdom gleaned from her past, allowed her to navigate these waters with a blend of optimism and practicality.

In this phase of her life, Emily encountered a variety of individuals, each bringing their own stories, personalities, and expectations to the table. Some encounters were fleeting – brief interactions that, while not leading to anything deeper, enriched her understanding of the diverse tapestry of human connections. Others offered more substantial prospects, kindling the excitement of potential romance.

One significant aspect of Emily's journey was her newfound ability to enjoy the process of getting to know someone without the pressure of immediate commitment. She appreciated the small joys of dating – the thrill of a first meeting, the discovery of shared interests, and even the awkward yet endearing moments that come with the territory of new connections. Emily learned to embrace these experiences, understanding that each one contributed to her journey, regardless of the outcome.

In her interactions, Emily placed a high value on authenticity and emotional intelligence. She sought partners who were not only intellectually stimulating but also emotionally available and empathetic. Her conversations delved into topics that were close to her heart – art, personal growth, her advocacy work, and her journey of healing. These discussions were not just small talk but pathways to understanding the values, depth, and compatibility of the person she was with.

As she met different people, Emily remained conscious of the lessons from her past. She was aware of the patterns she had fallen into in her previous relationship and was determined not to repeat them. This awareness made her more attuned to red flags and more assertive in expressing her needs and boundaries. She knew that a healthy relationship required not just mutual affection but also mutual respect, space for individual growth, and aligned life goals.

Emily also discovered the importance of balance in a relationship. She sought a partnership where both individuals could support and inspire each other, where their individual journeys complemented and enriched the shared path. This understanding came from her realization that a fulfilling relationship was one where both partners could thrive as individuals while growing together.

Her exploration of romantic possibilities was not without its challenges. There were moments of doubt, disappointment, and the familiar pangs of heartache. However, Emily faced these challenges with resilience and a deeper understanding of herself. She knew that each experience, whether joyous or painful, was a part of her journey, shaping her into a more rounded and empathetic individual.

Throughout her explorations, Emily maintained a strong connection with her passions and interests. She continued to invest time in her hobbies, her community work, and her personal growth. This balance ensured that her pursuit of romantic connections did not overshadow her individual journey but rather complemented it.

As Emily's story in exploring romantic possibilities unfolds, it becomes evident that her journey is not just about finding love again. It is about understanding the nuances of human connections, appreciating the journey itself, and growing as an individual. Her approach to relationships, informed by her past experiences, reflects her maturity, her depth of character, and her commitment to living a life true to her values and aspirations.

As Emily stood at this juncture of her life, reflecting on her past and contemplating her future, she outlined a set of goals and aspirations that reflected her personal growth and professional evolution. These objectives were not just mere targets; they were extensions of her journey, a roadmap for the future she envisioned for herself.

Professionally, Emily's ambitions continued to revolve around her passion for art and her commitment to community service. One of her primary goals was to expand the reach of the community art center. She envisioned transforming it into a more inclusive space that catered not just to aspiring artists but to anyone seeking solace, expression, or healing through art. To achieve this, she planned to introduce more diverse programs, including workshops for different age groups, art therapy sessions for people with mental health issues, and collaborative projects that brought together artists from various backgrounds.

Another professional aspiration of Emily's was to establish a scholarship program for young artists from underprivileged backgrounds. She understood the challenges faced by talented individuals who lacked resources and wanted to provide them with opportunities to pursue their artistic dreams. This initiative was close to her heart, as it resonated with her belief in the power of art to transform lives. To bring this goal to fruition, Emily started collaborating with local businesses and art patrons, organizing fundraising events and awareness campaigns to generate the necessary support and funding.

In addition to these community-centered goals, Emily aspired to further her own artistic skills and explore new mediums and forms of expression. She planned to attend advanced workshops and artist residencies, which would not only refine her artistry but also expose her to different artistic styles and cultures. This pursuit of personal artistic growth was part of her commitment to staying relevant and inspired as an artist and educator.

On a personal level, Emily's goals were intertwined with her journey of self-discovery and personal fulfillment. A key aspiration was to maintain a balanced and healthy lifestyle, where she could juggle her professional responsibilities with her personal interests and relationships. To achieve this, she continued her practices of yoga and meditation, which provided her with mental clarity and physical well-being. She also planned to travel more, both for leisure and for inspiration, exploring new places, cultures, and art forms.

In terms of relationships, Emily hoped to build a life with a partner who shared her values and aspirations. Her experiences had taught her the importance of compatibility, communication, and mutual growth in a relationship. She remained open to the possibilities of love, approaching her romantic life with a blend of hope and pragmatism. At the same time, she was determined not to let her romantic pursuits overshadow her individual journey or her commitments to her art and community.

Another personal goal for Emily was to continue her advocacy work in mental health and art therapy. She planned to collaborate with more organizations, broaden her speaking engagements, and write articles and possibly a book on the therapeutic benefits of art. These efforts were aimed not just at raising awareness but also at creating tangible changes in how art and mental health were perceived and addressed in society.

Emily's proactive and determined mindset was evident in how she planned to achieve these goals. She set clear timelines, sought collaborations and partnerships, and continuously evaluated her progress. She was not deterred by challenges or setbacks; instead, she viewed them as opportunities for learning and growth.

In setting her future goals and aspirations, Emily was guided by a vision of a life that was not just successful in conventional terms but was also rich in experiences, relationships, and contributions to society. Her plans reflected her multifaceted personality – as an artist, an educator, a community leader, and a woman with a profound journey of personal growth.

Emily's story, as it unfolds towards these future goals and aspirations, is one of continuous evolution and a testament to her resilient and proactive spirit. It is a journey that inspires not just in its achievements but in its approach – one that is grounded in self-awareness, driven by passion, and aimed at making a meaningful impact.

# Chapter 23: Reflections

In the quiet moments of introspection, Emily Carter often found herself pondering the tapestry of events and encounters that had shaped her life. From the serendipitous meeting with Michael in the golden hues of Alderidge's autumn to the present day, her journey had been a vivid mosaic of love, loss, resilience, and discovery.

The romance with Michael, brimming with connection and shared dreams, had been a significant part of Emily's life. It taught her the depths of love and the complexities of human relationships. Their parting, though laden with sorrow, served as a catalyst for Emily's personal growth. It propelled her into a journey of self-exploration, where she delved into the depths of her emotions and aspirations.

Post her relationship, Emily's life took on new dimensions. Her passion for art, which had always been her solace, became a medium of profound expression and healing. She poured her heart into her teaching, transforming her classes into spaces where art transcended traditional learning and became a tool for emotional exploration and expression.

Emily's professional life flourished as she embraced new roles and challenges. At the community art center, she became a beacon of creativity and support. Initiatives like 'Art for All' and 'Healing Through Art' were not just projects but reflections of her belief in the power of art to heal and unite. These endeavors brought her recognition and satisfaction but, more importantly, a sense of fulfillment in making a difference.

In her personal sphere, Emily's relationships deepened and evolved. The bond with her family grew stronger, marked by open conversations and mutual respect. Her friendships, both old and new, became richer, filled with shared experiences and mutual growth. Emily learned the value of nurturing these bonds, understanding that each relationship contributed uniquely to her life.

Her romantic life, too, underwent a transformation. Emily approached potential relationships with a blend of hope and wisdom, informed by her past experiences. She sought connections that were built on mutual respect, shared values, and emotional compatibility. Dating became an exercise in understanding and exploration, each interaction offering insights into herself and others.

Beyond her personal and professional realms, Emily emerged as a voice in her community. Her advocacy for mental health and the therapeutic power of art was driven by her personal journey of healing. She organized workshops, spoke at events, and collaborated with mental health professionals, using her experiences to advocate for change and support others.

As she reflected on her journey, Emily recognized the invaluable lessons each phase of her life had imparted. She had learned the importance of resilience, the power of self-expression, and the beauty of forging deep, meaningful connections. Her experiences had taught her not just to survive but to thrive, to find joy in the journey, and to embrace life with all its complexities.

Emily's story is a testament to the transformative power of life's experiences. It underscores the importance of embracing change, the value of introspection, and the endless potential for growth and happiness. Her journey from the first encounter with Michael to her current life is not just a series of events but a continuous process of learning, evolving, and becoming.

In the spectrum of her experiences, Emily found not just the narrative of her life but the essence of her being. Each moment, each challenge, and each triumph was a step towards understanding herself and her place in the world. Her story, rich with lessons and insights, is a reflection of the universal journey of growth and self-discovery.

Emily's introspective journey was akin to walking through a gallery of her own life, where each memory, each experience was a painting, each with its own story and emotional palette. As she delved into these personal reflections, she uncovered layers of change and realization that had shaped her into the person she had become.

The beginning of her introspection often took her back to the days with Michael. Their relationship, though ended, was a significant chapter in her life's narrative. It was her first profound dive into the depths of romantic love, a journey filled with joy, passion, and later, heartache. From this relationship, Emily learned the importance of emotional vulnerability. She realized that opening one's heart could lead to both immense joy and profound pain, but both were essential to experiencing the full spectrum of love. The end of this relationship was a pivotal moment for Emily, marking a shift from seeking validation in love to finding strength in solitude.

Her post-breakup period was a time of intense self-discovery. In the wake of her separation, she embarked on a journey inward, exploring the terrains of her heart and mind. It was during this period that Emily discovered the true extent of her resilience. She learned to embrace solitude, finding in it a space for reflection and self-growth. The art, which had always been her refuge, became her mode of expression, helping her process her emotions and experiences. This period was instrumental in shaping her approach to future relationships. She realized the importance of being whole within herself before sharing her life with someone else.

Emily's professional life, too, underwent a metamorphosis. From being an art teacher, she evolved into a community leader, an advocate for art therapy, and a mentor to many. Her career became a reflection of her personal growth, where her passion for art and her experiences intertwined to create a positive impact. Through her community work, Emily discovered the joy in giving back, in using her skills and experiences for the benefit of others. Her initiatives at the art center and her advocacy for mental health were not just professional achievements but were personal victories, reflecting her commitment to her beliefs and values.

As she reflected on her journey, Emily also pondered over her evolving relationships with her family and friends. She realized how these relationships had grown richer and deeper over time. The unconditional support from her family had been her anchor during her tumultuous times. Her friends, both old and new, had been her companions in joy and solace in sadness. These relationships taught her the importance of a strong support system and the value of nurturing these connections.

In her exploration of new romantic possibilities, Emily approached with a blend of optimism and wisdom. Her past experiences had taught her to look for a connection that was built on mutual respect, shared values, and emotional maturity. She sought a partnership that was an equal exchange of love, support, and growth. This approach to romance was a significant shift from her earlier days, reflecting her personal growth and her understanding of what a healthy, fulfilling relationship entailed.

Her advocacy work in mental health was another area of profound reflection. Emily saw how her personal experiences could be leveraged to help others. She understood the therapeutic power of art and used it to bring solace and expression to those struggling with mental health issues. This work was not just a professional endeavor but a personal mission, driven by her empathy and her desire to make a difference.

Emily's journey of introspection revealed to her the multifaceted nature of growth. She realized that personal development was not a linear process but a complex interweaving of experiences, emotions, and realizations. Each phase of her life, each challenge, and each triumph had contributed to her understanding of herself and the world around her.

As she looked back on her journey, Emily understood that change was the only constant. She embraced this change, not with fear but with anticipation, knowing that each experience was an opportunity for growth. Her reflections showed her the importance of living authentically, of being true to oneself, and of pursuing one's passions with determination and heart.

Emily's introspective journey was a testament to her resilience, her capacity for growth, and her unyielding spirit. It was a journey marked by moments of joy and sorrow, triumphs and setbacks, love and loss. But more importantly, it was a journey of becoming – of shaping herself into a person who was not only self-aware and compassionate but also strong and hopeful.

Through her reflections, Emily found not just a deeper understanding of her past but also a guiding light for her future. Her story, a rich tapestry of experiences and emotions, was a source of wisdom and inspiration, not just for herself but for anyone who had ever embarked on the journey of self-discovery and growth.

Emily's journey, marked by personal transformation and growth, significantly impacted her relationships with key figures in her life. Each relationship, be it with her family, friends, or Michael, evolved in response to the events and experiences that shaped Emily's path.

Family had always been a cornerstone in Emily's life, a source of unconditional love and support. However, as Emily navigated through her personal challenges and triumphs, the dynamic within her family shifted and deepened. Her parents, who had once been her protectors and guides, gradually became her confidants and advisers. The conversations with her parents evolved from mundane catch-ups to discussions filled with shared wisdom and mutual respect. They saw in Emily a resilience and maturity that went beyond their parental expectations. The support they offered during her breakup with Michael and her subsequent journey of self-discovery strengthened their bond, highlighting a family dynamic that was adaptive and nurturing.

Her relationship with her siblings also underwent a transformation. From the playful and casual interactions of their earlier years, they moved to a relationship marked by deeper understanding and empathy. Emily found in her siblings not just family but friends who were there to celebrate her successes and offer comfort during her moments of doubt. The trials and experiences Emily went through opened up new avenues of connection with her siblings, making their bond more multifaceted and robust.

The relationship with Michael, a pivotal part of her life's narrative, left a profound impact on Emily. Reflecting on their time together, Emily recognized the love they shared as a significant chapter in her life. It was a relationship that brought her immense joy and, later, deep sorrow. The lessons she learned from this relationship were invaluable – understanding the complexities of love, the importance of communication, and the necessity of aligning life's paths. Though their romantic relationship ended, the experience shaped Emily's approach to future relationships, making her more aware of her needs, desires, and the importance of emotional compatibility.

Her friendships, both old and new, played a crucial role in her journey. The friends who had been with her through various life stages witnessed the changes in Emily. They saw her evolve from the aftermath of her relationship with Michael to her steps towards personal and professional growth. These friends provided a support system that was vital during her times of change. Their interactions, filled with shared memories and new experiences, were a source of comfort and joy for Emily. The trust and understanding in these friendships allowed Emily to be vulnerable and authentic, providing a safe space for her to express and explore her evolving self.

New acquaintances, particularly those she met through her professional life and community work, brought fresh perspectives and dynamics into her life. These relationships were built on shared interests and mutual respect. They offered Emily insights into different worldviews and experiences, contributing to her personal growth. Her approach to these new connections was thoughtful and open, reflecting her maturity and the depth of her character.

The evolution of Emily's relationships highlighted the interplay between personal growth and interpersonal dynamics. Her journey of self-discovery, resilience, and transformation influenced how she interacted with those around her. It brought a depth and richness to her relationships, making them more meaningful and fulfilling.

Emily's reflections on these key relationships revealed the importance of empathy, communication, and mutual support. She understood that relationships were not static but dynamic entities that evolved over time, shaped by experiences and shared journeys. The impact of her story on these relationships was profound, marking a transition from dependence to interdependence, from seeking validation to offering support, and from love as a need to love as a shared journey of growth.

In sum, the evolution of Emily's relationships with her family, friends, and Michael was a reflection of her own journey. These relationships, influenced by the events of her story, became testaments to her growth, her resilience, and her capacity for love and empathy. They were not just aspects of her life but integral parts of her narrative, each contributing to the person she had become.

As Emily delved deeper into the nuances of her relationships, she realized that each one had played a pivotal role in her journey, acting as a mirror to her inner transformation and as catalysts for her growth.

The relationship with her parents, for instance, had evolved from a traditional parent-child dynamic to one of mutual respect and admiration. This change was particularly evident in the aftermath of her breakup with Michael. During this period, her parents provided not just comfort but also wisdom, helping her navigate through her emotions and decisions. Their support was unwavering, yet they allowed Emily the space to make her own choices and learn from them. This delicate balance of guidance and independence fostered a deep sense of trust and strengthened their bond. Emily's journey thus transformed her relationship with her parents from one of dependency to one of equality and mutual learning.

Similarly, Emily's bond with her siblings evolved significantly. They became her sounding boards, offering perspectives that were both grounding and enlightening. The shared history and the ease of their connection provided a comforting backdrop against the challenges Emily faced. Yet, it was their willingness to engage with her on deeper levels – discussing her career aspirations, her personal growth, and her reflections on relationships – that added layers of complexity and richness to their bond. The evolution of these relationships was a reflection of Emily's own maturity and her growing ability to forge deeper connections with those around her.

The end of her relationship with Michael, though a chapter closed, continued to influence Emily's approach to love and relationships. It was a relationship that taught her the intricacies of romantic love – the joys of deep connection and the pain of parting ways. This experience shaped her understanding of what she sought in a partner and how she envisioned her future relationships. It instilled in her a sense of self-awareness and clarity in her romantic pursuits. Her subsequent forays into the world of dating were marked by a sense of purpose and understanding, shaped by the lessons learned from her time with Michael.

In her friendships, both longstanding and newly formed, Emily found a diverse tapestry of support, joy, and learning. Her older friends were her anchors, offering stability and a sense of continuity.

Their shared memories and experiences were a comfort, yet their ability to grow together added dynamism to their bond. In contrast, her new friendships, formed through her professional and advocacy work, introduced her to new ideas, challenges, and ways of seeing the world. These friendships expanded her horizons and played a significant role in her ongoing journey of self-discovery.

Each of these relationships, whether with family, friends, or romantic partners, was a reflection of Emily's growth. They were shaped by her experiences, her evolving perspective on life, and her deepening understanding of herself. Through these connections, she learned the importance of empathy, the value of diverse perspectives, and the beauty of shared growth.

As Emily reflected on the impact of her journey on these key relationships, she realized that they were not just part of her story but integral to her evolution. They were mirrors reflecting her own changes, windows into different worlds, and companions on her journey. The evolution of these relationships highlighted the interconnectedness of personal growth and interpersonal dynamics, underscoring the profound impact of life's journey on the fabric of human connections.

Emily's story thus became a testament to the transformative power of relationships in shaping one's life. It was a narrative that illustrated the beauty of evolving bonds, the resilience in facing changes, and the joy in growing together with those around her.

Emily's professional journey, interwoven with her personal growth and experiences, was a testament to her resilience, creativity, and dedication to making a meaningful impact through her art and community work. Over the years, her career had evolved remarkably, marked by key projects and initiatives that not only signified her professional milestones but also mirrored her journey of self-discovery and growth.

At the beginning of her career, Emily was primarily focused on her role as an art teacher in a local high school. Her passion for art and teaching was evident in her approach to education, where she strived to inspire and nurture creativity in her students. This phase of her career, though fulfilling, was just the foundation upon which she would build a diverse and impactful professional journey.

The turning point in Emily's career came with her deepening involvement in the community art center. Here, she transitioned from a teacher to a leader and advocate for art's transformative power. One of her first major initiatives at the art center was the development of the 'Art for All' program. This program aimed to make art accessible to underprivileged communities, providing free classes and workshops. It was a project close to Emily's heart, reflecting her belief in the universal right to art and expression. The success of this program not only expanded the reach of the art center but also established Emily as a key figure in community arts advocacy.

Another significant milestone in her career was the establishment of the 'Healing Through Art' series. Drawing from her personal experiences with art as a therapeutic tool, Emily designed workshops for individuals coping with trauma and mental health issues. These workshops underscored the healing potential of art and positioned Emily at the forefront of integrating art therapy into mental health practices. Her work in this area garnered recognition from both the art and mental health communities, bridging the gap between these two fields.

Emily's professional evolution continued with her innovative approach to art education. She spearheaded initiatives to integrate art into the broader school curriculum, advocating for the importance of creativity and artistic expression in overall student development. Her efforts led to collaborations with educational institutions and influenced policy changes that recognized the value of arts in education.

A key project that marked a significant achievement in Emily's career was the organization of an annual art festival in Alderidge. The 'Canvas of Cultures' festival was a celebration of diversity in art, bringing together artists from various backgrounds and communities. Emily's role in conceptualizing and organizing this event showcased her leadership skills and her ability to bring people together through art. The festival not only enriched the cultural landscape of Alderidge but also highlighted Emily's commitment to promoting inclusivity and diversity in the arts.

Furthermore, Emily's passion for art led her to explore and embrace new mediums and techniques. She continued her personal artistic journey, experimenting with different forms and participating in various exhibitions. Her artwork, often reflective of her life experiences, gained recognition for its depth and emotive power. This personal exploration of art was not just a means of self-expression for Emily but also a way to stay connected with her roots as an artist.

Throughout her career, Emily maintained a focus on community involvement. Her projects often aimed at using art to address social issues, foster community engagement, and promote cultural understanding. This aspect of her work was not just professionally fulfilling but also deeply aligned with her personal values and her desire to make a difference.

Emily's professional journey was characterized by continuous learning and adaptation. She embraced challenges, sought new opportunities for growth, and remained committed to her vision of using art as a tool for education, healing, and community building. Her career path was not just a series of jobs and titles but a reflection of her journey as an individual – a journey marked by passion, resilience, and the pursuit of purpose.

In reflecting on her professional growth and realizations, Emily understood that her career was a crucial part of her identity. It was an arena where she could channel her experiences, her creativity, and her desire to contribute positively to the world. Her professional journey, with its ups and downs, successes and challenges, was a mirror of her personal journey – a journey of evolving, learning, and making a meaningful impact.

Emily's involvement in her community and her advocacy for mental health were not just extensions of her career but deeply intertwined with her personal journey and growth. Through these endeavors, she left a lasting impact on the community, turning her personal experiences into a catalyst for change and support for others.

At the core of Emily's community work was the belief that art could serve as a powerful tool for communication, healing, and bringing people together. This belief was born out of her own experiences with art as a means of navigating through her emotions and challenges. Her initiatives at the community art center were some of the first steps in her journey of community involvement. Programs like 'Art for All' and 'Healing Through Art' were reflections of her commitment to making art accessible and relevant to different segments of society. These programs not only brought art to people from diverse backgrounds but also established the art center as a hub of community activity and engagement.

The 'Art for All' program, in particular, had a profound impact on the community. It opened doors for individuals who might have never had the opportunity to engage with art due to economic or social barriers. By providing free access to art classes and workshops, Emily helped cultivate a culture of inclusivity and diversity in the arts. This initiative was a testament to her belief in the democratization of art and its role in fostering community spirit.

Emily's 'Healing Through Art' series was another significant contribution to the community. These workshops provided a safe space for individuals dealing with various mental health issues to express themselves through art. The success of these workshops highlighted the therapeutic benefits of art and brought attention to the importance of mental health. Emily's work in this area was deeply personal, driven by her own experiences with healing through art. Her advocacy in this field not only helped destigmatize mental health issues but also encouraged a more holistic approach to mental health care, integrating creative therapies into treatment plans.

Her community involvement extended beyond the art center. Emily actively participated in various community projects, often collaborating with other organizations and groups. She organized art exhibitions that addressed social issues, led community mural projects, and participated in cultural events. Through these activities, she fostered a sense of community, bringing people together to celebrate, reflect, and engage in meaningful dialogues.

Emily's role in organizing the annual 'Canvas of Cultures' art festival was another highlight of her community work. This festival became a platform for artists from diverse backgrounds to showcase their work, promoting cultural understanding and appreciation. The success of the festival under Emily's leadership showcased her ability to unite people through the universal language of art. It was an embodiment of her vision of a community bonded by creativity and mutual respect.

In her advocacy for mental health, Emily used her voice and platform to raise awareness about the importance of mental well-being and the role of art in mental health care. She spoke at conferences, wrote articles, and collaborated with mental health professionals, sharing her insights and experiences. Her advocacy work was impactful in bringing the conversation about mental health to the forefront in her community, encouraging openness and understanding.

The impact of Emily's community work and advocacy was multifaceted. It brought about a change in how art was perceived and used in the community. It fostered a culture of inclusivity, understanding, and support around mental health. Her work also had a ripple effect, inspiring others to engage in community service and advocacy.

Reflecting on her community involvement and advocacy, Emily recognized how these endeavors were intertwined with her own personal growth. Through her work, she found a sense of purpose and fulfillment. Her journey through challenges and self-discovery equipped her with empathy, resilience, and a deep understanding of the human experience, qualities that she brought into her community work. Her involvement in the community was a reflection of her journey – a journey of overcoming, growing, and using her experiences to contribute positively to the world around her.

Emily's story in the realm of community impact and advocacy is a testament to the power of using personal experiences as a force for positive change. It illustrates how individual journeys of growth and healing can extend beyond personal boundaries and contribute to the welfare and enrichment of the wider community.

Emily's journey, a rich mosaic of experiences, was replete with lessons and wisdom that significantly contributed to her personal development. Each phase of her life, each challenge, and triumph, imparted valuable insights that shaped her into a more resilient, empathetic, and self-aware individual.

One of the key lessons Emily learned was the importance of resilience. Her experiences, especially her breakup with Michael, taught her that resilience was not about avoiding pain or difficulty, but about facing them head-on and emerging stronger. She learned that resilience was about the capacity to adapt to changes, to find strength in vulnerability, and to keep moving forward, even when the path was uncertain.

Another significant lesson was the power of self-reflection and introspection. Emily's journey of healing and growth post-breakup was a testament to the transformative power of looking inward. She learned to understand and accept her emotions, to listen to her inner voice, and to be true to herself. This introspection led to a deeper understanding of her needs, desires, and values, shaping her decisions and relationships.

Emily also learned the importance of self-care and balance. Her involvement in activities like yoga, meditation, and art not only provided solace but also helped maintain her mental and physical well-being. She realized that taking care of herself was not a luxury but a necessity, essential for sustaining her ability to give to others and pursue her passions.

Through her experiences, Emily gained a deeper appreciation for the role of art in healing and expression. Her own journey with art, both as an artist and an educator, highlighted art's power to communicate, heal, and connect. This realization was not just a personal revelation but also formed the basis of her community work and advocacy for art therapy.

Another lesson that emerged from Emily's experiences was the value of empathy and compassion. Her interactions with various individuals, be it through her teaching, community work, or personal relationships, taught her to understand and appreciate different perspectives. She learned to listen actively, to empathize with others' experiences, and to offer support without judgment. This empathy became a cornerstone of her approach to teaching, her community involvement, and her advocacy work.

Emily's journey also underscored the importance of relationships in personal growth. Her interactions with family, friends, and romantic partners taught her about the dynamics of human relationships. She learned that healthy relationships are based on mutual respect, honest communication, and a willingness to grow together. Her experiences also taught her the significance of setting boundaries and the importance of nurturing relationships that are supportive and enriching.

An essential lesson for Emily was the understanding that growth is an ongoing process. She realized that personal development was not a destination but a continuous journey of learning, adapting, and evolving. This understanding allowed her to embrace new experiences, challenges, and changes with an open mind and a willingness to learn.

Lastly, Emily learned the value of giving back to the community. Her work in the community art center, her advocacy for mental health, and her involvement in various projects taught her that making a positive impact in the community was deeply fulfilling. This work not only benefited those she served but also enriched her own life, giving her a sense of purpose and connection.

These lessons, gleaned from her diverse experiences, contributed significantly to Emily's personal development. They shaped her into a more grounded, compassionate, and purposeful individual. Her journey, with its array of experiences, was a testament to the fact that life's challenges and joys are not just passing phases but opportunities for profound growth and learning.

As Emily looked back on the winding road of her journey, she couldn't help but pause at certain moments, those pivotal instances when her life had taken unexpected turns. Each of these moments had left its mark on her, shaping the person she had become.

One of the most profound changes had been her newfound strength and resilience. She vividly remembered the dark days after her breakup with Michael. The pain had been excruciating, and there were moments when she thought she might never recover. But she did. Through tears, sleepless nights, and countless hours of introspection, she had emerged stronger than ever. The scars remained, but they were badges of honor, reminders of her ability to endure and grow.

Her experiences had also deepened her understanding of relationships. She realized that love wasn't just about the euphoria of the beginning but also about navigating the challenges that came with it. Her relationship with Michael had taught her the importance of communication, empathy, and compromise. Even though they had chosen different paths, Emily was grateful for the love they had shared and the lessons it had imparted.

The support of her friends and family had been a lifeline during her healing process. She had learned that vulnerability wasn't a weakness but a strength that allowed her to connect with others on a deeper level. Her bonds with Sarah, David, and Ella had grown stronger, and she cherished those connections more than ever.

Professionally, Emily had blossomed. Her role at the community art center had evolved into a platform for her to inspire others through art therapy. The projects she spearheaded had touched the lives of many, and she felt a profound sense of purpose in her work. Art had not only been her solace but also her medium for healing others.

Community involvement and mental health advocacy had become second nature to Emily. She had seen the impact of her efforts on individuals who were struggling, and it fueled her commitment to making a difference. Her work was a testament to the idea that healing extended beyond the individual to the community at large.

As she reflected on her journey, Emily understood that life was a series of lessons. She had learned the importance of self-compassion, the value of embracing change, and the beauty of resilience. Her scars were reminders of her battles, and she wore them with pride.

And then there were the new romantic possibilities that had begun to surface in her life. Emily approached them with cautious optimism, knowing that love was a complex tapestry of emotions and experiences. She was no longer the same person she had been at the start of her journey, and her approach to love had evolved along with her.

Looking ahead, Emily saw a future filled with promise. Her goals, both personal and professional, were well-defined. She was determined to continue her work at the community art center, nurturing the creative souls who sought healing through art. Her vision extended beyond her current role, and she aspired to create a safe space for artistic expression and mental health support.

In the community and beyond, Emily's impact had been profound. She had shown that healing was possible, that growth was attainable, and that self-discovery was a journey worth embarking on. As she gazed at the horizon, Emily knew that her story was far from over. It was a story of resilience, of growth, and of the enduring power of self-discovery.

# Also by Michael Harbut

Love of My Life: Love Turns Deadly

Watch for more at https://bottom2thatopentertainment.com.

# Also by Michael Anderson

Love of My Life: Love Turns Deadly

# About the Author

Michael Harbut is an American Entrepreneur, investor, rapper, songwriter, record producer, and author. He has worked as an actor, movie producer, music video director and producer, celebrity booking agent, music industry adviser, public speaker, and entrepreneur. He has worked in shadows in the film, television, corporate world, entertainment, and music industries. He has collaborated with a wide array of people, including company owners, CEO's, actors, actresses, musicians, entrepreneurs, brands, celebrities, investors, big record labels, independent record labels, production firms, producers, politicians, and directors. He also collaborated with NBA, NFL, NHL, MLB, PGA, ATP, NASCAR, Boxing, and other elite sportsmen. He has experience working with a wide range of clients, including startups, Fortune 500 firms, tech startups, and more. Although he was born in Ohio, he spent his formative years in both his hometown and various locations across Southern California, and the Golden State.

Read more at https://bottom2thatopentertainment.com.